DARK MATTER

A STEVE NASTOS MYSTERY

DARK

MATTER

R.D. CAIN

ECW PRESS

Published by ECW Press
2120 Queen Street East, Suite 200, Toronto, Ontario, Canada M4E 1E2
416-694-3348 / info@ecwpress.com

LIBRARY AND ARCHIVES CANADA CATALOGUING IN PUBLICATION

Cain, Richard
Dark Matter : a Steve Nastos mystery / Richard Cain.

ISBN 978-1-77041-006-0
also issued as:
978-1-77090-256-5 (PDF); 978-1-77090-257-2 (EPUB)

Cover and text design: Ingrid Paulson
Printing: Trigraphik | LBF   5   4   3   2   1

The publication of *Dark Matter* has been generously supported by the Canada Council for the
Arts which last year invested $20.1 million in writing and publishing throughout Canada, and
by the Ontario Arts Council, an agency of the Government of Ontario. We also acknowledge
the financial support of the Government of Canada through the Canada Book Fund for our
publishing activities, and the contribution of the Government of Ontario through the Ontario
Book Publishing Tax Credit. The marketing of this book was made possible with the support
of the Ontario Media Development Corporation.

   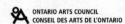

PRINTED AND BOUND IN CANADA

1

LINDSAY BANNERMAN LAY IN A heap, half-covered by a rat-gnawed blanket in a corner of a windowless basement that stank of musty potatoes, dampness and old things that had been stored for too long and forgotten. Afraid to move and almost too scared to breathe, she scanned the area. Concrete block walls and dirt floor. The ceiling was exposed floor joists and thick metal piping within arm's reach over her head. The only lighting came from a night light plugged into a receptacle that had been attached to the side of a joist above. There was another pile of filthy blankets at the far corner of the room with two distinct, human-sized humps beneath it.

She had no idea how she had come to be there. Her last memory was walking home from the bus to Abby's house; they were going to meet up with some boys, then go to a movie. *If I could just clear my head and remember . . .*

The feeling she had was familiar, high and weightless like vapour floating in infinite blue sky. She had tried oxys before and this felt similar. It was a warm, cozy feeling, like being wrapped in a warm blanket and having every inch of her body hugged by someone she loved. This kind of drug didn't appeal to her — she preferred the vitality and confidence that cocaine provided and stayed far away from opiates and the itching arms that came on their rollercoaster ride down to earth.

Summer school let out at noon, which was early. She rode the Lawrence Street bus to Meadowvale then walked north, oblivious to the crisp fall air, listening to her iPod. While scanning the song-list for Rihanna's "Disturbia," she caught a glimpse of the street ahead and for some reason, her heart dropped a beat. It was desolate, like always. This far east in the city had no commuter traffic, even during the morning rush. Something struck her as odd.

Before the song started she barely registered that there were kids in Wanita Park to her right. This part of Scarborough was like a disaster movie, where all of the people were dead and the streets vacant. Now she remembered thinking that exactly.

It was the van.

Something out of the '90s — beat up, powder blue with tinted windows. A rear tire was going flat. The van looked derelict and out of place, but there was no one around and Abby lived just up the street on Jean Dempsey Gate. Lindsay caught movement out of the corner of her eye and decided it was nothing, maybe a swaying tree, though the winds were calm.

She continued up the street, closing the gap between her and the van. The side windows were darkly tinted as well, making the back glass impenetrable. Hair on the back of her neck stood up as she passed the vehicle, and she let out an involuntary sigh of relief when she passed it, seeing that there was no one in the front. She remembered shaking her head and reaching into her pocket for her cell phone, but as the song on her iPod ended, there was a noise and she turned back to the van. The side door had slid open and the figure lunged out at her, arms reaching forward. Her knees buckled and she fell backward on her ass, head hitting pavement, and then he was on her. His second punch knocked her unconscious.

2

□ □ □

NOW, SHE REACHED AGAIN FOR HER CELL PHONE, FINDING HER POCKET empty. She shoved off the filthy blanket, stirring dust, searching for her bag although she already knew it would be gone too.

"Hey," a voice said.

Lindsay felt a jolt of fear, then watched as a young girl emerged from under the canvas blanket across from her.

Lindsay asked, "Who are you? Where are we?"

The girl's eyes darted furtively before she whispered an answer. "I'm Rebecca Morris. Some freak's keeping us here. What's your name?"

"Lindsay. What's yours again?"

"Rebecca. Don't worry; it takes a while for your head to clear."

There was more movement from under another blanket. Another young girl's face appeared, blank, peeked her way and then sank back under the blanket. Before she could ask, the girl said, "Don't mind her. She doesn't talk much."

"How long have you been here, Rhonda?" Lindsay began moving to get closer to the girl. Her head and jaw were aching.

"It's Rebecca." She smiled. "I don't know. What day is it?"

"Thursday? The twenty-seventh?"

The girl looked up as she did the math. "Two days then for me." She spoke as if to herself. "Holy shit. I didn't think I'd slept at all. I guess I must have."

The girl crawled over the short distance, although it seemed to Lindsay that she could have walked. "You seemed okay, so I just let you sleep. You've been here a few hours. Did he drug you?"

"Yeah, you?"

"Yeah, just the once."

A feeling of intense fear welled up inside her. "Has he . . . done anything to you?"

"No. I have no idea what the hell he wants, but it's not that. He opens the door and brings down food. He wears a mask — I've never seen his face."

Lindsay examined the ceiling. No creaking, no signs of movement. "Where's the hatch?"

"It's in that corner, but don't do it." The girl pointed. Her arms were stained with dirt, her nails filthy.

Lindsay crept in the direction of the hatch, squinting her eyes, slowly straightening her back.

3

"Don't do it." Rebecca said.

The night light plugged in between the floor joists cast a shadow over the hatch. She searched with her hands, wishing that her head was clearer. A joist had been cut away, making a flat area two foot square. The hatch was rough-cut lumber and there were sharp points, possibly exposed nails or screws.

When her hand grazed against the handle she felt the electricity rip through her arm. It was both cold and hot. She cried out, pulling her arm back and falling down to the floor.

Rebecca helped her sit up. "I knew you'd have to feel it for yourself. We're trapped here."

Lindsay stood, more determined. "I'm not staying here."

This time she was more careful. She traced her hands clockwise around the perimeter of the hatch, using the back of her finger, and the fingernail in the seam between the hatch and the frame, until she found what she was looking for: the electrical wires running a current across the bottom of the hatch. She slowly dug her fingers between the wire and the floor, splinters stabbing under her fingernails. Once she was past the second knuckle on two fingers she dropped her weight, pulling the wire down.

"Okay, here. Come and help."

The other girl stood next to her, peering into the darkness. "What do I do?"

"We're going to rip the wire right out so we don't get shocked when we open the hatch."

"I don't know. What if he's up there?"

Lindsay paused and listened. "I don't hear anything."

"Maybe it's just night and he's asleep."

Lindsay began pulling on the wire. "I want to go home."

Rebecca grabbed hold and put her weight into pulling. The wire sagged. Lindsay felt her way along and found a clip holding it in place. She put a hand on either side and pulled the wire sideways. It came loose and sagged halfway down to the floor. She repositioned again, this time bringing her foot up and stepping down on the wire. When it snapped, she nearly stumbled.

Rebecca asked, "Now what?"

"Now we work the handle." She tested the handle by grazing it with her arm; no shock, just metal, cold to the touch. She wrapped her hand around it and pushed and pulled. Nothing. Then she rotated it like the door to an airplane and it moved. She heard scraping and felt vibrations coming from the other side of the door. It was way too loud.

"He'll hear you," Rebecca said.

"Either he will or he won't — too late now."

Lindsay pushed the hatch up. She thought it would be heavier. The brightness from above stung her eyes. When she blinked, there were ghosts of every colour. She was too short to get the door to open far enough to keep it from falling back down again. It thumped back in place twice. Both times were loud.

"Rebecca, I need you to boost me up so I can —"

Heavy footsteps thundered over from the far side of the ceiling. The hatch was yanked open and both girls jumped back just in time to avoid being hit by the aluminum ladder that dropped down. A man groped his way quickly down the ladder. He was wearing construction boots, jean overalls and a bulky hoodie. Nylon was stretched over his face, distorting his features.

He never spoke a word, letting the cattle prod do the talking. Rebecca, immediately upon seeing it, ran to the far corner. Lindsay didn't know what it was until it was too late. More electricity ran through her body. It pushed her away from him, down to the cold earth floor. He charged two steps and pressed the prod against her throat, forcing her to lie down.

She had expected him to talk, to say something, but he didn't. Instead he breathed deeply, almost panting. He was jacked up and ready for a fight that Lindsay wanted no part of. She lay down and raised her hands in surrender. The man turned his attention to Rebecca, crouching down in her face and staring her down, but not before kicking Lindsay in the ribs with his construction boots. Lindsay couldn't control the yelp or the tears that followed.

The man turned back to the ladder and climbed up. The rattles and bangs of the ladder being pulled up after him echoed through the room, followed by the thump of the hatch slamming shut. The girls were left in near darkness. Heavy scraping and creaking from the floorboards above, moving toward the area of the hatch, shook dust from the joists. Particles floated weightlessly, reflecting in the nicotine-coloured light cast from the night light.

The scraping stopped; there were two thumps, then the sound of something rolling, piano keys struck accidentally, low ominous tones. The man had dragged a piano over the hatch.

Lindsay rolled over, clutching her stomach. "If I had spent more time thinking, if I'd been quieter, we might have made it."

"Not now. Now we'll never get out."

2

STEVE NASTOS SAT IN HIS HOME office hunched forward in a black leather swivel chair that creaked at the slightest movement. The walls were bare, his police memorabilia taken from the walls and shelves and deposited in the closet. The only evidence that he had been a cop was a photograph of him in his uniform, crouched next to his daughter, Josie, who was wearing his forage hat. Now he had his feet up on his desk and a phone to his ear; he'd been placed on Ignore ten minutes ago. Nastos entertained himself by reading the *Toronto Tribune*, the left-wing, cop-hating rag that made up as much news as it reported on. Only after the series of events that had led to his arrest for murder did he begin to consider that they weren't entirely wrong about their take on at least some of the city's cops.

The music on the other end of the line, a digital version of the latest Rihanna hit, stopped abruptly and the phone clicked. There was silence, then a woman's voice spoke to him. "MacPherson and Terrell Insurance, how may I help you?"

"This is Investigator Nastos; I need to do my monthly reconciliation."

He heard typing into a keyboard for what felt like an eternity. "And your reference number?"

"14-23-629-813."

"Your date of birth, SIN number and phone number, please?"

"What's the point of giving you my reference number if I just have to give you everything else anyways?"

"Mr. Nastos, I'm sure you understand the need for proper identification."

"Not really. I can't imagine there's a fraud ring going through my emails to get my reference number to report other fraudsters for committing whiplash frauds."

"Don't shoot the messenger, Mr. Nastos."

He provided the information. "Anyways, I just submitted the Ranatunga investigation. I sent it in last Friday, but haven't received the confirmation."

"Let me just take a look." She didn't put him on hold this time. He could hear chatter in the background, call centre noises.

"Yes, it's being sent back to you for completion."

"Pardon? I worked on that night and day for three weeks. It's complete."

"Actually, it's not, Mr. Nastos — you forgot to attach the new cover memo. Looks like you used the old one."

"You're kidding me, right? The only thing different is the date version of the form?"

"We try to pay attention to details, Mr. Nastos."

She was saying his name too much. She was a tightened-up bitch who'd be sure to say *Mr. Nastos* so she could think of herself as a consummate professional — too bad she didn't think it important to clear the contempt from her nasally voice. He opened the bar fridge and grabbed a Coke Zero. "Fine, I'll send the new one." He cracked the seal and took a sip after the hissing died down.

"Anything else, sir?"

"Yeah. How come I was only paid two thousand last week? I was expecting at least four."

She typed some more. "We've changed the remuneration schedule when there are only two vehicles involved."

"Are you kidding me? There were seven people in one of the vans."

"Sorry, sir."

"I sit in this ten-by-ten cell I've created for myself, investigating fraudulent auto accident rings. I'm here for ten hours a day, five days a week. Now, retroactively, you're telling me that my wage is being cut for no reason and I'm supposed to just sit back and take it?"

Silence.

"This is bullshit."

"Mr. Nastos, we have a policy about abusive or aggressive language."

"You think the word *bullshit* is abusive?"

"Yes sir, any profanity is abusive, according to our harassment policy."

"Oh, really. So *fucking* bullshit would really be pushing it?" He slurped his drink loudly.

"Yes, it would."

"And motherfucking, bat-shit crazy bullshit would probably be cause for termination?"

"It might, sir; I'd have to check with Human Resources."

"Well, don't bother, 'cause I motherfucking quit."

He pressed the button to hang up, then tossed the phone behind him on the couch. The overwhelming relief was quickly replaced by guilt. Money had been tight since he was fired from the police service, and the wrongful dismissal lawsuit had no end in sight. His wife, Madeleine, had been carrying the bulk of the financial responsibilities, which was stressful for her since she was a real estate agent and the market was all over the place.

The phone rang. After a moment, he decided to pick it up; if they offered, he'd take the job back and apologize. But the call display said it was his lawyer.

"Mr. Carscadden, I presume?"

"You presume correctly. How's the insurance business?"

"Well, they pissed me off, so I just quit. As in two minutes ago."

"Hey, good for you. You hated it anyway."

The vision of bills piling up on the kitchen table came to him,

Madeleine staring slack-jawed at a credit card statement that there was no money to pay. "Yippee, now we're broke. Maddy's going to kill me."

"Not so fast, buddy — how does ten grand sound?"

"You're not my type."

"Listen, I'll drop by. Put a suit on, we're going for a drive."

◻ ◻ ◻

NASTOS STARED OUT THE PASSENGER WINDOW, WATCHING PEOPLE and houses whiz past while Carscadden drove. His stolen life was out of reach; twenty-five years of being a cop had gone by just as fast. And while losing the job had been one thing, the separation growing between him and his wife was even worse. Getting fired had gone over badly; quitting the insurance company was not going to go over well either. It might even be what would put them in divorce court, assuming they could afford it. Feeling Madeleine slipping away in slow motion was the worst part of it all. It felt like dying.

High Point Road wasn't a bad street to live on — in the Bridle Path. The meeting was with a guy named Bannerman. He'd worked his way up in one of the big five banks and was obviously making some serious money. Why Carscadden needed Nastos there he wouldn't say. Nastos, unfortunately, had a good guess. These types of people had different problems than most. Maybe they were getting harassing phone calls or wanted a security audit of the mansion. In any case, getting out of the house for a change was welcome.

They drove in past the security gate. The estate looked to be worth about twenty million dollars as far as Nastos could tell — although Madeleine had never listed or bought a property in this neighbourhood. The Bridle Path was well known as the most expensive area of Toronto. Police were never called here. Nastos felt out of place. There was a time he could have driven around a few patrol zones and pointed out where every drug-dealing reprobate in a ten-mile radius lived without knowing where any bankers, politicians or multimillionaires were hiding. Carscadden, though, looked like he could get used to this. He was smiling, taking it all in.

Carscadden turned the car off in a rectangular area off the circular driveway, not far from the terrace entry. Nastos huffed himself out of the passenger side and they met up at the front door.

Nastos prodded Carscadden's shoulder. "Remember, you're here on business, right?"

"Cheer up, Nastos. You should be happy that old suit of yours is finally back in style."

Nastos watched as Carscadden smoothed out his off-the-rack jacket. In his late thirties, slim, with a recent haircut and ready smile, he was socially adept. He could even handle Nastos. "Yeah, it's just nice to see these guys can afford my new hourly rate."

Nastos shook his head. "Finally charging more than a plumber?"

Carscadden shrugged. "Didn't hear you complaining last year when you were looking at a murder conviction."

"Yeah, I guess." He smiled.

It was a stone mansion on at least two acres, marble pillars supporting a stone terrace — even the circular driveway was stone. The entrance alone was worth more than Nastos' entire house.

Nastos was expecting there to be a butler or armed security. There was neither, just a door ornate enough to cost ten thousand dollars, with its stained glass, wood carvings and gold inlay. Carscadden hit the buzzer, then quickly ran his fingers through his hair. He glanced at Nastos. "What?"

Nastos shook his head.

A middle-aged woman opened the door. She'd clearly been crying, but she had an easy smile despite her red eyes and seemed sincerely happy to see them. He thought she'd be wearing an evening gown like in the soap operas instead of jeans and a button-up shirt, and maybe sipping a cognac or Scotch instead of touching the discreet, white-gold crucifix hanging from a thin chain around her neck.

"I'm Claire. Please come in." There was an expression of hope on her face, making Nastos feel like he'd just been emotionally blackmailed into something. Carscadden led the way and Nastos followed.

He'd been on a White House tour back in 2000. This place made the East Wing look like a good start. They stood in a fair-sized foyer that featured a large flower arrangement and a double circular staircase with a fifteen-foot antique-looking crystal chandelier hanging down the middle. The artwork was all oil on canvas portraits, old, stern faces. A cat sat on a chair near one of the paintings that was unlike the others. It was of young girl wearing a flowing, blue Victorian dress reclining against a giant redwood tree. With a face bright with wonder, she stretched out to touch a fairy flying nearby. The fairy was little more than a smudge of light, obscured in a way that drew Nastos in closer. But he stopped, noticing that in the background the woods were foreboding and dark. The cat, a long-haired white Persian, moved in an exaggerated stretch then curled into a ball. Nastos noticed the off-white bandage around its front paw.

"What happened to your cat?" he asked.

Claire smiled again. "I don't know. She came in a few weeks ago bleeding. I think she stepped on something sharp and cut herself. It became infected. Had to take her to the vet."

Mr. Bannerman came around the corner. His suit was a charcoal Kiton; they started around six thousand dollars. He was lean with a military haircut and hints of grey. "Like the place?" he asked.

"This is unreal," Nastos replied.

"The bank owns it," he explained. "It's an executive perk. We have nowhere near this kind of money." He stuck his hand out. "Craig Bannerman."

"Too bad for you, about the money I mean." Nastos said, extending his hand to shake. "Call me Nastos."

"Nastos — that's Greek, right?"

"Yes, my dad's side."

"Sure," Bannerman nodded and turned to Carscadden. "And you must be Mr. Carscadden. We spoke on the phone."

Carscadden stepped forward. "I wish we were meeting under better circumstances."

"Thanks." Craig gestured toward a hallway. "Here, I'll show you to the living room."

Claire said, "I'll just take something out the oven and meet up in a sec."

Craig moved slowly. He was built like a boxer, with developed shoulders. Through the suit, Nastos could see the defined shoulders and arms. He must have just arrived home from work; he was loosening his conservative blue tie.

There was the dining room with a rough-cut sixteen-seater table that looked like it was out of a medieval castle. A sliding wall opened up to an entertaining room with a massive flat-screen TV, leather couches and chairs. More artwork, all of it real — no prints in a place like this.

"There's sixteen bathrooms, eight bedrooms, a den. We've only been here four years, took me two to find my way around." Craig smiled, almost apologetically. "This is all still pretty new to us."

Carscadden asked, "How long have you been with the bank? Twenty years, you said?"

Craig sat on one of the couches and indicated that Carscadden and Nastos should take their places across from him. "I started off selling mortgages in Shiloh, Manitoba — all they had there was an army base, a boxing gym, a Kmart and a Legion. Now I'm the executive vice-president of a bank." He shook his head like he couldn't believe it himself.

Claire came back into the room carrying a tray of drinks, chopped fruit and home-baked cookies. She put it down gingerly and smiled. "Help yourself, guys."

Nastos grabbed a cookie and bit into it — just to be polite, he told himself. "This is incredible."

Carscadden opened a bottle of water. "Great, thanks."

Craig slid a folder on the table toward him. He opened it to the first page. It was a full-body picture of a young girl: a thin nose, high cheekbones and full lips; her hair was blond with pink streaks. There was a resemblance to his wife, Madeleine. Maybe if Josie had an older sister . . . She stood next to Claire Bannerman in a kitchen, probably in this house. They both seemed happy enough; the girl was a little too thin to be healthy.

Craig waited till they had both spent time examining the picture. "My adopted daughter, Lindsay Bannerman."

Nastos understood when Craig confirmed the obvious. She looked nothing like either of them.

Carscadden had wanted to get into private investigation work. A lot of lawyers used the private sector. He had even gotten an agency license. Nastos wasn't sold on the idea himself; there were a lot of questions and details to work out. Being a wanna-be cop made being a civilian harder to bear. The hints he'd given to Madeleine that he had briefly considered it were met with a clear message: not a chance. The last thing she wanted was a return to the cop lifestyle of overtime and late-night call-outs.

Craig glanced between Carscadden and Nastos, taking a read of them, then he continued gingerly, like he knew he had to walk on eggshells with Nastos. "She was dating a young guy six months ago and when he dumped her, she kind of went off the deep end."

Nastos looked up from the picture. "What do you mean?"

"She started taking drugs and coming home late. It kept getting worse. She wouldn't tell us what was going on, where she was. We booked a psychologist, but she wouldn't go." There was something about Craig that was nervous; it was hard for Nastos to decide if he was anxious for help or hiding something — maybe even holding something back. It wouldn't be unusual for the parents to hold something back. Everyone lies — especially the victims.

Nastos asked, "Where do you think she was at night?"

Craig leaned back and exhaled. "Could be anywhere."

Nastos smiled to himself. *That wasn't a very good answer, Mr. Bannerman.* Nastos glanced at Carscadden, who still refused to say what was going on. "So what's the deal with your daughter, Mr. Bannerman? Why are we here?"

Craig exchanged a nod with Carscadden that Nastos found

himself resenting. "She's been gone for three weeks. No phone calls, no bank withdrawals, no school, no contact with friends. We don't know where she is and we want you to find her."

Nastos saw the anxiety this was causing Craig. From her corner armchair, Claire was silently hanging on every word, letting her husband the businessman, the deal broker, do the talking. He asked, "And the cops have done what, exactly?"

"Nothing. They say she's a habitual runaway, and she's seventeen."

Nastos agreed. "They get ten thousand missing persons a year. If she's a habitual, they aren't going to go looking for her. They just put her in the system, then wait till she comes back on her own or turns up doing something stupid. And they can't apprehend her, she's over sixteen. It's not like she was abducted."

Carscadden asked, "So no holds barred, get her home as soon as possible? That's what would you'd like us to do, Mr. Bannerman?"

Bannerman gave his wife a meaningful look, like this was one of the secrets he finally felt comfortable enough revealing. "Don't bring her here. When you find her, take her to the Bellwood for drug treatment."

Nastos knew the place. "The private live-in rehab centre. That's not far from here. I just don't think they'd even take an eighteen-year-old. They look for a certain amount of mature commitment to the process that I don't think a girl her age could muster."

Bannerman's tone was flat. "They'll try for fifty thousand dollars."

"Yeah, they probably would," Nastos agreed. "It's not a locked facility; if we get lucky and actually catch her, she can just get up and leave whenever she wants." Nastos rose to his feet slowly. "I don't think we're the best people for the job." He avoided eye contact with Claire — not that it mattered; the weight of her gaze clung to him anyway. He looked at Carscadden and waved for him to step out with him for a moment, then excused himself, thanking the couple for their time.

He heard Carscadden, behind him, say, "Just give me a minute,"

15

then Carscadden followed him through the foyer and out the front door onto the terrace. Without turning, Nastos said, "I don't think so, Carscadden."

"Why not?"

He felt a hand on his arm turning him around. "I feel like a bottom-feeder."

"A bottom-feeder, for helping a lost little girl?"

"Seventeen, Carscadden — she's only as lost as she wants to be."

The lawyer's mind was calculating his counter-argument. Nastos wondered for a moment if for Carscadden, it might be about the money.

"You said it yourself, Nastos: the cops aren't exactly going to kick down every door until they find her. Don't you think she's a bit too young to be alone? You saw the picture; a lot of guys would want a piece of her. One might want it a little too much. And what are you doing, anyway? You quit your job, you're unemployed, you need the money and you have the skills. You're just going to sit at home and rot? Going to watch the afternoon soap operas until you die on the couch at eighty-five? Sounds like a fun forty years of waiting. You need to keep yourself busy. Let's find his little girl."

Nastos paused a moment to consider his options. He'd known Carscadden was getting a private investigator's license and didn't exactly try to stop him. Working at Canadian Tire wasn't a very attractive option. Finding people was something a cop could do in his sleep.

Changing his tone, Carscadden asked softly, "So what's this really about, Nastos? What's holding you back?"

Nastos felt anger and conflict subsiding. He was ready to admit to himself what was stopping him; it wasn't just his wife. "Maybe it's that she's not in a very nice place. What if we find her dead? That's not very appealing to me, especially when it comes time to head back here and tell the Bannermans the terrific news. Death is one part of the job I am happy to leave behind. I guess my gut is telling me that there's only bad news at the end of this story; maybe the cops should just take this one."

"You're just making excuses. You may not know it, but you

need this. I know you're worried about feeling like a glorified security guard after having been a cop for so long, but this is you taking your life back — cleaning up a mess that the cops left behind."

Nastos shrugged.

"You've locked yourself down in that dungeon, punishing yourself for everything that happened to Josie. Now that piece of garbage is dead and rotting in hell. So maybe this is an opportunity to show her how to survive and put things behind you. Step back into the world and accept what you are."

"And what's that?"

"You're the guy who can find that man's daughter. You said it yourself: the cops aren't going to do anything for a habitual."

"Maybe they'll arrest her for hooking, and everything will turn out okay."

Carscadden looked at the ground, nodding slowly to himself. "Nastos, why did you quit the insurance job after only a few months?"

"I told you before, sitting in an office photocopying police service reports wasn't very exciting."

"Or fulfilling, you told me that too," Carscadden reminded him.

"Dumpster diving for children isn't my idea of fulfilling either." Nastos turned away, wanting to end the conversation. Carscadden silently moved to a position beside him.

Nastos surveyed the neighbourhood. The Bridle Path was a quiet, well-treed winding road dotted with multi-acre properties and modern-day castles. Nastos saw more than the sheen of surface glamour. Through coloured maple leaves, he examined a nearby mansion. It had dark fieldstone walls, honey-stained wooden window frames, tall black wrought-iron light fixtures. For the most expensive real estate in the country, it was beginning to look like something from Amityville.

"Nastos, they need help. How many kids have no one to love them? They love Lindsay and are going crazy to get her back. I don't know how we can turn our backs on them. Unless — if this is about Madeleine . . ."

Nastos had to smile; the lawyer had snuck it in. Carscadden

17

hadn't kept a girlfriend, or his ex-wife, for more than two years, and now he was the woman expert? Nastos on the other hand had been married for fifteen years and he knew that once kids arrive, as anyone will tell you, everything changes. "I'll tell you, Carscadden, constantly telling your wife that you are going to do one thing, and then doing the complete opposite, is a good way to get divorced."

Carscadden paused like he had nothing to say, looking down at his shoes, hands in his pockets. "But she didn't hate the cop part. She hated the you not being there. This is private work. We choose the hours and the pay is a lot better. And you know no one's going to find her if we don't do it."

Nastos shrugged again. If they could confine the hours to nine to five, maybe it would be enough — besides, Canadian Tire would always be there. "Okay, let's see what we can do."

Carscadden led the way back into house to the living room and they both sat back down. Nastos wasn't hungry until he examined the food tray. He grabbed a wedge of pineapple and another fresh-baked cookie — couldn't be too polite. "Tell me about your daughter," he said.

Nastos noted that Claire had moved and was now sitting next to Craig on the couch. They both seemed relieved that Nastos had returned. "We adopted her when she was seven years old. Single mom had committed suicide, by hanging. There was no one else in the picture."

Nastos asked, "No boyfriend for the mom?"

"Some loser — he disappeared shortly after she died. Lindsay was on her own. A girlfriend of the mom's contested the adoption. She wasn't a family member and was herself a drug addict. We adopted Lindsay less than a year afterwards. Most adopters want infants, but we saw her and it was love at first sight."

Nastos noticed how Claire tensed when Craig referred to the boyfriend as a loser, touching her crucifix again. She probably thought he was being harsh, non-Christian. She said, "We prayed so long for children; I guess God had different plans for us. Then we were blessed with Lindsay. And now she's gone."

If there was a rift in the marriage, in Nastos' estimation, it was regarding the church. The loving couple with home-baked cookies seemed to angle away from each other once Claire brought up praying. Craig was obviously more of a realist than she was. Nastos used the silence in the room to consider how much money, or realism, was spread around to speed up the notoriously slow adoption process. She probably had no idea he had greased the wheels for her.

Craig began again. "Since her boyfriend broke up with her, she's been staying out late, using drugs and stealing everything that wasn't nailed down: jewellery, cash — she even tried to get the car out of the garage but I had the alarm set."

"I'd like to start with a list of her friends, phone records, if you have them —"

"Here," Craig interrupted. "Her Facebook password, all of her phone records — we still pay the bill. If you call it goes to voicemail."

Nastos had seen the paperwork and was surprised that Craig had an entire dossier ready to go. "You have a total file all done?"

"This is everything the cops said they'd want and never bothered to pick up."

Craig slid it over and Nastos flipped through a few pages. "You even have stuff on the woman who contested the adoption?"

Craig's face creased. "Jessica. I put the adoption information in there when I saw that she had added Jessica as a Facebook friend. You think it's important?"

"I have no idea." Nastos checked through the phone records; there were quite a few numbers. "When exactly did Lindsay take off?"

"September twenty-seventh, three weeks ago." Bannerman's eyes didn't waver, but the corners of his mouth turned down.

Nastos scanned through the phone numbers on her billing record. There were a few numbers that Lindsay had called regularly right up until she left.

"You ever get this to the cops?"

"Copies of everything. I had to actually go in and hand it to them myself. I guess I should look for her myself too. Jesus Christ, I pay enough property taxes to have three personal cops assigned to me twenty-four-seven, and this is all the help I get."

Nastos flipped pages, keeping his face blank. If the house was a perk, why was Craig paying taxes? It was as if he felt uncomfortable revealing the extent of their wealth. He decided that as long as he had a sense of what Craig was holding back, it wouldn't pose a problem. Returning to the page before him, Nastos felt he had everything they'd need: a dozen pictures, birthmarks, blood type. With her phone number, they could trace her phone's GPS in about five minutes. Nastos closed the file.

"Does she have access to money?"

"She has a bank card; it hasn't been used since she disappeared."

Nastos rested the file on his lap while Craig continued. "The police did the report over the phone; no one came here. They told me to bring in the phone records and they'd have a look at them when they got a chance. They're not returning calls."

Claire Bannerman spoke up. "I can't believe that a child can go missing and the police don't do anything about it."

Out of habit, Nastos found himself trying to defend his former colleagues. "The city is full of kids — most are just out having fun. Cops are overworked and just assume that she'll cross their paths if, like I said, she's doing anything stupid. She's on the system. That means she hasn't gone to a hospital or been arrested."

Claire was lost between angry and sad. "You think she joined the army, Mr. Nastos? Is she competing in a top model search and too busy to call? She's not a nobody. There are people who love her."

He didn't want to say what he thought she was doing besides drugs. After she couldn't sell stolen merchandise from her house, she'd have to find something else to sell. He remembered her face from one of the pictures, the blue eyes and innocent smile. "I think she's shacked up with people she shouldn't be with, Mrs. Bannerman. Friends probably think they're doing her a favour."

Claire replied by folding her hands in an unconscious gesture of prayer and looking thoughtfully at nothing.

Praying wasn't going to be the answer for Lindsay. Nastos continued. "We're going to have to track down some of the cell numbers in the records."

Craig handed several business cards to Nastos. "I know a few of the executives at Rogers and Bell Canada. They know what's going on and are expecting your call. They're anxious to help, so don't hesitate." Nastos read the cards. Two vice-presidents and a president. Bannerman kept good company.

After some more questions, Craig handed over a twenty-thousand-dollar deposit cheque to Carscadden. They shook hands with him and Claire, then left for the car.

Carscadden pulled out of the driveway and waited a few minutes before asking, "What bothers you most about this?"

Nastos still had the file in his hands. He spun around and put it down on the back seat. "I don't think they were completely honest. I bet she's been a nightmare for them for a long time. Hell, the adoption was likely a mess from the beginning. And three weeks missing, that doesn't sound so good."

Carscadden stopped at the intersection of Lawrence and High Point. "This pays a lot more money than the insurance business."

Nastos pulled out his cell phone and started dialing. "Taking their money makes me feel kind of dirty. Twenty grand is a lot of money for this."

"They want her back. If we can do it fast, I'm okay with returning some of their deposit."

Carscadden had his issues; however, the accumulation of wealth didn't seem to be a burning desire after all. Nastos said, "I'm calling a buddy still on the force. I want to see what kind of story they have on Lindsay. Maybe she has a longer history with the police than they felt like revealing. If she's been picked up before, we can get an idea of where she hangs out."

"Good idea."

"Twenty grand; may as well try to deserve it. Drop me at home, then I'll meet you at the office."

Carscadden turned left toward Bayview. "Want to go to Frankie's for lunch?"

"Kalmakov's bad news — I'd rather stay clear of the guy."

"After everything he's done for us?"

"I appreciate that you successfully defended him from a triple-murder conviction, so he holds a certain place for you in his heart. You just need to remember that he's a Russian mobster, not the kind of guy we want to owe anything to. Besides, I have to consult with Madeleine about all this. I might be a while."

3

MADELEINE NASTOS WAS A born interrogator. She asked the kind of questions that had only incriminating answers. And in the amount of time Nastos required to consider options and mull over an escape route, she would read the pensive, maybe even lost, expression on his face as weakness and hit him with more questions.

"You know what my uncle went through to get you that job?"

They were at the kitchen table, where she was drinking herbal tea. She stirred the spoon one way, and just when things started going smoothly, she'd abruptly stop and stir the other way.

"Maddy, sitting at a desk all day isn't for me. I gave it a solid six months — most retired guys only last two years anyways. We'll be okay for money."

Her disappointment masked the real issue: money. The wrongful arrest lawsuit against the police service was still pending and cash was tight. Nastos wasn't old enough to collect the police pension and he couldn't be hired back because he'd served time in jail briefly for breaching his release stipulations while he was on trial for the events at Cherry Beach.

"So what are you planning to do now? The trial really hurt us."

This was going to be the fun part. He sat next to her and put his hand out. She accepted reluctantly, her fingers interlacing with his. *Start with the good news.*

"Today Carscadden and I picked up a cheque for twenty thousand dollars; we split it fifty-fifty."

She liked the sound of twenty thousand dollars. "What did you have to do for it?"

Here we go. "There's a banker — he lives in the Bridle Path, in a mansion."

She perked up; this was sounding promising.

"He and his wife couldn't have children, so they adopted. I don't think it was an easy integration, and the girl has taken off from home a few times. Now she's gone again. Here, look." From his pocket, Nastos produced the picture of Lindsay with her mom in the kitchen for Madeleine to see. Lindsay looked more like Madeleine than either of the Bannermans.

"How long has she been gone? She's a skinny little thing."

"Three weeks. He's asked us to find her and get her home."

"That's a lot of money."

"Bridle Path — you'd have a stroke if you saw the place. It's worth twenty million, easy."

She did the math. "That's one hundred thousand in commission."

"Twenty for us to find her, another fifty to get her into a treatment centre; it isn't much for them. What would you pay to get Josie back?"

"It depends on the day." Madeleine started to smile, then her gaze turned to the patio doors and the sky outside. She began spinning the spoon back the other way. "You just can't give it up, can you? Saving all the little girls of the world. You have a hero complex."

"The only thing I'm qualified to do is be a cop. There aren't a lot of transferable skills; one of them is finding people."

"I thought you were ready to finally leave it all behind you. You're not getting any younger. You're planning on chasing teenagers around Toronto for the next five years till your pension comes in? Josie's growing up so fast. This time off could all be worth it if after the settlement you were spending more time with her, while you still have it to spend."

"This money will get us closer to the settlement from the lawsuit; one step at a time. Looks like I'm now in the world of sales and promotion, like you."

She wasn't buying it and kept staring out the window, lost. Her blond hair was pulled back in a ponytail, revealing her long neck and tense shoulders. The reflection in the glass was like she was half-gone to another world where he couldn't touch her without his arms going right through. It had started with her staying on the couch downstairs to read; then came the end of flirting, the end of intimacy. The more they worked to get Josie past what happened, the more Madeleine seemed to be turned off sex completely.

Nastos persisted. "I'll have less competition than you, though. You don't see private investigator signs up everywhere like there are for real estate agents."

She looked at him, having heard not a word of what he had said. "Quitting was a bad idea, Steve. Josie needs stability. Here you go again; you'll be gone all hours of the night, sleeping half the day —"

"It's too late now."

She began drumming her fingers. "Just pick up the phone and get your job back. We can't afford this. We can't afford to have you out there feeling emotionally fulfilled when we have a mortgage to pay." It was the kind of anger that she sometimes reached, where she didn't have to shout. She had detached herself from him, like she was giving advice to a stranger.

"No, I'm not going back to insurance. I don't think they'd take me anyways."

"Huge mistake. Huge."

She looked into the living room, then to the front foyer as if she was looking for something urgent that needed her attention. She was looking for a reason to get away from him. What she wasn't saying was that she had known all along that it was just a matter of time before he pissed somebody off or did something stupid. He had to admit that he'd done both.

"Sorry about your uncle."

"He'll get over it."

Nastos stood up and stretched. "How long before Josie comes back from her friend's house?"

"She's staying for dinner. They'll call when she's ready."

He took a chance. He grabbed her hand and led her around the corner to the living room couch. He lay down and pulled her on top of him; she resisted only reluctantly. He ran his hands through her hair.

She said, "Steve, not now."

"Yeah, sure. Maybe some other time."

◦ ◦ ◦

NOT LONG AFTER CARSCADDEN AND NASTOS LEFT HIS HOUSE, Craig was able to get time away from his wife. It was easy to explain; he had taken the afternoon off work to meet with them and now he needed to head to the basement office. It was cool and quiet there.

For a house this size, it was a small room, barely twelve by twelve, lined with bookshelves and warmed by a gas fireplace. There was a network plug-in for his laptop. His wife wouldn't bother him down here and she rarely used his laptop; nonetheless, he employed the usual security precautions.

He used Firefox in private browsing mode, and when he wanted to look up something especially secure — the kind of thing that he absolutely never wanted the IT guys at work to see — he used Google Chrome and kept the browser hidden in an innocuously named file. He deleted the browsing history after each session. He didn't care so much about himself, but Claire didn't need to know about anything that would make her upset.

He never bookmarked a single site, relying instead on his memory. He brought up the Toronto escort directory on one tab; then in another he opened the RedLightEscorts Erotic Services page. He spent at least an hour a day scanning the images of the girls, the young blonds. Some obscured their faces with Photoshopped blurs, forcing him to study their bodies instead.

26

He reached for his cell phone and dialed a number. She answered, but the voice was wrong. He hung up. He scrolled all of the pictures that were new since yesterday — nothing. Nothing so far he'd have to keep searching.

He closed the screen and checked his email. Both of his connections at the cell carriers were helping. They had set up electronic surveillance on Nastos' and Carscadden's cells as well as Carscadden's business number. All phone calls would be recorded as MP3 files and emailed to him with a one-hour lag time. There were no messages yet. He planned on paying close attention to the progress of their investigation. If they were getting close to anything, he needed to know.

◻ ◻ ◻

CARSCADDEN STRODE INTO HIS OFFICE, FINDING HOPKINS AT HER DESK, a phone jammed up to her ear. She smiled upon seeing him. She was older than him by seven years, but didn't show it. Her dark hair was trimmed to her chin to accent her heart-shaped face. He placed some Indian takeout on the counter in front of her. She stood, smoothing out her skirt, then raised her hand to stop him in his tracks. "I have to let you go, Mom, Kevin's back and we have to go over something. Okay, bye, Mom."

She eyed the food. "I'm starving. Here, trade ya." She slid a file over the counter and spun it so he could read the name Viktor Kalmakov at the top, then began ripping into the stapled brown paper bag from Raja's Indian Food. "Ummm, good choice."

Carscadden picked up the file. "How many did he kill this time?"

"He wants a limited partnership set up."

He sighed. "Taxes, corporate law — how exciting."

Hopkins came around the counter and peeled the file from the counter. "Let's go through it. You're going to like the numbers, if you can handle it."

"I can do it with my eyes shut. Please, eat, you practically deserve food anyways."

27

She ignored most of what he had said. "Are taxes the only thing you can do with your eyes shut?" She puckered her lips, leaving him no choice but to kiss her.

"No, it's not." He opened the door to the office that he now shared with Nastos. Hopkins followed him in, closing the door behind her. She sat at Nastos' desk, opened the file and handed Carscadden the first page. He read it.

"Twelve million dollars equity. Nice. I could use some partners like that."

Hopkins rolled her chair over next to his. She pointed. "That's our cut there. Cash *that* check and I'll be shopping by this afternoon."

Carscadden read the payout. "That's more like it." He flipped to the second page in the Kalmakov file. "That's too much money; what's the catch?"

Hopkins pulled over the rest of the file. "He came here personally to drop this off. Look at the names of the partners. They're all trouble."

Carscadden only recognized one name out of the six listed: Liuzzo, a knee breaker.

"Viktor must have said half a dozen times that it involves some close friends and it's a sensitive matter. He's getting into the shipping business, barges."

"Expanding the garbage business, probably. If it's for waste removal, it might include hazardous waste, international shipping — it could get complicated with insurance and permits."

Hopkins asked, "Do dead bodies count as hazardous waste these days?"

Carscadden mulled it over. "Only if they are politicians." He closed the file and set it on his filing cabinet. "Well, that'll be a nice paycheque."

The front doorbell chimed. Hopkins stood to answer it, but Carscadden stopped her. "Hey, one sec." She turned to him as he approached her. He grabbed her ass with one hand and kissed her hard on the lips. He cupped his other hand at the nape of her neck and released her when she started kissing back. "Hey, hey, what kind of place do you think this is?"

Her face scrunched up. "You started it."

"See that? That backtalk? That's what I'm talking about. Tonight I'm taking you home and teaching you a lesson, young lady."

"Oh, really? Well, I might just teach you a lesson of my own. And I might not wait until we get home." She left the office, pulling the door closed.

Carscadden opened the top drawer of his desk and sucked back a long pull from his vodka bottle. He was living the clichéd detective life and loving it. He had the hot secretary he'd been dating a few months now, the bottle of booze in the top drawer and until recently he had been flat broke. Being his own boss, free of his former corporate shackles, was a freedom he had never experienced before in his adult life.

It was Polish vodka. The label was a black with the white outline of an ox pulling a plow under the guidance of a farmer walking behind with a whip. Carscadden decided he would be the farmer. With hard work, he would pull the treasure from the earth by working hard and being his own man. All he needed to do was give Nastos, the big dumb ox, the odd whip in the ass to get moving. He smiled. Nastos was turning into the best friend he'd ever had.

When Carscadden heard Hopkins talking to Nastos in the front room, he put the bottle away and went to the washroom to swish with mouthwash. The Indian food would take care of the rest of the alcohol breath.

4

ANTHONY RAINES SAT IN THE brown leather armchair nearest the fireplace in his office. He gave a thumbs-up to the muscular man who, upon receiving the signal, pressed a button on the timer and slipped out of the room, leaving Anthony alone with his client. She was leaned back in the crook of the couch, her eyes closing, the book and its blank pages drooping away from her.

"I want you to relax while we go through this next part. Lean back on the couch and just let your muscles relax. You're going to hear my words as I speak to you directly. And you'll recognize the voice you hear as the voice of your internal monologue — that instinctive voice you've listened to your entire life. And that's fine, because in a sense it's really going to be you talking to yourself."

"I've gone over your chart and your signs and spent a good amount of time studying up on you. So let your hands hold the stiff spine of the book in place, and let's get started. I know you've worked hard for your career. I see a solid worker who is appreciated by the smarter co-workers, but undervalued by some minor petty person you have to deal with. Too busy to hold grudges — that's not your style; you believe destructive people get theirs in the end anyways, sooner or later, usually later. You're independent but strike a balance when others want your company.

"You're a protector, a person who cares, a defender of weaker people. With your sign you prove to be a difficult adversary after the first confrontation, and I see here you're balanced and only go for the throat when it's justified. Your sign can be highly skilled in many different fields, cooking, reading people's body language; I see a strong intuitive ability, on the verge of psychic at times.

"You've settled into a pattern of life that, if you think about it, has so many more pluses than minuses. I do, however, feel an interest in changing things up a little. There is a part of you that is like a lone wolf. You are on this journey where you are ultimately alone, soldiering forward to great unknowns. I can tell you that everything is going to work out fine if you just keep moving forward.

"You're never really satisfied and always strive for self-improvement. You'd like an exciting getaway, just yourself, a week of reinvention and recharging. Your sign needs what I call quality alone time. And a new geography would do you wonders spiritually.

"You're at a stage in your life when you have a lot of practical advice to offer those around you. If you were to take the time to think about it, you'd recall that you've helped a lot of people over the years with your insights and observations. Your spirit is at times a lot more mature than your peer group. You're mature enough to know when to let loose and have a bit of fun; I see, though, that you often hold yourself back out of a sense of responsibility.

"How am I doing so far?"

Mrs. Simmard closed the book she was holding and placed it gently on the table. She didn't say anything — they usually couldn't, not right away. Her eyes turned to the digital recorder he'd told her to bring. The red light was flashing; it had recorded everything he had said.

Anthony swirled the teacup in his hands, now leaning forward in the leather chair. He finished the last of his cooling drink, savouring the dregs at the bottom of the cup, where the strongest flavour from the bitter leaves and the honey had settled together.

The timer chimed three tones, and Anthony thought of Chavez, his life partner, who had set it when she sat down. Simmard's reading was half-over; it would chime again in another fifteen, then again when her time was up.

Anthony paused a moment to visualize Chavez, his thick forearms that rippled as he reset the clock, his voice, deep and coarse. He would be heading to the gym now with a mutual friend. Bruce Townler was a veterinarian they were close to. A bald, thick man who was increasingly by Chavez's side. Anthony wouldn't say he was feeling crowded out; he'd never say that. Chavez could do what he wanted. He had always come back before; this would be no different. Chavez had an errand to complete. Anthony considered that if he did a good job, he'd put Chavez, or Bruce, or both, to work in his bedroom here.

The client, Mrs. Simmard, was a nouveau riche from Rosedale; she was sitting on a fortune. White hair dyed blond, well-dressed, thin, with large dark sunglasses hiding practically invisible bruises from a recent cosmetic surgery and a slightly ostentatious amount of jewellery. Anthony corrected himself. Not *thin*; rich women like these would use the word *slender*. Anthony did a quick once-up-and-down as she lay back on the couch. She knew he was gay, so he threw out a "great outfit" to explain his glances so she wouldn't realize that he was doing such a thorough physical inventory.

"Thank you," she said. "You have a relaxing way of speaking."

Every detail was critical to a true reading. At times he had wondered if he was a fraud. Was he doing what anyone could do by making such observations? He had learned to accept that his psychic abilities were real. He turned his mind to people and studied them at a level of detail that few could; the gift put it all together.

What separated him from the fakes was the way he meshed the gift and the ability to read people with the "third element" he had learned from stage magicians. Magicians performed their shows in three distinct stages: the *pledge*, the *turn* and finally the *prestige*. He'd pledge to give them a minor reading, he'd turn it with information gleaned from clandestine background checks or subtle personal networking, then he'd hit them with the prestige, the information from beyond the grave, things he could know only if he was authentic.

At sixty, she was still attractive — she had clearly been beautiful her entire life. She would be impervious to flattery related to her appearance, likely seeing it as retail manipulation. To get inside, he used his understanding that her soul craved validation of the type of person she had become.

Tasteful, coordinated clothing, upright posture, poise. He went through the options: modelling, real estate, entertainer, singer. She had an authentic personality that ruled out real estate. Singers catch more attention than models and they're usually smarter, deeper people. Artists were more attracted to people in his line of work.

He noted the mole over the upper lip. She had the money to remove it and didn't. She took it as a beauty mark; she would have a few more on her back. Again it meant confidence. There were faint red discolourations on her hand between the thumb and wrist; she'd been testing makeup. Her perfectly coiffed hair indicated a recent trip to the stylist.

Anthony made these calculations rapid-fire, with a calm demeanour. He was out of practice with the showmanship side of readings. The analysis of people — that gift he used every day. Now he felt it brewing up inside him, the moment of prestige.

"Shall we continue, Mrs. Simmard?" He gestured for her to take a cup of tea from the tray. He had poured two cups while he gave the first portion of the reading. He explained how she should swirl the leaves around while she drank so he would have more to work with.

"You know, Mrs. Simmard, I have a few friends who have crossed over into the afterlife, and sometimes they tell me the strangest things."

"Oh, really?"

As much as he was confident with himself, he threw out the showstopper in a way that could be both right and wrong. If she said yes, he'd be a legend; if she said no, he'd use the declining negative technique of *no, that wouldn't be a good fit for you.* "One of my friends, from the other side — you weren't a singer, were you?"

Her head dropped slightly, her eyes staring into his, wide in surprise. It was a home run on the first swing.

"That was over thirty years ago, in Montreal." There was no hint of an accent, but she would be bilingual. Anthony did more calculating. Montreal thirty years ago — the 1980s, the '70s to be safe; his mind searched through the Rolodex of memories and demographic movements: the FLQ, John Lennon.

"Well, a reading is really about me telling you what I see, then a certain portion of it is for you to interpret the meaning. Some things I'll tell you might seem elusive or off the mark; you have to remember that they may just be symbols for us to decipher together."

"Of course."

She was receptive; her advance payment of seven hundred and fifty dollars told him that. He went through the basic themes in his mind: money — she was set. Love — her man had just died and left everything to her. Career — it was behind her. And then there was health. She appeared fit; however, there were telltale signs of historic smoking, the lines around the mouth. He exploited that one easily.

It was never bad to tell them what they wanted to hear. But it was far more effective to confirm their worst fears; that was particularly galvanizing, especially if you provided them with an escape route. "I see a medical problem developing in your chest, some kind of blood vessel problem, but that's not going to be for a long, long time." Her eyes opened wider. "The kind of thing walking, yoga or any kind of fitness could stave off if you're able to be consistent."

"I walk every day and go to yoga three times a week."

"Then you're doing all you should need to age gracefully."

"How do you see my future going without William?" There was fear and concern in her voice, more than she would have intended. Anthony responded as if it was a casual question.

"I see some unwanted advances coming your way from men. One man — I can't describe him, but I feel that his forwardness is a little uncomfortable, like you've known him a long time and never thought of him that way. You should just take it as flattery, Mrs. Simmard. If you shrug it off, so will he. Men are fools around beautiful women, but you already know that, don't you?"

After the final chime, Anthony led Mrs. Simmard out. He put the cash she had given him into a pottery jar on the mantel. He was sure she'd tell her friends about him and he'd get the money rolling in again.

He followed a basic script in his readings. He encouraged her to work with him to decipher the messages he received and, while his credentials practically spoke for themselves, he still gave her a brief history of his experience. He always provided clients with pre-emptive excuses for failure, explaining that he wasn't perfect; ghosts could be elusive or vague in their transmissions.

Next it was always about the games of language. Rainbow ruses, statements that attributed both a trait and its opposite at the same time. *You're independent, but strike a balance when others want your company.* Barnum statements were so general they applied to everyone. *You're at a stage in your life when you have a lot of practical advice to offer those around you.* He encouraged her to work with him. *Well, a reading is really about me telling you what I see, then a certain portion of it is for you to interpret the meaning.* It could also be called forced teaming.

There were so many other ways inside a person, and so many profitable things to do once you were there. While the readings provided a reliable income, after an unnerving event — the vision — they were necessary evils to further the real calling of his life.

Chavez didn't come back in time to say goodbye, leaving Anthony alone and feeling incomplete, which he didn't like. He preferred to mirror the emotions of the people around him. He enjoyed the goodbyes as much as the hellos, even just for the small rituals of sharing a life with someone.

He went to his study and opened his laptop. His browser was

still open to his website. He clicked the link to go to his bio, where it had all begun. In 1985, he had been only twenty-eight years old when he had led the police to the body in the field. A man, young — in the prime of his life — with a lean body and bright future was found half-naked, his figure twisted in a shallow grave. His discovery had made Anthony famous. After that shameful waste of life, the media was all over him — TV shows, celebrities, everyone wanted a piece of the action. Back then, four hundred dollars an hour for psychic readings was a lot of money; and yet they paid. None of it would have been possible without Chavez in his life. Strong, confident, handsome — it all came together when they met.

Still, at times he would admit that he had felt like a fraud. From the outside looking in, he would have thought it would feel like more of a passive process to be psychic as opposed to the painstaking observations, the labour of creating an empathic connection to strangers.

He was reading people's appearances, behaviours, making judgments based on socioeconomic class, recycling it through a basic narrative structure: love, money, career, health, ambitions, hopes and dreams. He had developed it over time, and with basic manipulation techniques, he made sure he covered all of the essential passageways that we all walk through on our journey through this world.

Many times, ideas came to him from his dreams. What came to him almost one year ago was a dream like nothing he had ever experienced before. He dreamed he had died and been reborn into a new world. The dream was like living an entire life in the afterlife. He spoke to people there who explained the universe to him. They explained the core things that humans are meant to learn in their short lives. They were frantic for him to take the message forward. Humanity depended on it. He awoke with a singular purpose that day: to get the message organized, then out to as many people as possible. And sharing the vision was what he was going to do at next month's show at Casa Loma, both for the need for money and the need to bring humanity together with one singular vision of faith.

He exited the bio page and tabbed over to his Excel program. His financial situation was a horror show of overdraft and re-mortgage. They had come so close to having the house paid off; now it was mortgaged up to eight hundred thousand dollars. Keeping up the appearances of his lifestyle was getting expensive. It wasn't a spending problem; it was an income problem. He let out a deep breath and closed the spreadsheet.

With the remote he turned on the TV to CP24, the twenty-four-hour news channel. The ticker at the bottom rattled off useless information. The Don Valley Parkway was shut down on the weekend for construction, a car accident on the Gardiner. The Leafs were playing the Rangers tonight. And a young girl was missing, hadn't been seen in weeks. *Hmmm. Wonder if they'd want to hire a psychic?*

It had all begun for him when he helped recover the dead man. The image of the sun-bleached cadaver flashed in his mind less often over the years. But if he could travel back through time and speak to his young self, how would he do it differently? He'd played it over in his mind on many penniless and sleepless nights. Could it be done again with a conscious attempt to maximize the good old bottom line? He made a note of the missing girl's name. A wealthy, grieving family might pay good money to find her before she died. His windfall had lasted for years after finding a dead body. What could saving a girl's life with his powers bring him?

Anthony opened a bookmark on the computer that took him to the Casa Loma page. The castle was one of the city's most pictur-esque landmarks, built at a cost of three and a half million dollars in 1911, back when that was a lot of money. He dialed the phone number. Booking the entire castle actually hadn't been that expen-sive, less than ten thousand for the evening with everything included. The TV crew was almost the same price. For someone almost one million dollars in debt, it was a gamble. If the money didn't start rolling in within seven days, he'd be bankrupt, and an audit would find the income tax games he'd been playing for the past decade. Ultimately, he just had to have faith that the message of the truth would bring earthly rewards. Bankruptcy and jail for the rest of his life, or freedom fifty-five with more fame and money then he could ever imagine.

The booking agent answered the phone on the third ring and Anthony made the final arrangements. He hung up and the phone rang almost immediately. He was surprised to see it was Dr. Bruce.

"Hey, Anthony. Getting excited about your show?"

"That's one word for it. I confirmed the booking for Casa Loma. Chavez is gone to drop off the cheque now."

"And the TV people?"

"They're booked too. It's all ready to go."

"You sound nervous, Anthony. Do you want me to swing by with something to help you relax? More Atavan, Paxil? Maybe something stronger?"

Anthony shook his head. Bruce made more money selling drugs to his friends than to his clients for their animals. "I still have pills left over from before. Isn't Chavez with you?"

"No, he called and said he wouldn't have time for me today. I think he's in a mood."

"Yeah, I know what you mean." Chavez had been aloof lately. "He's playing his tricks again. He tells you he's with me and tells me he's with you."

"You know," Bruce said, slyly, like he was going to reveal the biggest secret of his life. "I was going to work out today but I'm not into it. What's your afternoon like?"

The idea of rolling around in bed with Bruce wasn't the worst offer he'd ever had, but it wouldn't be enough to make him forget about what was at stake. And it was Chavez he needed reassurance from, not Bruce, no matter how well intentioned. Bruce just didn't know the full story.

It was like Bruce felt the stress through the phone lines. "Don't worry, Anthony; you're great at what you do. Chavez and you make a good team. With him behind you there's nothing you can't do."

Anthony smiled. "Well, he's not behind me now — why don't you get over here and get behind me?"

"I'll be right over. I just have to do a few quick post-op exams."

38

5

NASTOS OPENED THE DOOR TO Carscadden's office, allowing his friend to be first inside. It had been renovated since he'd first seen it, new carpet, paint, better desks. It wasn't that long ago that people would walk in, take a look around and hire Carscadden just because they felt sorry for him, but he was doing better now. Hopkins greeted him with a sweet smile. "Back so soon? Did you get yourself arrested again?"

He rolled his eyes — *here she goes.* "No, but I'm working on it. I could use the downtime to work on my memoirs."

"Well, before you get locked up again you should invite us over for dinner." She filled her water glass up from the Culligan jug and had a taste. Nastos noticed the shape of her legs in the skirt and heels. "Nice outfit."

"Thanks — it's nice to finally have some extra money for shopping. In fact, I'm going to give your wife a call and see if she wants to come along."

"You'll have to put that plan on hold until your heel-dragging boyfriend gets my lawsuit with the city settled. Until then, Holt Renfrew's going to have to wait."

She made a purr that sounded like disappointment. Nastos counter-offered. "Dinner we can do. How's Sunday night? Josie wants you guys to see her new princess dress."

"Hey, that's a great idea. Make your Szechwan back ribs."

"Slow-braised beef, it is."

She made that sound again, throwing in a pout for good measure.

"For you, though, I'll do Szechwan back ribs. I'll make a few different appetizers too. You guys are in charge of margaritas and wine."

"We need to do this weekly."

"Madeleine wouldn't mind. Anything to get me cooking more." Nastos glanced at Hopkins' tapered waist. "You know that young boy-toy of yours would appreciate it if you wore something tight and revealing."

"Really?"

"Oh, yeah. Something that jacks the breasts up, you know? Something tight, revealing — and classy too. He loves that stuff."

"Is he the only one?"

Nastos smiled. "Probably not, no."

"No, I didn't think so."

Carscadden was standing at the door, smiling. "Hey, if you two are done, babe, can you hold the calls for a while?"

Hopkins had slid her paperback aside and started cleaning up what was left of her takeout food. "Don't worry, hon; I'll hold the hordes at bay."

Carscadden had added a second desk for him a few months ago when he first dreamed up the idea of a detective agency. Nastos' desk was off to the side, making an L shape with Carscadden's. He watched the expanding mess as Carscadden flipped the file open and spread the papers out, pushing aluminum takeout bins of Indian food off to the side. Nastos fired up his computer and logged in to his email. "My old partner from Sexual Assault, Jacques Lapierre, emailed me everything he had on Lindsay from her previous runaways. Jesus, it looks like he included the investigation into her mom's suicide."

Carscadden glanced over. "Did I ever meet Jacques?"

"No. I'll invite him by. I'll tell you right now, he's a Habs fan."

"That's okay. As long as he hates Washington."

"Oh yeah, he hates Washington."

Carscadden pointed to the computer. "That should make for interesting reading." He rolled his chair over to get a better look.

Nastos thought he detected the odour of alcohol on Carscadden's breath. He sniffed the air, but couldn't be sure. "I'll read through the police reports and pass over anything that seems interesting. The mom's name was Tabitha Moreau."

"Stripper name," Carscadden said to himself. "You enjoy the reports — I have to get through this Kalmakov deal, then make some time for your civil case against the police service. I meet with them this week for round one hundred."

On the surface, Kalmakov was nice enough. Nastos still felt the creeps, though. He might be a quasi-reformed Russian gangster, but Nastos wasn't yet convinced he was reformed enough. And after the "waste disposal" help the old man had provided them with the dearly departed James North last year, he still seemed more than eager to relive some of his glory days. "You know, the problem with the Russian mob is that once you know too much, you can become a liability."

Carscadden grabbed the remote from the desk and turned on the TV, ignoring what Nastos had said. "I need some music; I'll put on the satellite radio." Carscadden found an '80s rock channel and dialed down the volume.

Nastos printed out all fifty pages of the reports, most of which were useless to him; he was able to narrow it down to a dozen pages of text. Few had anything nice to say about Lindsay's clichéd upbringing. There was the abusive dad who disappeared, followed by the mom's abusive boyfriends. Mom was of course a druggie. She eventually hanged herself — that wasn't part of the cliché. Jacques was kind enough to include the soco's — scene of the crime officer's — pictures of the hanging, just in case Nastos had any doubts.

Nastos read that the friend who fought for custody, Jessica Taylor, was as bad as the mom and eventually gave up on Lindsay shortly after the Bannermans were short-listed as prospective parents. Nastos could practically smell the payoff after that. He made note of the name Jessica Taylor. He had her date of birth and an old address from Flemingdon Park.

Nastos turned back to the death photographs. Something about them was wrong. Whatever it was that caught his attention wasn't readily apparent when he studied each picture one at a time. He must have made a noise because Carscadden rolled his chair over to look. "What have you got there?"

"Lindsay's birth mom hanged herself."

"Jesus, what a mess."

"Yeah. If people knew they crapped all down their legs after hanging, fewer might do it."

"So what's the deal? Something catch your eye?"

Nastos scrolled through the various pictures. They were in order and together they told a sad story. A picture of a run-down, practically derelict, apartment building. The next one was of the room number, 501. The following photo showed the door open and then came various shots of the apartment. The place was a mess. Overflowing ashtrays, takeout boxes, a sink full of dishes. There were ragged and dirty stuffed animals scattered around, some with amputated limbs as if chewed by small dogs — or rats, Nastos corrected himself. Rats would have done that.

Then the camera showed the outside of a bedroom. The next picture peeked inside at the mess. Clothes, linen, shoes and empty liquor and beer bottles were everywhere. This shot was the first to show a glimpse of Lindsay's mom: her arm, out of focus, at the edge of the picture's frame. The next photo showed how it had happened. She had tied rope to the handle of the closet door and slung it over the top. She had tied the dangling end around her neck and sunk her body weight down, asphyxiating herself, her feet never leaving the ground. Naked, skinny, both knees bent, slumped to the right.

There were tight pictures of the knot she used as well as of scrapes at her neck, signs of buyer's remorse. She had two broken fake fingernails. The last shot showed the rope where it went over the door, her weight gouging into the cheap particle board.

Carscadden stated the obvious. "All she had to do was stand."

Nastos countered, "Or let's say she did stand. She still had to untie the rope. Maybe that's when she clawed at her neck, but she passed out before she got it loose. Blood toxicology shows she was very drunk. How many auto-erotic asphyxiations go wrong? Those people do it this way and they don't want to die — she apparently did."

Carscadden nodded. "Yeah, maybe she did try to stand. It wouldn't take long before she dropped right back down again. And the drop of her body would only crank the knot tighter. So the theory was that she got the rope ready, got drunk, looped it around her neck and by the time she changed her mind she was too weak to do much about it."

Nastos handed the stack to Carscadden. "I've seen it before. Still though, something struck me as odd. I just can't put my finger on it."

Carscadden snatched at the mouse. "Here, let me take a look." He began going through them. "She was pretty, just like her daughter. How sad."

Nastos asked, "Any idea what you're looking for?"

"Not really."

Nastos said, "I'll start with the phone numbers."

Carscadden grunted acknowledgment, already immersed in the pictures of death. Nastos spread out the business cards that Bannerman had given them. "Rogers security, Bell security, Telus security — this guy knows everyone." He flipped to the cell numbers on Lindsay's phone bill. There were fourteen that repeated over the last two months. The first business card was Rod at Bell Canada.

"Rod speaking."

"Hey Rod, this is Steve Nastos. Craig Bannerman said I should give you a call."

"Right, Lindsay — no sign of her yet?"

"No," Nastos said. "We just started on this thing."

"Well, give me the phone numbers; if they're ours, I'll get you the subscriber info."

Nastos went through the numbers one by one. Rod was able to help out with seven; thankfully, none were pay-as-you-go numbers.

"Thanks, Rod."

"Call back anytime. And hey, if I'm not here, write down my personal cell. Call me twenty-four-seven. If you need anything to find Lindsay, call anytime, day or night."

"I appreciate that."

"No one here's going to be giving me crap for trying to help out Craig Bannerman."

Nastos called Jim at Rogers and found the same level of co-operation. With Rogers, Nastos now had the registered names and addresses of every phone number on Lindsay's record. The two pay-as-you-go numbers Jim identified became the most promising because they could be registered anonymously by purchasing cards with cash at convenience stores instead of over the phone with credit cards.

"Hey Jim, can you ping the pay-as-you-go numbers and see where they are?"

"Actually, Steve, both of the phones have GPS. One sec."

Nastos waited a moment on the line. "Jim, don't the phone owners have to activate the GPS? Can't they turn it off?"

"Oh, hell yeah, they can turn it off. They don't know I can turn it back on from here. It's easier than triangulating towers and they'll never know I did it." Nastos heard fingers tapping on a keyboard.

"I can get within ten metres with our system. One sec. Okay, one number's at Windon Road, near Saint Dennis and Eglinton, that's Courtney Love. Obviously a bullshit name. The other's in Scugog Township — wherever the hell that is. Check out this name. Anita Bonghit."

"Can you repeat that?"

Jim chuckled. "When you see it spelled out, it doesn't seem like anything. When you say it, you realize it's a pseudonym. I need a bong hit. Anita Bonghit."

"What a loser." Nastos heard more typing.

"Here, Steve. I'll email you the billing address, since it matches the GPS hit. It's a bullshit name but it seems like the real address for Anita."

"Great, thanks. Do you know where Scugog Township is?"

"By GPS, it's north of Oshawa."

"And Jim, what else do you have for Courtney Love?"

"Her billing address? Let's check here." There was a pause before he came back. "That looks like the real address too. They were smart enough to use fake names but these geniuses both seem to use real addresses."

When Jim read out Love's address, Nastos flipped to the front of the Bannerman file and saw a match. Courtney Love and Jessica Taylor were likely one and the same — or at least they lived at the same place.

"Can you email me everything you have for both of them? Address, everything?"

"It's on the way. You probably already have it."

"Perfect. Thanks."

"Well, you have my number. If you need anything, call anytime. Day or night."

Nastos hung up. He had made rough notes on scrap paper while speaking on the phone and gave the information a once-over. Lindsay Bannerman had called Courtney Love, who was more than likely Jessica Taylor. It wasn't a coincidence. Anita Bonghit was still an unknown, but at least he had an address.

Nastos logged into Lindsay's Facebook account. She had an open profile that listed five hundred and twelve of her closest friends. There were messages and messages from people asking her to come home. Of the names that the cell companies had provided, neither Anita Bonghit nor Courtney Love were listed, but Jessica Taylor was. Nastos looked over at Carscadden, who was still studying the suicide pictures. In his hands was the blown-up image of the rope over the top of the door.

Carscadden shook his head. "Nothing so far. Good pictures, though."

Nastos nodded. "Yeah, the photographer did a good job. Great detail."

A close-up of the knot that had been tied. The woman's weight had gouged the wood. If it had been a solid wooden door, Nastos might not have noticed anything, but it wasn't solid. It was a cheap piece of garbage, built with strips of particle board around the perimeter of the door, with another strip across the middle, like the digital presentation of the number eight. The veneer was thin, revealing everything Nastos needed to see. "Stop there. Yeah, there it is."

Carscadden held the picture farther away. "And we're looking for?"

Nastos grabbed a pen from the desk and used it as a pointer. "She positioned herself in the closet and flipped the rope over the door. She had the length close enough, then went to the other side of the door and tied the rope on the door handle. Then she came back inside the closet, put the rope around her neck and dropped her weight."

"Yeah," Carscadden agreed. "She lifted her feet to hang and choked herself out. After a while, she died."

Nastos pointed at the groove the rope had made over the door. "What's wrong with this picture?"

Carscadden squinted, seeing it. "The groove in the door goes the wrong way. The splintered wood goes backward, not forward."

Nastos summarized. "She didn't sag down to choke herself, she was lifted off of the ground, then the rope was tied off from the other side of the door."

Carscadden studied the picture. "She was killed." He scrolled through the others again. "Minimal claw marks at her neck from trying to get the weight off the rope, no bruises on her arms from banging on the walls. No kick into the drywall in front of her."

Nastos knew he didn't have all of the answers. "Drugged, I don't know. All she thought of was the rope around her neck. She was a user. I don't see any pictures of the closet wall, maybe it *was* smashed in."

"Do you think it was the boyfriend? He killed her, then disappeared?"

Nastos shook his head. "It's always the boyfriend."

Carscadden stood and stretched. "Well, that sucks for her, eh? Listen, buddy, I'm beat. Hopkins and I are going to have an early night tonight, so let's shut this down till tomorrow."

Nastos knew what that meant. "Oh, you two are going to have sex tonight. Good for you."

"What can I say? She gets me home and treats me like a beast of burden. What are you guys doing tonight?"

Nastos was reluctant to say it was family counselling for Josie. It might ruin his mood. "Slow night, I hope. We'll meet up with Jessica and Anita Bonghit tomorrow. I'll just give Jacques a call and give him the good news about Lindsay's mom."

He picked up the phone and dialed Jacques' cell number.

Jacques answered by saying, "Jesus, now what do you want?"

"You just solved a cold case."

"Good for me. Which one?"

"This girl we're looking for, her mom — Tabitha Moreau? It wasn't a suicide. My guess: it was the boyfriend at the time, who bolted. Darius Miner." Nastos explained about the pictures while Jacques went through them on his end. "Tabitha Moreau didn't commit suicide. She was murdered."

6

CRAIG MADE SURE CLAIRE had extra wine at dinner, then told her that he'd follow her up to bed after the third period of the hockey game.

As he sat in the basement office, he listened for the sound of water running in the bathroom. After it stopped, he peeked up the staircase every few minutes until he saw the bedroom light go off. He watched a bit of the game for another fifteen minutes, ensuring that she was sound asleep before he turned off the door chimes and went outside through the basement walk-out.

The car was parked on the far side of the house beside the garage. He had left the handbrake up two notches when he arrived home, so when the car started the headlights would remain dark. Bannerman slid silently into the driver's seat and engaged the ignition. The BMW's three-month-old engine barely made a sound as he crept out of the driveway.

He pressed the remote to open then close the gate, then turned to take Bayview Avenue south to downtown.

It was ten-thirty and he was tired from the wine. He opened the glove box, grabbed a five-hour energy drink and guzzled it down fast, hoping to sober up quicker. He didn't have to worry about work tomorrow, as he had taken the rest of the week off. In the morning he would put on a show of leaving for work, then get a hotel room to sleep away his exhaustion.

The streetwalkers might not be out until midnight, and they moved around. They weren't the same girls every time but most girls tried to make it out on Fridays and Saturdays, the big money nights. They were a different breed of gentleman's company. They were the hardcore drug addicts, homeless or practically homeless, and less attractive discount fare. Bannerman knew he'd have to wait around somewhere for the time to pass. He considered going to the office, then changed his mind. The card swipe system would keep the record. He couldn't even sober up in the underground parking lot, for the same reason. He found a quiet side street, a one-way with houses in darkness — except for the occasional blue blur from a TV screen.

He rolled down his window, put the heat on low and let the car idle. His laptop was in the back seat. He slid it out of its case and powered it up. At least he could play solitaire to while away the time. When the wifi icon turned green, he smiled. An unsecure signal. Perfect. Bannerman forgot about solitaire and got to work.

He started scrolling the escort sites again on RedLight. For the most part, the girls were self-organized by race. Bannerman focused on the Eastern Europeans on local pages. They were most likely to be white girls.

Image after image, naked body after naked body. He began to notice that often the same girl would be in various ads — different poses and outfits, different rates. Just like supermarket chains, they marketed the same products at different price points.

His cell phone had a memo feature and he had begun using it to keep track of the information because there was too much. Too many naked women for anyone to keep track of.

He studied every picture from the escort site before going to the *Toronto Today* website. The only logical search parameter he could think of was geographic. The massage parlours and Asians were north of Sheppard Avenue. There were more places near the airport in Mississauga. He went highway exit by highway exit from Morningside to Highway 7, to the Gardiner. He then checked Hamilton, Brampton, the GTA.

It was all just passing time, reading dirty ads by the women who promised to be dirty girls. Imperfect bodies were twisted, with arched backs, in awkwardly angled, self-snapped pictures. He scrolled the pages slowly. They were like a bouquet of wilted flowers rolling up the screen as he dug further down, the thoughts of their offers and promises at first began to arouse him. Almost instantly, he thought of Lindsay on the streets confused and desperate, and he felt physically ill. It was at that moment that he hated the sliver of darkness that he had felt welling up within himself. He felt ashamed and angry. An image of his wife first leading Lindsay into her new room all those years ago came to him. The wonder on her young face, the hope in her eyes. He was overcome with a desperate longing and reaffirmed his promise to find her at any cost.

When the clock on the radio read midnight, he was sober, alert from the caffeine drinks and ready to get started. He patrolled the streets of Church and Wellesley, noting that most but not all of the "girls" had Adam's apples. The Shuter Street girls were out; nothing interesting there.

It wasn't until his third pass up Parliament Street that his heart began to pound. This girl was young, thin — maybe too thin — leaning into the passenger side of a car. Bannerman quickly ducked from the road into a parking space, leaving his car out wide enough to watch the girl and the driver. She was smiling, her hair down, but in the dark he couldn't tell whether it was blond or dirty blond. She seemed a little reluctant, averting her eyes — maybe he was trying to talk her down too much. If the man had known the strip, studied it as much as Bannerman, he'd just pay whatever she asked. Her beauty was a rarity here and wouldn't last long. She looked like Lindsay.

When she opened the door and climbed inside, Bannerman followed. His heart felt like it had come alive, unable to let her out of his sight. He jotted down the licence plate, just in case, and recorded that it was a tinted-windowed grey Honda Civic.

He followed them to a dark alley, where they parked under a tree that blocked the flickering streetlights.

Bannerman waited a few minutes, then found the nerve to get out of his car slowly, the door closing with just the slightest click.

He approached with quiet steps, cautious, and angled toward the passenger side. He crept closer and closer. When the palm of his hand touched the cold body of the car, the sensation of touching a rigid corpse crept up his arm.

And the car quivered. It jostled slightly as if by unwanted contact, as if it could feel him intruding. He was low, his ass to the ground, only peeking up to catch another glimpse of her. He had to know.

When the driver's door burst open, Bannerman thought he was imagining it. The man — Mediterranean, with broad, thick shoulders — looked enormous when he came around the car with outstretched arms, his face a death mask. Bannerman had little time to rear back. He tripped over a parking curb, hands scuffing the damp pavement, and found himself jammed against a recycling dumpster.

"You some kind of fucking freak?" The man didn't wait for an answer. Bannerman thrust his arms up to cover his face as the man grabbed the collar of his shirt and began pummelling him. He squirmed and twisted, not to avoid the strikes — no, he wanted to catch a glimpse of the girl as she ran away. He shouted, "Wait, come back! Wait!"

◻ ◻ ◻

Tuesday, October 23

LINDSAY, REBECCA AND THE OTHER GIRL — HER NAME WAS ANDREA — awoke to the sound of heavy footsteps creaking across the floor. Their slow, measured tempo made Lindsay's blood run cold with fear even though the man hadn't hurt them . . . yet. The girls slept together, as far from the hatch as possible, which meant that the first footstep they heard each morning was right over their heads.

The joists creaked and sank under his weight. The man rolled the piano aside; dust drifted down from the ceiling. Every time more dust fell, she felt more forgotten, more buried, more dead. The damp caused her to cough. Her water bottle was empty and she was reluctant to ask for more.

As the hatch peeled back, blinding natural light shot through the semidarkness, revealing that it was mid-morning in the real world. The ladder gave a rattle reminiscent of a steel anchor being released into the ocean. Silence. Then footsteps. Steel-toed construction boots, insulated overalls, work gloves and this time a balaclava all came down the ladder, slowly into view.

He was carrying a plastic bag from Shoppers Drug Mart. Before tossing it to Andrea he removed a piece of paper and handed it to Lindsay. *Another one of his stupid handwritten notes.* She snatched the paper and read it while Andrea went through the shopping bag. Tampons, baby wipes and toilet paper. He stood waiting for Lindsay to read the note out loud, as was protocol. There were no secrets here among the girls. *Is this everything you need?*

"Yes," Andrea replied.

The man turned and left, taking with him the bathroom area garbage can filled with used tampons and pads. He climbing up, pulling the ladder away and slamming the hatch shut. Andrea went over to the toilet to freshen up. The toilet was in the corner nearest the night light. There was an iron tap mounted to the ceiling with a drain under it for a shower. They had analyzed the jailkeeper's behaviour countless times. He'd been nicknamed the Mute, Fuck-Face, the Warden and other names. No matter which name they used, it was spoken with fear and hatred, making it clear who they were talking about.

Is he going to keep us forever? What does he want with us? If there's a ransom, why don't my parents just pay it? Don't they want me back? It was no use, it just went in circles.

Andrea came back over to the warmth of the other girls. "I think that puts me at twenty-two days here, maybe more."

Lindsay said, "We have to get out. We can't sit around and die of old age."

Rebecca was finally coming around. "I don't think old age is what's going to get us." Her voice trailed off. She was trying to make sense of the situation and didn't like where her mind was taking her. "Nearly a month here. There's no sign he's going to let us go. I think he has plans, but it's like he's waiting for something."

Lindsay said, "It must be ransom. He hasn't raped us. We have no idea what he looks like. He could let us go after he gets his money and we'd never be able to identify him."

Andrea pulled out one of the baby wipes and began wiping her face clean. "My parents don't have any money."

"Mine do." Lindsay said. "He'd know if he checked my driver's license. I live in the Bridle Path."

Rebecca said, "Are you serious?"

Lindsay nodded.

Footsteps creaked again. He'd be getting breakfast ready. Bottles of Gatorade with mini dry cereal boxes. He always made sure he collected everything he brought in. Lindsay hiked her pants up. There was no use denying that she was losing weight. Her waist was two inches smaller. *What I'd do for a cheeseburger and fries.*

She glanced at the toilet and a plan came to her.

Lindsay peeled her shirt off and ran her fingers through her hair. Weeks of built-up grease from the lack of soap made it impossible to thicken it up.

Andrea asked, "What are you doing?"

"We're getting out of here. Andrea, go get the lid from the top of the toilet tank and put it down there." She pointed to the floor. "Cover it up with one of the blankets. We're going to smash it over his head."

Rebecca said, "We can't overpower him."

Lindsay considered taking her pants off to really sell it, but she wanted the protection of jeans during the fight. "We're going to distract him like we planned."

Andrea asked, "Planned?"

Lindsay conceded, "Okay, like how we talked about. Then I'm going to smash him over the head with that porcelain lid."

The hatch opened and the ladder rattled down. She refused to accept imprisonment. Lindsay reached back and gripped the weapon, glancing to the two girls, who were exchanging terrified expressions. With pleading eyes, they both looked at her and shook their heads "no."

7

AS THE WARDEN DESCENDED, he took a cursory glance around the opening of the hatch. As he climbed down farther, he checked the corners of the room, where any surprises might come from. The dark nooks, where threats could hide, were the toughest parts of the room to see from the entry point. Secure in the knowledge that they were all accounted for, he reached back up, and brought the breakfast tray down.

He stood straight and turned to the girls. They were ready for him in the established way, except one girl had chosen to take her top off. He noted the ugliness of the lumps of flesh hanging from her frail body. And he could smell the fear.

Lindsay spoke. "I know you won't answer," she began. "But we're really hungry."

He shook his head. They had no idea about the meaning of the word hungry. They needed to get out more, to other countries where you had to fight for one meal a day. He came closer, put the tray down and began to turn away. He had no interest in their pleading.

"Wait, wait, just one sec."

He sensed that she had moved toward him, just a step, but that could not be tolerated. A message would have to be sent.

He paused to let her finish.

"Listen, like I said. We're all hungry. I know I'm young and inexperienced. But, listen — this is tough to say in front of the other girls." Lindsay paused, trying to sound sincere, trying to conjure what would sound authentic but also match what he might expect to hear. "But . . . it's been a while since I've been with a boy." Rather than trying to read his behaviour to see if the act was working, she tried to produce tears. It wasn't hard, not with the stench from the dirt floor and their unwashed bodies, let alone the prospect of dying in this place. "Anyway, if you'd be interested, I wouldn't mind."

She traced fingers from her right hand down her bare chest and tried to smile.

They were all attractive. It had been a while since he had taken a woman, and when he did, she looked like these girls. And it wasn't really sex; it was more like punishment. He glanced around the room, searching for anything out of place, anything that could be used as a weapon. Nothing. With a gloved hand, balancing the tray of cereal on the other arm, he slowly gave her the finger.

Lindsay knelt down and pulled the other girls down by their arms so they were next to her. "We talked about it last night." She looked at the other girls. "We're all hungry." Lindsay reached her arms out to him. "Come here, I'll make you feel good. Please, I'm hungry."

He looked back over his shoulder and shook his head. Maybe next time. Besides, he had a new prisoner waiting upstairs, someone more to his liking.

He put the tray down on the ground and turned toward the ladder. It was a silver aluminum A-frame that might not hold the weight of both him and the new addition. He noticed a shadow cross over it; then he heard the footsteps charging toward him. He was able to get an elbow up, but the weight of the porcelain lid smashing over his head carried enough momentum to bring him to his knees. His head felt like an egg that had been dropped to the floor, fractured, with aching fault lines.

He tried to get up, stumbling forward and making a noise. His amateur assailant swung again, with both hands as hard as she could. The flat part of the lip struck the back of his head, the porcelain shattering. It would have done more damage had it stayed intact. He dropped to the ground and rolled onto his back.

Lindsay turned a fragment in her hand, overjoyed to see it was razor sharp, and lunged at him. Though the Warden was dazed, he still kicked her away easily and staggered to his feet. He shook his head to clear the cobwebs, then counter-charged. She couldn't back up fast enough. The Warden shoved her backward and punched the right side of her face twice, then grabbed her by the shoulders and shoved her back into a wall. She stumbled, tripped and her head slammed into the concrete. Rebecca had run over, aimed for his balls and kicked with all of her strength. She managed to graze him, but adrenaline masked the pain and her kick only made him angrier. Knowing he could easily outpower and outfight all of the girls at the same time he paused a moment, sucking in air for the next round of action. When he rose to his feet, Rebecca began to back away, her hands up in front of her, pleading for mercy. Andrea had been cowering in the corner the whole time.

The Warden produced the cattle prod from his belt and when he hit Rebecca with the voltage, she squealed like a beaten pig. He couldn't suppress the smile he had under the mask and giggled like a little boy playing. He crept toward Andrea and while she begged for mercy, he kicked her to the ground. He turned to Lindsay, the leader of the uprising. As she struggled to get to her feet, he smashed the prod over her head, ripping her scalp open. A red, sticky coating of blood streamed through the blond hair and down the back her neck.

The Warden stood in the middle of the room for a moment and eyed the captives. They wouldn't try that again — not with what he had done to them, and certainly not with what they still had to come.

Andrea crawled over to Lindsay, staying close to the wall. Andrea was the only one with any brains. He couldn't tell if he was bleeding from the head or not. His balls ached, and he felt nauseous.

The next captive would be tending to that issue; the girls could all sit together and maybe offer each other technical pointers. He grunted and went upstairs, leaving the hatch open and pulling the ladder back out. He lumbered out the back door to the porch.

◌ ◌ ◌

THE STRONG FALL SUN CREPT ITS WAY UP IN THE SKY, STILL OBSCURED by forty-foot evergreens that ran around the property line, guarding the shack. Any person entering the backyard had to either walk up to the front door or cross the treeline, both of which would leave trespassers in an open shooting gallery for some distance.

Chavez loved the smell of these evergreens. They dripped sap that to him smelled like Canada. Long-dead pine needles coated the backyard, starved from green to orange. Beyond the trees, at the back of the property, ran a small stream. During the spring melt, it became a torrent of white water and violent undertows. Now, in mid-fall, the water had become perfectly still, like a dormant ana-conda. It reminded Chavez of the *encantados* of Brazil — mythical shape-shifting serpents that had stalked him in his childhood. A lone crow, black as onyx, sat in a tree and watched the stream.

When he was ten, he had been taken from his home by a United Nations child protection worker. She was tall, white, thin, with long blond hair. He had never seen such a being in his life. She led him out of his house by the hand and told him that he couldn't be with his parents anymore because they had gone with God. She brought him to another house in the village. They were a family he knew vaguely, because they had two boys of their own who had bullied him many times.

Whenever he could escape from his new home, he'd wander up and down the dusty streets, overhung with jungle trees and lined with wooden shacks made from scrap wood, rock and poured mortar, searching for his true mother and father. In his imaginary world, his parents were waiting for him in a big house filled with toys. If he could only find them, he would be free from the man he was forced to call *Tio* — Uncle.

There would be no more slaving in the woodshop, crafting junk to sell to tourists. He wandered the village, speaking to everyone from policemen and soldiers to vagabonds and banditos — all strangers.

Tio had used the folklore of the *encantados* to control him and keep him from wandering — but it was too late. After one of Chavez' failed excursions to find answers he overheard a businessman speaking to his wife. As they walked hand in hand out of a village bar, the old man whispered to her that "the worthless little runt will be looking a long time," that his father had shot his mother in a drunken rage when he found she had tried to sell their son — him — for much-needed money, then shot himself after an altercation with the police. "That little boy will find nothing but misery in the truth," said the man. "The boy is like a *cuervo perdido*," a lost crow.

Now he knew why he had been moved in with this family, and forced to call the man Tio. Tio also used the *encantados* to keep him silent about the nature of their relationship. At fourteen, after years of secrets and abuse, he realized that no invisible man in the sky named God was coming to save him. Soon after the Christian god was condemned to the same fate as the forgotten gods of Mount Olympus, so fell fictitious devils and *encantados*. He came to understand that gods and devils were nothing more than mythological scapegoats used by men. Men like Tio, who manipulated and preyed on the young and naïve. The world was a place where men helped men, or men hurt men; ghost stories, like those that told of the *encantados*, were for children. Chavez had been through too much to be considered a child any longer. This realization became a launching point for action when he decided to free himself.

After serving three years in the Colombian army, Chavez returned home with a rifle and a mission. Tio, his wife and his sons were the first in a long line of betrayers and complacent enablers to hear his rifle speak his rage. When Tio had reached for a knife, Chavez had chopped his hand off with the machete that hung from his belt. There was less blood than he had hoped. Tio begged for his life before taking the final bullet in his pleading, pathetic face.

Only the strong survived in the world. For the weak, like his mother who had tried to sell him, and even for his abusers, he had nothing but contempt. The only one to escape was the blond child protection worker, who was busy throwing other orphans to sadistic predators. And one day she too would go screaming to her imaginary god.

Young Chavez had dragged the four bodies out into the backyard and counted the crows that fed on their flesh. Their caws, their earnest screeches calling others to come and enjoy the feast, was like nothing he had ever heard before. In broad daylight, they picked into Tio's eyes and drove their beaks into his fat protruding tongue. Chavez vowed that day that he would never again be anyone's victim.

The call of a crow pulled him from his daydream. A tree bough dropped, then sprang up as the bird took flight. Chavez looked down at the boy who lay unconscious in the shade. He was still covered by a painter's sheet that had dropped away from his face. Smooth perfect skin, blond hair, hazel eyes partially open in the half-sleep of anesthesia.

Chavez inhaled a long pull of air with his nostrils. Underneath the boy's Axe body spray and hair gel, he could smell his sweat. He could smell what a dog smells when it remembers a person forever.

He heaved the boy's limp body over his shoulder. His footsteps, although heavier now under the extra weight, were still sure and effortless. Arriving at the hatch, he dropped down the ladder and gingerly extended a foot while bracing the body with one arm on the nearby wall. He started down into the basement, ducking around the floor as he angled down into the cool, dark room.

The girls were all together now, using the tampons and pads to clean the blood away. Tears and dirt caked their faces. He smiled under his mask. He dumped the drugged boy at their feet, stopping to make sure he was breathing. They were the unwanted. If they had been cared for, properly coached, they would not have fallen into the hands of a man like him. He stood tall over the boy until all eyes settled on him; then he did something he had not done before: he spoke.

"For what you did, one of you bitches is going to die." He looked at Lindsay and removed the mask so she could see him smile.

NASTOS MET CARSCADDEN AT
the office at nine-thirty. They had only two names to check
out; it looked like it was going to be a quick day. They sat into
Carscadden's Ford Escape and headed out for the morning.

Carscadden shifted into drive. "First stop is Jessica Taylor, I
take it?"

"Jessica Taylor. Yeah, I'll put the address in the GPS."

"Let's just go up through town: north traffic won't be too bad."

"Sure thing, we have all day. Besides, I doubt she's an early riser."

Carscadden stopped at a red light and leaned over to get his
sunglasses out of the glovebox. Nastos caught the smell.

"Jesus, boy, you take a little nip out of your flask this morning?"

"What?"

"You okay to drive, for fuck's sake?"

"I had a small swig to finish off a bottle for the recycling bin.
You my mother now?"

Nastos smiled. "Yeah, wouldn't want to keep the recycling guys
waiting."

Carscadden's hands tightened on the wheel but he remained
silent. Nastos decided not to press the issue for the rest of the drive.
He'd let it go for now, but he'd keep an eye out for a problem
resurfacing.

Jessica's address came up as a row house; Carscadden parked a short distance down the street.

Flemingdon was a notoriously bad area. A maze of red-brick and brownpanel townhouses lined the private roadways on both sides. From where they stood Nastos could see that a few residences had cracked windows; more had bags of garbage left out front. Near the laneway entrance into the townhomes on the right, there was a dumpster overflowing with garbage — it stank from fifty paces. There wasn't an automobile in sight born in the current decade, and many had expired val-tags from years ago. Most people here would be on drug squad watch sheets and street checks. Claire Bannerman might say that this was where the other half lived.

They had gotten out of the car and locked it before Carscadden realized he'd forgotten his BlackBerry on the dash. Moments later, the device safely in Carscadden's pocket, they began their search for Jessica's house. As they turned a corner and began walking down the main driveway, Nastos noticed a Toronto Police cruiser parked at the far end of the complex.

Carscadden checked his BlackBerry for the address. "That's too far down. Jessica's just here on the left."

"Good. The fewer cops, the faster this will go."

A brown Chevy Impala pulled in off of the street and began driving behind them at a crawl. Nastos tried to ignore it. He found the number they were looking for and had started up the driveway when the car drove up to the curb behind them and jerked to a stop. The passenger window slid down and a thick freckled hand waved them over. "As I live and breathe — Steve Nastos."

Nastos stiffened at first, then relaxed as his mind searched to link a face to the voice. He turned and approached the car's window with Carscadden following. Nastos recognized Detective Brian "Hollywood" Dennehy. No one ever referred to him as Hollywood except himself. Dennehy was a thirty-year vet who considered himself a movie star and never went anywhere without his partner, Brad Byrne. Byrne would be the obscured man in the passenger seat.

Nastos smiled a greeting at Dennehy. "Got yourself a body up at the end of the street there?"

"Yeah, looks like an OD." Dennehy poked his head out the window with an uncontainable smile. "Here's a better question. What the hell are you doing here, revoking someone's car insurance?" The obscured mass in the passenger seat shook and laughed.

"Can't you tell by the suit? I've gone Mormon. We're offering multiple wives if you sign up today."

Dennehy's grin turned into a scowl. "You and your stupid fucking jokes, Nastos. Good riddance."

Nastos visualized his fist mashing into Dennehy's face. It was far from the first time he'd done so — only now he didn't have to worry about getting demoted or transferred to the traffic unit. He clenched his fists. Carscadden grabbed him by the upper arm but Nastos broke free easily and forced his way into Dennehy's face.

"Why don't you get out of the car, Dennehy? Stretch your legs a little."

Dennehy pulled the door handle and barged out, Nastos stepping deftly to the side of the swinging door. Byrne bolted out of his side of the car and came around. Dennehy and Byrne had the same crewcuts, thick bellies and dark suits. Carscadden squeezed between Byrne and Nastos.

Dennehy and Nastos were now nose to nose. The other man was taller, peering down, his face flushed. "Here I am, tough guy. You've got a big mouth. Now take your shot."

Carscadden had to put both of his hands on Nastos' shoulders to pull him back from Dennehy.

Dennehy smiled. "That's the second time this lawyer has saved your ass."

Still staring at Dennehy, Nastos let Carscadden de-escalate the situation.

"C'mon, Nastos, he's not worth shit. Let it go."

His eyes still locked on Dennehy's, Nastos' lips curled in a slow smile that would make the hair on the back of anyone's neck stand on end. "Some other time, Dennehy."

"I don't have time for pieces of shit like you. And hey, Inspector Koche sends his regards. Bet you didn't know he made inspector, courtesy of you."

Koche was the cop who had had Nastos charged with murder. The news that Koche had gotten promoted by ruining Nastos' life only made him angrier. "All the more reason to crawl under his desk, eh, Dennehy? Good for you. You're blowing a real somebody."

Dennehy produced a middle finger and slid back into the car. Byrne went back to the passenger side, sneered at Nastos and spit on the ground toward him. After Byrne poured himself in, Dennehy hit the gas, squealing the tires as the Impala peeled down the lane of row houses.

Carscadden said, "Saves me having to tell him to screw off."

Nastos straightened his jacket and tie. "Save it for next time."

Carscadden began walking for the townhouse and Nastos followed. Nastos remarked, "You know, he's a devout Catholic. Goes to church all the time."

Carscadden scowled down the laneway. "Guess there's no commandment stopping him from being an asshole. And what's the deal with those guys? Same suits, same hair, same attitudes. Tweedle Dumb and Tweedlefucking Dumber."

They stopped at the small alcove by the front door. A rusted black mailbox hung on the brick wall, its lid stuck open.

"They've worked together for years and years. They've always gotten transferred together — that never happens for anybody."

"They have friends higher up?"

"They must. They're like Frick and Frack. They spend their time off together, get their haircuts together —"

Carscadden's face contorted as he considered this. "Heterosexual life partners."

"Yeah, that sounds about right."

Carscadden pressed the doorbell. "Well, if we start finishing each other's sentences —"

Nastos pulled a few letters out of the mailbox, checking for the name Jessica Taylor. They were phone bills and flyers for pizza places. He dumped them back in.

There was no sound from inside, so Nastos pounded on the door. "Don't worry, if we start finishing each other's sentences, I'll push you in front of a subway car."

Nastos was about to peek in the side window when the door shook and rattled open.

"Who are you?" The woman was white, skinny, with hair bleached blond except for three inches of brown and grey roots, held back in a bun. Her face was red and blotchy with yellow areas, like the back side of wallpaper.

Carscadden said, "We're not cops. We're looking for Jessica Taylor, hoping she can help us out."

"With what?" Her weight shifted to one side, causing her bony hips to poke out the top of her white track pants. Her fake D-cups rocked from side to side in her tank top.

Carscadden held up a photograph. "This is Lindsay. She's seventeen now."

Jessica looked at the picture. "She's pretty. Sorry, I haven't seen her."

"But you've been speaking with her for at least four months. She's been calling your phone. You've probably called hers."

Jessica bit her lip for a second, then raised a defiant chin, brushing a few stray hairs back. "We met up on Facebook and I told her some stories about her mom."

Carscadden shook his head, "Heavily redacted, I hope."

"Huh?" Her face twisted at the foreign word. "She should know about her mom if she asks, don't you think?"

Carscadden tried to poke his nose in the door. "We don't give a shit if you've talked with her, we just want to know she's safe. Is she here now?"

Jessica put her arm up to stop him. "No, she's not."

While Carscadden was talking, Nastos focused solely on her body language. She seemed mostly honest, but only mostly. Nastos asked, "If you were Lindsay, would you take off? She had it pretty good with the Bannermans."

Jessica scoffed. "Oh, sure she did. Private school, designer clothes and all the sex she could handle from the old man. Yeah, she had it really good."

Nastos shared a look with Carscadden. "He was having sex with her?"

Jessica brushed her hair back again. "She never came right out and said it. Just the warning signs were there. He had this way of looking at her. My stepdad used to look at me like that. And that was when I left too."

Nastos wasn't going to discuss the allegation with Carscadden while Jessica was standing there. It was best to show confidence in her, to build trust and get her to say more.

"Listen, we'd appreciate it if we could just come in, look around and make sure she's either not here, or that she's safe. She doesn't have to go back if she doesn't want to."

"Yeah, I know. But she's not here." She looked Nastos up and down, reluctantly stepping back from the door. "Go ahead. Look. She's not here."

It wasn't so bad that they had to hold their breath. Jessica's place was cluttered, and the threadbare carpets looked as if they had never seen a vacuum. Stale cigarette smoke clung to every surface, adding another layer of despair to the already derelict condition of the house. Walking stirred dust up from the floor and the sound of compacting sand ground under each step where there was carpet. There were two bedrooms, one of which had been turned into a sewing room full of tacky quilts and pillows. A sewing mannequin stood in the corner, a tape measure draped around its headless form. The second bedroom was where Jessica plied her other trade. There was a plain mattress on the floor and a chair in one corner next to a plastic garbage bin. A night stand stood in the other corner, likely full of sexual accoutrements that Nastos preferred not to contemplate. There was no sign of a teenage girl living there.

67

Nastos asked, "So, Jessica, she found you on Facebook, or you found her?"

"What do you mean?" Jessica produced a cigarette and placed it in her mouth, leaving it to dangle annoyingly when she spoke.

Carscadden said, "You contested the adoption to the Bannermans. You've known Lindsay a long time."

"She tracked me down. She said she wanted to know about her mother, that was all."

Nastos asked, "You know where she would be?"

Jessica grabbed a lighter from the top of the refrigerator and lit her smoke. "No." She took a long hard draw, sucking the smoke so hard her cheeks caved in, and exhaled in their direction. "And you two can leave now." She pinched the filter between two fingers.

Nastos waved his hand in front of his face to waft away the smoke. "Does Lindsay know what you do for a living?"

Jessica put her hands on her hips. "Screw you."

Carscadden thanked her for her time, then he and Nastos left. Dennehy was still parked down at the end of the row houses. Carscadden broke the silence as they walked back to the car. "How old would you say she was?"

Nastos considered it. "Maybe close to forty."

Carscadden shuddered. "Whatever happened to forty being the new thirty? She makes forty look like the new one hundred. And legs like pipe cleaners."

"With her, it's not the years, it's the mileage."

Carscadden slid into the driver's side and started the car. "What's your take on her allegations against Bannerman?"

Nastos slammed his door shut. "I have serious doubts about anything Jessica would say. Bannerman was pretty cool about things when we were there. You know him better than I do; what do you think?"

Carscadden drove out of the townhouse complex and turned toward the Don Valley Parkway. "If he had been assaulting her, there might be emails, statements to friends, maybe some kind of evidence at the house."

Nastos knew where Carscadden was going with this. "If he's a molester, or a kiddie porn guy, from my experience, there would be images or files on his computer. He'd have a private hard drive where he'd keep it all. That what those guys do. He could have made and distributed files. There would be ways to find out. But —" Nastos stopped himself. "I've been wrong before, but with Bannerman, I just don't think he's the type."

Carscadden agreed. "But we have to at least ask him about it, right after we look into number two on the list. I don't know about you, Anita Bonghit."

9

THE ADDRESS FOR ANITA
Bonghit was north of Oshawa. It was a long drive, up the 404 to
the 401, east to Simcoe Street in Oshawa, then north, all the way
through town into Scugog Township. Toronto's metropolitan high-
rises became low-density sprawl. The flat geography of Oshawa
near the lake changed as they entered its urban south-end ghetto of
derelict buildings housing methadone clinics and Cash Converters.
Then the landscape evolved into million-dollar historic buildings and
subdivisions.

Once they drove out of Oshawa, there were rolling hills and
rural estate bungalows, with long, winding driveways lined by
maples. Toronto had transformed into something from *Anne of
Green Gables* in a little over an hour. They turned on a concession
road and found the house on the south side, atop a ridge. At night
the city lights would line the horizon, just before the great lake.

The house wasn't dilapidated or cramped by its neighbours. It
was a grey brick with dated white aluminum trim over the windows matching the garage door and deck railings. It looked like the
kind of place where an elderly couple would live. Parked beside the
garage, with no other vehicle in sight, was an ATV. Carscadden
turned the ignition off and pulled out the key. "Time for a Bonghit."

Nastos let Carscadden lead the way to the front door, hanging
back and surveying the countryside.

Carscadden hit the doorbell. "How in the hell would Lindsay have met up with this person?"

Nastos brought a hand up to his forehead and squinted into the bright sun. It might have been an acre of fenced land, backing onto two acres of crown land filled with maples, birch and evergreens. Peeking around the side of the house, he saw a sixty-foot-long Quonset-style greenhouse. There was ample room for growing pot, and Bonghit's hothouse, or pot house, would be perfect for drying and packaging.

Nastos pointed to a basement window that was blacked out. "Who blacks out their windows?"

Carscadden shook his head. "And we are in harvest season."

No one was coming to the door. Nastos made sure there were no obvious surveillance cameras as they checked around the back of the property.

Nastos sniffed, but smelled only fertilizer. There were no signs of neighbours. Two squirrels chased each other through the back-yard. The road was quiet.

Carscadden said, "Jesus, Nastos, let's just look and get it over with, I can see the curiosity is practically killing you."

"Yeah. Not being a cop has its advantages. No rules of evidence. I can do an illegal search and the evidence won't be tossed out. The worst I can get is a ninety-dollar trespass ticket. No reports, no supervisors with grade-four reading levels telling you they don't understand what I wrote."

Nastos started toward the greenhouse, coming around the house and starting into the yard. Nastos noticed that, despite the direct sunlight, there was still dew on the lawn, wetting their shoes and pants. When he looked down he saw worse news and pointed at it for Carscadden to see. "Watch your step — dog shit."

"Great. These shoes cost two hundred. Could you imagine if —"

Nastos later recalled that the scariest part about the whole thing was that the dog never barked. It never tried to call other dogs or alert its master. It had basically decided that it could take them both on its own. And no wonder, really — it was a one-hundred-and-fifty-pound Rottweiler. It was fast for a dog its size. It came from around the Quonset hut, running full speed in a wide arc, like a base runner passing third and coming into home. Only the front incisors showed through the tight, vicious snarl. Small, beady black eyes, white froth on its chin.

It didn't take months of watching *Dog Whisperer* or extensive study of animal psychology to understand that to stay standing there with looks of horror frozen on their faces was suicide. Both Carscadden and Nastos turned at the same time in a panicked, frantic sprint for the SUV, parked a short eternity away.

Nastos rounded the corner first, cutting the angle, which put Carscadden firmly in second place. And as the saying goes, you don't have to be faster than the dog — you just have to be faster than your friend.

Carscadden was taken down hard, but to his credit he never turned to look back. The goal was the car, and second best was not an option. When teeth closed on his ankle, he kicked and twisted his left leg while he crawled forward, scrambling quickly to his feet. Thank god it wasn't going for his throat, he thought wildly, or the release of blood would have made a mess of his shirt. Nastos had made it to the Escape and popped the truck while Carscadden kicked and flailed.

Nastos rounded the car armed with a fire extinguisher. A blast of cold, thick air sent the dog retreating. White carbon dioxide powder coated the car, the dog, the driveway. The dog stopped only ten feet away then started barking with a thick heavy voice, thundering through the air like the bass drum at a Led Zeppelin concert.

Nastos shouted, "Move!" and Carscadden clearly thought it was the best idea he'd heard all day. He bolted for the car, leaving a shoe and sock behind. Nastos retreated to the SUV, went around to the driver's side and closed the door after himself.

Carscadden panted. "Fucking thing was going to rip my foot off."

Nastos hit the gas, revving the engine. The dog didn't budge; it had retrieved Carscadden's shoe and sat on the driveway with its one-hundred-dollar trophy in its slobbering mouth.

Nastos spoke almost to himself. "Well, that answers that question."

"What?" Carscadden asked.

"What's black and tan and looks good on a lawyer? A Rottweiler."

"Funny guy. You know, if you'd taken the corner a little wider I might have made it. Asshole." Carscadden checked his foot and ankle. There was no blood, just thick, frothy saliva. He tried to wipe it off with a lone napkin he found in the glove box, but the serviette was quickly saturated.

Nastos had to smile. Carscadden's sense of humor was at its best when he was pissed off. Nastos saw a King Cab pickup truck that resembled a garbage scow — mostly green and rust, and a door didn't match — driving down the road. It slowed at the end of the driveway, then turned in. There were two more Rottweilers in the pickup's bed. The truck stopped beside them. The sneering driver was so big he had to pry himself out.

Nastos opened the window for Carscadden. "You can't get out looking like that. Stay here. I'll talk to him."

"Sure." He pointed to the dog. "And tell him the Land Shark can keep the shoe."

The driver was six-four, close to three hundred pounds, in his fifties, with a dirty grey-white beard, deep wrinkles and red patchy skin. He might have been a redhead at one time in his life. The Rottweiler with the shoe in its mouth wiggled over to him, the shoe dripping with slobber. It ignored Nastos when he slowly exited the car.

Nastos stuck his hand out. "Steve Nastos."

The Rottweilers in the back of the truck began pacing, then jumped down on their own and lay down near their master's feet. The huge man didn't seem very interested as he looked Nastos up and down with apprehension. "Fine. What do you want?"

"I've been hired to find a girl, Lindsay Bannerman. Don't suppose you know a person named Anita Bonghit?"

The man's eyes briefly flashed surprise, then returned to anger. Nastos knew he'd found his guy.

The man's face squinted into a fake confused expression. "Who?"

"You have each other's phone numbers."

Bonghit didn't answer right away. He seemed to be stalling. He pulled the shoe out of the dog's mouth and inspected it. It was soaked and full of puncture marks. "Well, your buddy's not going to want that back." He put it back in the dog's mouth like he was sticking a plug in a bathtub.

Carscadden shouted over. "You can keep it."

Nastos smiled.

Bonghit turned back to Nastos. "Remind me how I know her? Your friend, I take it?"

"Sort of. Her parents hired us to find her."

"Parents? How old is she? What kind of guy do you think I am?" He glanced from Nastos to Carscadden, going from shock to anger.

Nastos produced a photograph of Lindsay. "This is her."

Bonghit looked the picture over a few times. "I haven't heard from her in a while. She's sure as hell not here."

"Mind if I have a quick look around so I can cross you off the list?"

The man's voice boomed. "Yeah, I do mind. I said she's not here." He took a step toward Nastos. "Why don't you go before Daisy here decides she needs a matching shoe?" The dog perked up at hearing its name, then turned and sat next to the man so she could see Nastos better.

Nastos didn't react to the challenge. "I don't know if you have kids, but there's a guy out there who just wants his daughter back. Is there anything you can suggest to help us find her?"

"Yeah. I suggest you quit wasting your time here."

Nastos pulled out a business card and handed it to the man, who ripped it from his hand and stuffed it in his pocket without looking.

"Okay, bye." Bonghit said it like he was saying "Fuck off." He stood there glaring at Nastos, waiting for him to avert his gaze first and leave, like a submissive dog.

Nastos didn't waver. "You sold her pot. Was that it?"

Bonghit didn't even flinch. "Yeah, the odd time, for her migraines."

"How'd you meet up with her?"

"Craigslist. Happy?"

"I'd be happier if I knew where she was."

Carscadden pulled himself up on the open window and sat up on the frame so he could look over the roof of the car. By the look on his face, he was still furious. When the dog came over to bring his shoe back, he waved her off and said, "Keep it, Daisy. The score's one–nothing for the dog." He turned to Bonghit. "So what's your deal, anyways?"

Bonghit wasn't impressed. "Watch yourself."

"Who the hell are you? You live up here at the North Pole with your team of satanic Rottweilers, coming down to the city to sell pot to the good girls and boys like Ganja Claus."

He didn't smile. "That's funny."

Carscadden kept going. "Yeah, well, tell you what, Ganja" — Daisy came over again, and he shooed her away — "we have this girl to find, so do you know anything or don't you?"

Bonghit eyed Carscadden up and down, finally beginning to soften. "Tell you what," he said. "I remember her. She's pretty, tough to forget. The fact is she's a good girl and if she's gone, like you guys say, then it's probably bad news. All she did was pot, nothing serious. I don't even think she drank."

Nastos asked, "Was anyone bothering her or did you get a read on her relationship with her parents?"

"Just the usual stuff with parents. There was some woman, though — not her mom, maybe an aunt."

Nastos asked, "Jessica?"

"Yeah, I banged her every time I was in town."

"You paid her in pot for sex?"

"No, I paid her in pot to shut up and never tell me what to do with my life. Anyways, she was putting some kind of pressure on your girl, I don't know what for. All I did was give her a good price on a quarter-ounce. You can check out the greenhouse if you want, you'll only find drying plants."

Nastos checked with Carscadden, who looked satisfied. "No, that's fine. Thanks for your help."

Bonghit shook his head. "Ganja Claus. Nice one."

Nastos put the car in drive. They remained silent, Carscadden rubbing his ankle, Nastos with his hands resting on the steering wheel. As they came down from the rolling hills and returned to the flat urban cityscape of Oshawa, Nastos felt more comfortable away from the country and back in the confines of the urban landscape.

Carscadden asked, "What's your take on Bonghit?"

"He had no idea what we were talking about. He was genuinely confused. If anything, he made me want to know more about the pressure Jessica was putting on her. Maybe Jessica saw her as a meal ticket — access to guilt money."

Carscadden thought it through out loud. "Guilt for escaping the thug's life while Jessica lived on the margins. I dunno, feels kinda weak."

Nastos checked his blind spot and moved into the middle lane to get around a slower driver. "Yeah, you're right. But it makes me want to look for more all the same. Jessica is hiding a lot more than Ganja Claus."

Carscadden asked, "What about Bannerman?"

Nastos thought for a moment. "Good point. Bannerman probably paid Jessica off during the adoption process. He might be pissed if she slimed her way back into their lives, but that would make him mad at her, not Lindsay."

Carscadden reached into the back seat and grabbed a water bottle. He offered one to Nastos, who waved it off. "Nastos, if he was hurting Lindsay, and she was ready to talk, let's say he killed her — I just don't see that. He just didn't seem the type."

"Yeah, I know."

"Or if he was mistreating her in some way, abusing her, maybe she just ran away and in twenty years she'll surface in the Yukon, waiting tables."

Nastos had worked many cases just like that in the Sexual Assault Unit. The worst cases of abuse never came from 911 calls. Instead, the women just appeared at the front door of a police station, often years or decades after the abuse had happened, and dumped the saddest, most horrific stories of exploitation on the unsuspecting front desk officer. It was a strong possibility.

Nastos dialed Rod, the Bell Canada contact.

"Rod here."

"Yeah, Rod, it's Nastos calling."

"Hey, Nastos, what's up?"

"That Taylor woman I asked about, did you clone her phone for me?"

"Yeah, she's wired. Why, you think you have something?"

Nastos checked with Carscadden to make sure he was listening. "Yeah, we were at her place today asking about Lindsay. If she knows anything, she may have incriminated herself on her phone by now. I was wondering if someone could email me recordings of all of her phones calls so far today. I'd like to listen to them."

Rod asked, "You think dropping by was enough to get her talking?"

"Oh, sure. Cops call it tickling the wires. Whenever cops have a situation like this, a disappearance or kidnapping, we tap the phones, then release the reward money for anyone with information. It always gets people talking if they have something to say."

"Sure, I'll have it sent to me, then I'll forward it to you."

"Perfect."

"Still need the phone tap for the next week, Nastos?"

"Yeah, we better play it safe. Thanks, Rod."

"Anytime."

Nastos had nearly the same conversation with Jim from Rogers about the trace on Bonghit's phone. He thought back to how many police investigations he had led that were stymied at every turn by the telecom companies. Only the influence of Bannerman had them behaving co-operatively. If either Bonghit or Taylor had said anything about Lindsay, he'd know about it right away. Hopefully

Rod or Jim wouldn't listen to the audio files. If there was bad news, it had to be confirmed and delivered the proper way, not by over-anxious friends who thought they were helping.

When Nastos saw the Oshawa hookers out in broad daylight, he knew he was close to the 401. Good riddance to "the 'Shwa." He turned from Simcoe Street onto the highway back to Toronto.

Nastos looked over at Carscadden. It was quiet on his side of the car. "What's with you?"

"I was just thinking about some crap I need to deal with for Kalmakov, some offshore stuff."

"Umm" was all Nastos could say as a reply. "I've been thinking about what Taylor had to say. You know, about the abuse. When we go to Bannerman's, we should check the drains while we're there, just to be sure."

Carscadden stared forward with a blank look on his face and agreed. "I was thinking the same thing. If he molested her, like Taylor suggested, then we should check all the house drains for blood."

10

ANTHONY RAINES STOOD OUT-
side the Toronto Police headquarters at 40 College Street. The
building, composed of glass and brick, looked like a pyramid that
a child would make out of Lego. It had been years since he had
been inside, but he was sure little would have changed. He would
encounter professional skeptics, cynical people who were not open
to the spiritual world around them. He wiped his cold, sweaty
palms on his pants and focused on slowing down his breathing.
It's go time. Reaching into his side pocket, Anthony removed the
piece of paper he needed. Wrinkled and moist both from his sweat
and from the humidity, the sheets, which he had pulled from the
writing pad he kept by his bed, twitched in his hands.

He'd always had unusual dreams and liked to record them
before they retreated back to that unreachable place in the cobwebs
of his mind. Every detail of this dream had been jotted down in a
frantic mess; he hadn't wanted any detail to be missed. Rather
than rewriting it more clearly the next day, he had left it as it was,
as if the frenzied script communicated the urgent body language
of the message.

Memorizing the information wasn't going to be enough; for his
interview with the detective, it needed to sound conversational. He
would be more comfortable with the notes in his hands, though.

He passed through the front doors. Inside, the station was a large, open place with glass elevators and marble flooring. A quick scan of the foyer revealed the receptionist at her desk; straightening his back, he approached. Overweight, over-accessorized and wearing entirely too much makeup, the receptionist hung up the phone and flashed a sincere smile at Anthony. "How may I help you, sir?"

"Yes, my name is Anthony Raines, R-A-I-N-E-S."

"Yes, sir?"

"I need to speak with Detective Bob Blake of the Homicide Unit."

The receptionist's face revealed a micro-expression of surprise. "One moment, please." She picked up her phone and dialed a number.

Under the counter, out of her sightline, he wiped the sweat from his hands again. "I'm not a suspect. I have some information that may help."

"Okay." She smiled a little more easily.

"The last thing I killed was a pound cake."

A broad smile. She could probably relate. He glanced at his notes and put them away for good.

She glanced away while she spoke. "Yes, Detective, I have someone down at the front counter who'd like to speak with you regarding a case. He says he has information. Sure thing." She glanced at Anthony. "Which case?"

He cleared his throat. "The missing girl."

She relayed the message, vague as it was, then hung up. "He says he'll be right down. You'd never find your way up; it's a bit of a maze."

"Thanks" — he read her name tag — "Joan." He smiled and sat down to wait on a nearby bench.

He recognized Detective Blake from his research. *Up a few pounds, Detective, not that I would kick you out of bed over it.* He extended his hand and Blake accepted it with a warm smile. "Good afternoon, Detective. My name is Anthony Raines, R-A-I-N-E-S."

"Yes, and how can I help you today, Mr. Raines?"

"Sir, if we could just go up to your office? I have information I would rather share in private. It's regarding the missing Bannerman girl."

Blake turned and motioned with his hand for him to follow. They went up the elevator and around the perimeter of the building. Raines observed the glass walls, private offices, conference rooms and squad rooms. Blake opened a door that read Homicide Unit and sat at his desk. Anthony slid out the chair nearest Blake.

Anthony asked, "Is your computer connected to the net?"

"Yes, it is."

"I want to give you a lead on a murder, one that hasn't been reported yet. I just need you to go on the internet and see something with your own two eyes so you don't think I'm some nutcase."

Blake's patience was beginning to wane, like he was thinking that very thing. "Sure, but can you make it quick? I was just going to leave the office."

Anthony gave the detective his personal website address.

There was a delay as the detective read the information. "You're a psychic? You're *that* Anthony Raines?"

"Yes, sir, I am. I wouldn't come here in person unless I knew I could help. This is a risk to my career if I'm wrong."

Blake opened the top drawer of his desk and withdrew a notepad. "Okay, what do you have to tell me, Mr. Raines?"

"Detective, I can tell you're very skeptical. Virgos are very analytical; you wouldn't be one, would you?"

There was a pause. "Actually, I am."

"You know," Anthony visualized the notes that were hidden in his pocket. "If you tell me the colour of your car, I can tell you what year you were born. If you told me the hour you came into this world, I could tell you all kinds of things to try to make you feel more at ease about trusting me."

Blake quickly scanned the office like he was wondering who was seeing him with this lunatic. "No, thanks, I'm not a big believer — I'd rather you just tell me the information you have for me and I can have it checked out."

"You were born in '64, I think."

The detective was silent.

"You're probably methodically going through all of the ways I could have gotten that information. I assure you, my means aren't fully understood, not even by myself." Anthony waited till the detective spoke.

"You could have gotten that from Facebook or something."

"Okay, how about this one, Detective? The first job you ever had in your life, you got through a lucky break. Someone older helped you out or it would never have happened. That was after the close call you had in the water when you were younger." Anthony knew this described ninety percent of the world's population. No inexperienced teenager obtained their first job without a lucky break from an employer willing to take a chance.

"You have medication in your desk that's expired and you've been hitting the bottle pretty hard lately. And your diet is out of control."

The detective didn't say anything.

"I'm not doing a reading here. It's just that I know things about people. If I knew more about you, Detective, trust me, what I could tell you would be most impressive. I do this for a living."

Blake spoke unemotionally. "Who put you up to this?"

"A young girl went missing a few weeks ago, Detective. Thinner than most, long hair, pretty, not Hollywood beautiful. Any boy her age would date her, though."

"That describes about a million people, Anthony."

"True. Only this one has been murdered, Detective. I'll be honest with you — spirits from the other side haunt my sleep. They can only tell me about the past, never the future, and they are asking me if we have found her yet. They tell me her soul is suffering until her body can be recovered. They hear her screaming, Detective. We have to find her to stop her pain."

"You're telling me she's dead, though, right?"

"Yes, sir, it's her soul that's suffering."

Anthony noticed that the detective was picking at his nails, a habit Anthony considered worse than smoking. He tried to relax. Helping the police find this girl was a stepping stone to finding the next one, hopefully alive.

"Where is she, Mr. Raines?"

"Along one of the city trails, near a university. I see a bridge and a gentle creek, long grass, a paved trail. Forgive me, but there *are* flies there, and they've started their nasty work. I can't actually see *her* — I just hear the buzzing."

"How do you know it's a girl then?"

"I said before, Detective, those who have passed over speak to me. They described her as I relayed to you, not a few moments ago."

"So you're telling me that you know where a body is for a girl that hasn't been reported dead yet? And you don't think that maybe this is going to draw a certain amount of police attention your way?"

"This has happened to me once before, Detective. Check my bio on the website; you'll see I helped the police locate a body twenty years ago. I know what to expect, and I don't care about the intrusion on my life . . . We just have to find her."

"Well, there are miles and miles of trails throughout the city, Mr. Raines . . ."

"You're going to find her, Detective; it's not a place a body can go unnoticed for long."

Anthony went through his mental checklist. He'd covered everything. And that was the easy part.

Anthony answered all of the usual questions about himself: name, date of birth, address, phone number. Blake led him back to the front lobby. The cop didn't notice the woman with the camera, but Anthony certainly did. He checked his watch. Right on time. *Toronto Today* magazine just landed an exclusive.

Looks like I'm going to get back on the front pages again.

◘ ◘ ◘

CARSCADDEN PUT THE RADIO ON CP24, THE TWENTY-FOUR-HOUR news station, and leaned back in his seat. Just as Nastos turned up the volume to hear the traffic report, the female host interrupted with a news bulletin. "Toronto police have found the body of a young girl in the area of Morningside and Lawrence, in the city's east end. Information is sparse in this developing story, but CP24's Glenn Barrett is reporting from the scene."

Nastos and Carscadden shared a look. Carscadden was the first to say, "Holy shit."

Nastos agreed. "Holy shit is right."

"A young girl, a fifteen-minute drive away from where she lives — it's her, Lindsay."

"It's just your worst fear that it's the girl we were hired to help." Nastos pressed a little harder on the gas pedal. "We better get cleaned up and head over there."

◻ ◻ ◻

SPORTING HIS OLD SUIT AND SHOES FROM THE OFFICE CLOSET, Carscadden found himself once again in the driver's seat, while Nastos brooded over a picture of Lindsay Bannerman. A long line of police cars was parked on the east side of the road across from Morningside Park. As Carscadden turned in, he saw a command post Winnebago, Forensic Identification Unit vans and detective cars.

A uniformed officer waved them to a stop and Carscadden put his window down. "ID," he said.

Carscadden showed his bar association card. A smirk spread across the cop's face. "If you're chasing an ambulance, you're a little late for this one, pal."

"Wrong card. Gimme a sec." Carscadden rummaged through his wallet and found his private investigator's identification. "There. We were hired to find a missing person. We might be able to identify the body, save you guys some time."

The uniformed cop didn't look overwhelmingly receptive. "No, thanks, we got it."

Nastos hung up his phone and leaned over to the window. "Yeah, I was just talking to Detective Jacques Lapierre; he said if we park here at the front, he'll come over and meet us."

"Jacques? Didn't think he was here." The cop straightened up and looked around. "Park by the FIU van — they won't be back here for a while."

Carscadden found some shade between the large forensics van and a tree and parked there. The afternoon heat was coming on strong. Multi-coloured leaves rattled in the wind. They slammed their doors shut; Nastos leaned back against the car, his head tilted enough to look straight up at the maple tree above. Carscadden joined him. The leaves were spotted black from some disease he had noticed in older trees. Yellow, red and burnt orange leaves fluttered against the backdrop of the clear blue sky. Carscadden was jolted when the side door of the FIU van swung open and Detective Dennehy squeezed out of the narrow frame. Dennehy saw Nastos and smiled.

Carscadden sighed. "Just had to be that asshole."

Under his breath, Nastos said, "Yeah. Let's keep it professional and hope he does the same."

Dennehy was in good spirits. "Hey, Nastos. Working hard at doing nothing, I see."

"Suck a dick, Dennehy."

Carscadden sighed. *So much for being professional.*

Dennehy's smile only broadened at Nastos' comment as he drew closer to them. Byrne came out of the van behind him. Dennehy stood with his feet well apart, broadcasting a narcissist's level of confidence with his grin.

Dennehy said, "You and your boyfriend planning on playing catch in the bushes? You'll have to go someplace else."

"Thanks." Anyone in the world would be easier to deal with than these idiots. "Listen, guys, we may be able to ID the body."

Byrne asked, "How's that?"

Nastos produced a photograph of Lindsay Bannerman. Dennehy examined it, his eyes wrinkled and his lips pursed thin.

"Blond, pretty, thin, young. But no," he shook his head with a mirthless smile. "Not her."

Carscadden had come around the car. "Thank god."

Byrne reached out for the picture and took a look. "Looks a lot like her — who's this?"

Nastos said, "A missing person we're on."

Byrne didn't look up, still studying the picture. "So you've gone private? Great."

Dennehy shrugged, looking at Carscadden. "I guess you did good work on the trial."

"Yeah." Carscadden eyed Nastos. "Sometimes you just have to make your own luck."

Carscadden felt an awkward moment when he considered whether to extend his hand to shake with Dennehy, but the cop didn't appear to be in the hand-shaking mood.

Byrne's radio squawked and he answered it. "Go for Byrne."

"We got an ID. You near the FUI van?"

Byrne turned his radio down and opened the door to the van behind him and shouted in. "Yeah?"

A cop's head emerged and smiled. "Sneaky fucker. Yeah, we got the prints back. Her name is Rebecca Morris. She's on CPIC as reported missing."

"Good work, guys. That was a weird one."

The cop's head disappeared and the door closed. Byrne turned back to Nastos and Carscadden. "Well, there you go, it's official."

Carscadden said, "I guess we can get going to Bannerman's, then."

He turned to go, but Nastos didn't budge. He was looking at Byrne. "That look on your face back there, Byrne, what was it?"

With a glance, Byrne checked with Dennehy, who reluctantly gave his approval. "The crime scene was a bit unusual is all. Actually the girl, she was a bit of a mess. Marked up."

"Like how?"

"Like he carved something on her chest. The word *Sorrow*."

Nastos' blood ran cold. "Fucking serial killer."

"Yeah, you'd think. And there was a '30' written on her left wrist."

Dennehy put his hands up. "Easy, guys. This could be some pissed-off boyfriend who watched one too many Hannibal Lecter movies. It could be misdirection."

Nastos silently processed this new information. It wouldn't be the first time some genius tried something like that. "I take it the ID and the carving are on holdback for now."

Dennehy said, "Yeah, you know the drill."

"And the number 30?"

Byrne said, "You heard the man." Byrne pointed toward the police tape, then waved at Carscadden and Nastos before leaving.

Nastos took the picture back from Dennehy. "Lindsay looks similar. Same hair, same age —"

Dennehy put his palms up to stop him. "Hey, hey, Nastos. We both know there's a dozen missing girls that look just like her on any given day. It's too early to make that kind of call."

Nastos shrugged and turned toward the police tape. He looked up at the trees again and watched the heavy black branches swaying overhead, blocking the light. He had one thought running through his head. *Lindsay Bannerman, where are you?*

11

NASTOS LEANED BACK IN THE
passenger seat as Carscadden drove to the Bannermans' estate. He
watched as Carscadden leaned out the driver's door to push the
button at the gate. Soon enough, the gate clicked and swung open
and Carscadden ducked back into the parking area near the main
door. Nastos noticed a small black Honda Civic parked near the
front door that he had not seen before. The personalized plate read
DRBRUCE. There was someone sitting in the driver's seat. Taking it
all in, Nastos thought to himself, *If there's a neighbourhood that
still receives home visits from doctors, it would be this one.*

Carscadden hit the doorbell, and before long, Craig Bannerman
answered. Upon seeing Carscadden and Nastos, he let out a breath.
"Thank god."

Before Nastos could inquire about the Honda, Craig abruptly
turned away from the door and jabbed a finger inside. Nastos
barely had time to wonder what had pissed him off when he heard
a man talking inside the house. Craig led them into the living
room, where Mrs. Bannerman was speaking to someone Nastos
didn't recognize. He was in his fifties, soft and chubby with brown
hair and a roundish face. He was expressive with his hands and
the inflection of his voice. When he turned to see who had come in
the room, his eyes scanned up and down Carscadden twice. He
came over, extending his hand.

"Anthony Raines, pleased to meet you."

Carscadden and Nastos introduced themselves.

Craig Bannerman said, "They're the two guys I hired to find Lindsay."

Anthony looked like he was being asked to make the most important decision of his life. He nodded. "Good choice."

Nastos noticed that Claire seemed relieved by Anthony's assessment.

Nastos asked, "And what is it you do, Mr. Raines?"

"Oh, call me Anthony. Everyone does."

Nastos took note of the non-answer. "Sure, Anthony. Are you going to be helping me and Mr. Carscadden?"

Anthony ignored the minor slight. "I do feel that I can be of some help here, yes. Mrs. Bannerman was kind enough to give me a call."

Craig shook his head; he obviously thought Anthony was a lunatic.

Carscadden asked, "So you're a private detective, too?"

Anthony smiled. "No, I'm a psychic. I've helped the police with this sort of thing before."

Claire smiled at Anthony; Craig shook his head, looked at the ceiling and exhaled.

Nastos asked Anthony, "A psychic? You're kidding me, right?"

Claire Bannerman's jaw dropped. "Don't you come into this house with that type of attitude! He's here to help."

Nastos didn't back down. "I have some tough questions coming, so I'd appreciate it if you invited him to leave so we can get some work done."

Craig made no attempt to protect his wife, as though he wanted her to hear it, whatever *it* was. Nastos wasn't convinced. *He might not be so receptive to what I'm going to say.*

Claire said, "He's not going anywhere."

"Okay," Nastos relented. "But don't say I didn't warn you." Nastos waited a moment. Anthony could have done the polite thing and left; instead he held his ground.

Nastos made a direct accusation, pointing at Craig Bannerman. "There's no doubt in my mind that you molested Lindsay."

Craig's eyes widened in horror and surprise. "What?"

"Shut up and listen, Craig. You were molesting her and she couldn't take it anymore, so she ran away. Now you'll never see her again."

There was a moment when Craig's body went slack. His shoulders sagged; he looked broken. Nastos thought he had scored a direct hit. The guilty have a tough time coming up with a quick lie. Craig was speechless and it was almost a sad moment for Nastos — he liked Craig. Now he would have to think of him as a creep and add him to the list of people that he would like to see dead.

But then Craig changed. He sucked in air, his eyes narrowed, his fists clenched and a vicious snarl spread across his lips. "I'll . . . fucking . . . kill you." He charged at Nastos, lunging for his throat. It took both Carscadden and Anthony to hold him back. Craig swung fist after fist and when he was too far away to punch, he tried kicking at Nastos. Through clenched teeth, he hissed, "You lying sack of shit, get the fuck out of this house."

Anthony was wide-eyed, his head poking forward, glancing from Nastos to Craig, unable to take his eyes away from the men.

Nastos turned back to Craig, who was now ten feet away, still restrained by Carscadden and Anthony. Nastos had to deliver the line realistically, so he shouted back, "You did it — I know it for a fact."

Craig's face was purple. "You're full of shit. I pay you to go find my girl and you come back with nothing but lies and bullshit? You incompetent fuck, you worthless piece of garbage."

"Deny it then."

"You're goddamned right I deny it." Bannerman went slack again. His hands flew up to cover his face and the flood of tears let loose. "Oh god . . . this is a nightmare. Lindsay . . . where are you? Come home, please just come home."

Claire shoved Carscadden aside and wrapped her arms around her husband. Her eyes seemed to have grown in size.

Anthony looked ill at ease, and with a sense of guilty

satisfaction, Nastos realized that he was wishing he had left when he had the chance. The sobbing made Nastos uncomfortable too, since the only thing he could do to relieve the couple's pain was to find Lindsay. However, he thought he had perceived something else. Anthony had something else going on inside, an emotion that Nastos couldn't name.

Anthony looked at the miserable husband and wife. He didn't seem to know what to do. He whispered, "I should go," to Claire and slipped out the door.

When Nastos said, "Good riddance," Claire spun toward him.

"I thought you were asked to leave. Twice." Nastos raised his hands in surrender.

Carscadden approached the Bannermans slowly. He cleared his throat to speak, but Nastos beat him to it.

"Craig, we know that you never hurt Lindsay. We knew right from the start. But accusations were made and we needed to be sure. We needed to be rock solid on that one before we could move forward."

Claire said, "So this was some kind of joke? Some kind of dinner theatre?"

Nastos said, "I have a daughter. I love her so much it actually causes physical pain. My heart nearly explodes out of my chest when I see her. I know what you are going through. I think about Lindsay at night. I think about how it would feel to be you, and have my girl out there. And I made a decision, a contract with myself. Despite the fact that you are paying the bills, Lindsay is my client. I'm telling you right now, I will do what it takes to get her back here as soon as possible. You've seen first-hand that I'm even prepared to go after you. It's like I have obsessive compulsive disorder and I have made getting her my life's mission."

Carscadden added, "What that was, was an interrogation. Nastos started with a direct accusation. A 'behavioural observation question.' Guilty people react in a variety of ways; innocent people usually get really, really mad, just like you did. This is ugly work, but it's necessary."

Craig asked, "So police normally accuse parents like this?"

Claire interjected, "Who made these accusations?"

Carscadden answered, "Jessica Taylor."

Both Bannermans were visibly disgusted at the mention of her name. Claire said, "You'd listen to something out of that tramp's mouth?"

Nastos stepped forward and crouched down. "We had to be sure. And now we are. I'm sorry we had to do that."

Carscadden asked, "Have you listened to the news much today?"

Claire answered by turning her back further on Nastos.

Nastos continued, "Well, it wasn't Lindsay. But there was a young girl's body found today. Carscadden and I went by and confirmed it — the police found a dead girl near Morningside Park this morning. I wanted you to know that it isn't Lindsay, but the police aren't releasing the name yet. I don't want you to be in a state of limbo over any delays."

Craig answered. "I guess I appreciate your consideration." He seemed to read the hesitation on Nastos' face. "But . . ."

"But she was a lot like Lindsay — young, blond, skinny. She may have been murdered by someone who will kill again."

Craig's face turned pale. He checked left and right, looking for something. Claire reached for the box of tissues from the table and handed them to him. He rubbed his hands on his pants, then ran fingers through his hair.

Nastos continued. "She'd been reported missing too. How long has it been for Lindsay?"

Craig couldn't do the math. Clearly his mind was reeling.

"Twenty-six days?" Nastos asked. "Something like that?"

Craig's voice cracked. "Oh, god!"

"Carscadden and I are going to do everything we can."

"You think somebody has her someplace? God, he could be doing —"

Nastos put a hand on Craig's shoulder. "Don't think like that. There was no sign this girl was abused. Don't let your mind play tricks on you."

It was an awkward silence. Carscadden said, "Listen, it's time we went." He added, "Craig, can we talk to you quickly outside the door?"

"Sure." Craig blew his nose and stood up, still shaken. He stocked up on a few more tissues and followed Nastos and Carscadden into the hallway.

Carscadden turned to Craig. "That Anthony character, all he'll do is waste your money. But there's a chance he will help your wife feel better, like everything is being done."

"I guess."

Craig asked Nastos, "You ever heard of this Anthony loser?"

"No, should I have?"

"I've been on his website. Looks like he did help the police find a body years ago. Since then, he's been a psychic to the stars. He had a radio show for a while. But he's slowly slipped off the face of the earth. In a few days he has Casa Loma booked for a TV show. He's sharing some revelation with the world."

Nastos considered this. "You think this helping you is just some publicity stunt?"

"Yeah."

"Well, looks like your wife wants him in. So I guess you're out-voted."

Craig shrugged. "Marriage is all about winning battles and losing wars."

Nastos asked, "How did your wife get a hold of him?"

Craig shook his head. "She didn't. There was a flyer in the mail, I think. I'm not entirely sure. She says she called him; I'm not pushing the issue. Apparently he says he can probably help us find our daughter."

u u u

ANTHONY RAINES CLOSED THE DOOR BEHIND HIM AND SUCKED IN A breath of the fresh fall air. Courtesy of Mr. Nastos' provocations, it looked like the Bannermans were ready to pay someone else through the nose to get their daughter back. This was working out perfectly.

He made note of the license plate on the Ford Escape in the driveway. The validation tag on the plate was December, which likely meant Carscadden was a Sagittarius. Bruce had kept himself busy surfing the web with his iPad in the front seat of the Civic. Leaning against the Escape, Anthony pulled out his BlackBerry and did a Google search on Nastos. He was surprised by the length of the return, for a nobody. He sat in his car and read through a few pages. He recalled the story about a cop charged with murder; he hadn't realized that that was the man he had just met. He was a celebrity, of sorts. Anthony read through a few articles looking for something useful, personal information.

Cops always protect their home address, though he did find the street name. Then Anthony read that his wife was a real estate agent. He brought up the Toronto Real Estate Board website and did an agent search for Nastos. There was only one. Madeleine Nastos. He clicked the link and found a picture that showed Madeleine standing in front of her car, a grey Honda Odyssey.

Anthony's concentration broke when he realized that there was a photographer outside the gates, snapping away in his direction. *Forgot I hired her again.* He had managed to get the photographer from *Toronto Today* to take pictures of him leaving the Bannerman residence. Sliding into the Civic's passenger seat, Anthony ignored the photographer and instead concentrated on getting to Nastos' residence. *Time for a little reconnaissance.*

From the driver's seat Bruce asked, "Back home?" He smiled, running his eyes down Anthony's body.

"Not your turn, loverboy — we have a stop first."

◌ ◌ ◌

HOMECREST WAS A QUIET STREET ENDING IN A CUL-DE-SAC TO THE east of Meadowvale, south of Lawrence Avenue. Driving past the house, Anthony had gotten lucky and seen the Honda Odyssey in the driveway. It was a nice place: red brick, white shutters and a well-maintained lawn with flowerbeds filled with seasonal plants.

Curb appeal. Anthony smiled. *His little lawyer friend has a bit of curb appeal too.*

Anthony noted the license plate numbers in the driveway and the validation stickers. It looked like Nastos was Pisces, Madeleine a Taurus. He made a mental note. Movement caught his eye in the rear-view mirror; it was a car stopping just behind him. It was Carscadden and Nastos. Nastos exploded from the car and charged Anthony's window. "What the hell are you doing here?"

Anthony wanted Dr. Bruce to just hit the gas, but it was too late for that. *How the hell did he get here so fast?* He rolled down his window and produced a smile. "I was going to drop off a flyer for your wife. Do a free reading." He didn't have any flyers and Nastos didn't look as if he'd be too receptive to taking one anyway.

"It's disgusting, what you're doing to that family. Leave them alone."

Anthony could see he'd be lucky to leave with all of his teeth. "Just trying to help. You're a non-believer — I get that."

"They're going through hell, pal. Leave them alone. And if I ever find you in front of my house again, I'll cave your face in."

"Sorry." Anthony rolled up the window and then Bruce did hit the gas. *What have I just done?*

12

ANTHONY WAS STILL THINKING about the confrontation with Nastos when he saw that on his own street — no, at his own house — something was wrong. At this time of day there were never so many cars parked on the street. People around here had money and weren't the type to throw parties during the day for no reason. As he drew closer, he saw the occasion. A contingent of unmarked police cars was parked in front of his house. There was a squad car in his driveway and a uniformed officer standing outside his front door with a clipboard, writing stuff down and checking his watch.

Bruce said, "Looks like you're famous again."

He tried to sound flirtatious. "I can think of worse things than a house full of cops."

Bruce pulled to a stop at the side of the road a few houses back. "Yeah, well, I'll let you out here, if you don't mind."

Anthony gave Bruce's hand a squeeze and exited the car. He turned his attention to his house and the show the police were putting on.

Oh my god, Greta. Anthony nearly had a stroke when he saw Greta, the neighbour from a few houses down, on his front porch. A bored stay-at-home housewife, she liked to take Anthony's dog Ginger for walks. Sometimes in the summer she'd come over for the dog but they'd end up getting drunk on margaritas by the pool. He confronted the officer standing at his door. "This is my house."

The officer didn't look up from his writing. "Good. They'll want to talk to you. One sec." He smiled at Anthony, then spoke into his radio. "Detective Blake, your guy is at the front door."

Greta turned from the officer and spoke to Anthony. "When I saw the commotion — well, I thought it would be a good idea to get Ginger out of everyone's way."

Anthony was relieved. "Thanks, Greta." He could see that she wanted to know what was going on but didn't want to ask. So he told her.

"I helped the police find a missing girl today. My information was so accurate they have to make sure I wasn't involved."

She looked at the cop with the clipboard, who shrugged. "Yup, that's why we're here."

She was impressed. He had shown her some of his skills in the past, but this was going to make him a legend. "Anthony, I wouldn't believe it if I hadn't seen what you can do for myself."

He shrugged, trying to play the reluctant hero. Greta tugged on Ginger's leash. The dog had never turned down an extra walk.

There was no verbal response on the cop's radio, just the sound of two clicks of the mic being pressed. Moments later, Detective Blake came to the door.

"Come on in." Blake smiled broadly and waved for Anthony to follow.

"Nice of you to invite me into my own house."

"Like you said in my office, you've been through this before."

Blake led him into his own home office, taking at seat at Anthony's desk. He opened a manila envelope and spread out the contents, sheets of printed paper.

Blake produced a pen from his inside pocket and gestured for Anthony to have a seat. Anthony scanned the room. The books on the shelves had all been knocked over, the couches had been dragged out of position and the cushions tossed. Anthony pulled the leather chair over and sat.

Blake smiled. "Yeah, we kind of had to have a look around."

Anthony asked, "For blood?"

"Any kind of human tissue, electronic records. I have your phone records here, the last two months' worth. I'd like you to go over the numbers with me. I'm also going to need an account of your time over the last forty-eight hours. You know, all the basics for a case like this."

Anthony suppressed a smile. With his words, Blake had given every impression that it was just procedure, and that he had no expectations; however, Anthony saw behind the veneer. There was something behind Blake's lingering eyes. *If he's trying to get a read on me, he's out of his league. Detective Blake, you're in the presence of a master.*

Blake spread out the phone records. "Why don't you tell me who these people are you're calling?"

Anthony pulled out his cell phone and brought up the address book. In fifteen minutes, Blake had made notes on every number.

"And now your itinerary for the last two days?"

Anthony reached over Blake, grazing his thigh while opening the desk drawer. His appointment diary was gone, and everything else in the drawer looked like it had been gingerly put back in place and reorganized by drunken orangutans.

Blake opened his jacket and produced Anthony's scheduler. "I think you're looking for this."

Anthony wondered how much of the book he'd been through. There were men listed in that book, powerful men, who wouldn't want it known that they had a relationship or an arrangement with Anthony. "Good thing you found it. It's important to me."

Blake flipped through a few pages. "I haven't called these people yet, but if it checks out, it looks like your time is accounted for."

"Go ahead and call them."

"Who would have thought so many people came to see psychics."

Anthony refused to eye the book in the detective's hand. Blake was watching him closely, looking for nervousness — which of course Anthony would not let him see. A strong man had come in here, in control, and had invaded his space. This man was running the show. At any moment the man could use the power of his badge to force Anthony into the bedroom, onto the couch, even against the door, and there was nothing he could do about it. The fantasy provided Anthony the perfect diversion. Blake probably anticipated that Anthony would crumble under the pressure. Anthony considered the reality that Blake didn't know how right he was.

Blake smiled and averted his gaze, looking instead at the laptop on the desk. He pressed the button and the screen came to life. His face wrinkled. "Password, eh?"

"Must you?"

"I must."

"Elton. The password is Elton."

Blake kept smiling, saying nothing. He typed in the password and the desktop icons appeared.

Anthony came around the desk, standing next to Blake. "If I knew what you were looking for, maybe I could help?"

Blake opened the web browser and bought up Google Maps and MapQuest in separate tabs. He jotted down the recent addresses that had been looked up in his notebook. Anthony said that none of the addresses were going to be significant. Blake asked, "We went through the entire house. You live here all by yourself?"

Anthony knew the delivery was critical. It was easy to lie after you have convinced yourself it's the truth. And just to be sure, he gave Blake something else to think about. "Yes, I do. Maybe if I get lonely, I could give you a call, Detective?"

Blake's perma-smile broadened. He knew Anthony was just trying to make him uncomfortable to be funny. "No, thanks. I have everything I need." He stood up, leaving the computer screen on, and put his notebook in his jacket pocket. "Just once and for the record, Mr. Raines, how did you know the body was there? I'm guessing you were out on a walk and happened upon her. Maybe you dreamed up this psychic revelation to help your business along? Did you just get lucky or something?"

He considered allowing Blake the victory for just a second. But the plan was the plan and Blake's clumsy charms, unintentional as they were, were not going to work.

"I told you, Detective. I had some disturbing dreams the other night. It's happened once before, I hope it never happens again. I could smell her — the air was so thick, in my dream, that I could taste it. I can still see the image in my mind . . . feel her tortured soul."

Blake shook his head. "Well, that's a hell of a problem you have."

◻ ◻ ◻

AFTER THE COPS WERE GONE, ANTHONY GRABBED A COLD CORONA from the fridge and sat it down on the table in his study. He slid the drawer open and lifted out a box that contained his tarot cards. He dried the condensation from the cold beer on his pants and opened the box, setting the lid aside and folding back the black satin cloth that covered the deck. He lifted them out and spread the cards out in his hands with the face sides away from him, then slid them back together, just to get a feel for how the cards were moving.

Cold readings were so much more difficult. As experienced as he was, every good chance guess was still a guess. Every trick, angle and manipulation was part of a complicated balancing act between showmanship and divination that in some ways seemed to become more difficult over time. The raw skills he had, the ability to keep the magic fresh, was a different story — that was innate. Tarot was so much easier with its science — he liked to let the science carry the burden from time to time.

Shuffling the cards, he reflected on the difficulty of having faith in himself, and how it had never been easy. Then the dream came that changed everything. Now he was on a frantic mission to save the world. Making life and death decisions was something he hated; no matter how sure he was when sacrificing a few to save many, it was still a responsibility he would readily abdicate.

Turning his attention back to the matter at hand, Anthony concentrated on one thought as he slowly manipulated the deck: Nastos. He divided the tarot deck in two, then carefully folded the piles together on the table. Next he held them all in one hand and slid out large sections with the other, putting them in somewhere else. He did this exactly three times. There was one awkward card; he removed it and set it aside without a second thought. Last, he sequestered small sections out of the deck and turned them upside down, all while keeping the faces of the cards looking away from him. He placed the deck face down on the table and spent a moment imagining the face of Nastos as best as he could recall.

Anthony was going to use his six-card spread, a Celtic cross. The first card was the centre; the second card went on top of it, rotated ninety degrees. He put a card to the right, one at the bottom, then on top and on the left side. As he might have suspected, the centre card, the card at the heart of the matter, was the Magician.

The Magician is a transformer. Through will power, he can manipulate the elements into any substance, into the materials of life. From nothing, he can create something. His number is one. The Magician is a man to fear. From the card's position, Anthony understood him to be a threat.

A man with near-divine power to transform himself, as if he were in fact a conduit for a higher power. While performing the tasks of deities, he would appear to those of this world to be practicing magic.

The cards above, below and to either side were just as troubling to Anthony. They made up the shape of the cross and signified what the Magician was willing to sacrifice for. The top centre card was the card of Justice.

The card of Justice ensures that certain laws cannot be violated, only enforced. The first is the law of cause and effect; the second is the law of karma.

Cause and effect ensure that all events of the present are the result of all past states. Karma signifies that all your actions return to you eventually.

As I sow, so shall I reap. The thought sent shivers down his spine. Nastos was going to sacrifice everything — more than he would even know himself at this stage — to bring Anthony down to the master *he* served: Justice.

Anthony felt his shirt sticking to his back from sweat; a large bead of wet salt slid down the side of his face. He eyed the deck of cards. The next card was the most important. It had been laid sideways over the middle card and it signified what, if any, action he could do to stop the fate that was coming to him. It had to be laid sideways because it represented taking a chance of angering karma, which was already conspiring against him. He closed his eyes and flipped the card, pausing only briefly to touch it, hoping to feel something good was on the way. All he felt was the waxed back of the deck, cool and unreadable.

He closed his eyes and revealed the card. When he opened his eyes, he was looking at the card he dreaded most. The image was of a man wearing black armour, holding a black flag and looking down onto a battle from the heights of his pale horse. Death. The card of transformation to a new life.

Death is going to visit you, Mr. Nastos. The spirit world is calling your name.

13

Wednesday, October 24

NASTOS ROCKED THE FRYING pan, rolling the diced vegetables in the oil and spices. He dialed the heat to medium, then cracked three eggs, pouring the yolks into the sink to be washed down, and put the whites into a small mixing bowl. Madeleine wouldn't eat yolks because of the cholesterol, but he and Josie liked the flavour, so he squirted in some Dijon mustard. The Dijon brought back the original egg colour and gave a creamy texture with few added calories and no cholesterol, just the way Maddy specified. He sprinkled in some grated cheese and poured the egg over the sautéed vegetables.

Josie was in her pyjamas at the kitchen table. Madeleine seemed distracted. She was wearing a business suit and standing next to Josie, going through yesterday's mail. The toast popped and Josie went over to get it; toast fetching and drink pouring were her contribution to breakfast.

Nastos slid the cooked eggs onto the plates. "Ready for the ROM, Josie?"

"Yeah, I'm ready." Josie finished pouring, then put the juice jug back in the fridge. Nastos saw her glance at her mom and pick up on the fact that she wasn't being herself. She seemed disappointed.

Nastos asked Madeleine, "So, what is it?"

She slid a letter over to him. It was upside down; still, he could tell from the handwriting that it was from his mother. She told him, "Write back, it's been long enough."

He didn't want Josie here for what might be coming. "Hey, Jo, go get changed real quick, would you?"

"Sure, Dad." She left, giving him a look that told him she knew he was trying to protect her from an argument. It was beginning to happen a lot lately.

He turned the burner on the lowest setting and picked up the letter, examining it. He felt it for thickness and twisted it to see if it contained any pictures. No, only paper. He dropped it unopened into the recycling box.

"I've been in touch with them on Facebook, Steve."

The mere thought of his parents made the kitchen feel like it had just shrunk. He was never going to allow them to be near Josie. The first memory that came to mind was the trip to Niagara Falls when he was thirteen. Mom, Dad, Steve and his little sister, Carrie, were planning to hit the wax museum, take the *Maid of the Mist* boat tour and walk under the falls, just the four of them. They had looked forward to it all week. The kids were told to pick out their own clothes because their father was busy in the garage, getting the car ready for the long drive.

Nastos chose jeans, running shoes and a T-shirt. He and Carrie waited out in the car; then Mom brought out a bag of food for the car ride, and then Dad came out. Horn-rimmed glasses, a collared golf shirt and perfectly polished black shoes.

They laughed and sang songs on the drive. Dad pointed out cars he liked; they ate snacks and drank pop. When they parked near the falls two hours later, they exited the car and gathered together. It was then that Dad went crazy. "Is that what you choose to wear? There's no colour on your shirt. What if you get wet from the Falls? Where can we bring you dressed like that?"

Carrie had made the mistake of wearing running shoes. Dad freaked out even more on her. People were going to think she was a boy, *or worse*. Whatever *worse* was, Nastos had no idea until he was much older. Anyway, they left. They all filed back into the car and drove straight home. For two hours, their father lectured them about how they had ruined the trip for their mother, who cried into her hands, seeming to reinforce what he was saying.

After the grounding, when he had tried to apologize to his mom for something he still didn't understand, she kept changing the subject. Just like she always did, she changed the subject. At the time, he had felt abandoned; now he saw that she was just trying to pretend that the family wasn't in constant chaos. She was living in a dream world where everything was perfect and Dad wasn't half-crazy. Nastos' father had obsessive compulsive disorder, and unless you were a mind reader, sooner or later you'd do something that set him off. That last thing Nastos wanted to do was give his parents a chance to do to Josie what they had done to him.

Nastos turned to Madeleine. "I know you've emailed them, but I never will. You've heard the reasons. People like that never change."

Josie came into the room full speed. She skidded to a halt and grew concerned when she felt the mood in the room had only gotten worse. She spoke quickly. "Dad, the sheet says I have to be at school early today because the bus leaves early!"

"Jo, you're still in pajamas."

"I know, but I mean for breakfast, will it be done in time? I don't want to be late."

He smiled, "Jo, go change, I'm serving it out right now."

He wondered if maybe she was checking on him, making sure Maddy wasn't being too harsh.

As she left he added, "And it's going to be cold this morning, so wear something warm."

Madeleine sipped her oj and returned to her argument. "Yeah, I've heard the stories. It's just that they're in their seventies. Wouldn't it be nice to have an understanding with them before they're gone? Do you want to hate them the rest of your life?"

Nastos served the omelettes onto the plates. So much of this had come up while they were in counselling for what had happened to Josie. The psychologist Mills was a decent guy and had sided with Nastos. Now Nastos just wanted the mood to brighten up, for Josie's sake. "You know, maybe you're right. Maybe I'll see Dr. Mills about it."

Madeleine appeared to take no enjoyment from her victory. Josie ran down the stairs wearing jeans, running shoes, a long-sleeved T-shirt. She slid into her chair at the kitchen table, grabbed a piece of toast and started on the eggs. Nastos rubbed her back. "You look great. Stuff your face and we'll get you to school."

◻ ◻ ◻

IT WAS NINE-THIRTY IN THE MORNING WHEN NASTOS MADE IT TO Carscadden's office, across from Moss Park. The office was in darkness. Nastos found the key on his key ring and slid it into the lock. The alarm chirped when he pushed the door open and he typed in 1967, the last year the Leafs won the Stanley Cup. Carscadden was a Leafs fan and liked the code because it was easy to remember. Nastos liked it because it was the one password that wouldn't have to change for the rest of his life.

He flicked on the foyer lights, relocked the door and left the phone on bypass. Carscadden's office was unlocked. Nastos sat at his own desk and opened the ever-thickening Lindsay Bannerman file. A picture of her was clipped to the first page. She was sitting against a blue background — standard school picture fare. She was posed. Her hair wasn't perfect, but it was close. She looked both happy and mischievous through a crooked little smile. A younger version of Lindsay could be Josie's sister.

He pulled out the scrap paper with Jessica Taylor and Anita Bonghit's names on it, then remembered that he'd been sent MP3 files of their phone intercepts by Bannerman's buddies at the phone companies. A quick reverse lookup of Bonghit's address returned the name Dean Bunting. He wrote the new name next to Bonghit.

Phone taps, which would normally take specialty warrants

signed off by judges and cost a police service thousands and thousands of dollars in administration fees, Nastos could get for free by whispering the password *Lindsay*. Nastos turned on his computer and realized he should have grabbed a coffee.

He logged in to his Gmail and listened to the intercepts. Jessica's phone was active every few minutes. They were always incoming calls and it was always men. The average conversation was Jessica saying hello followed by a man asking if she had any time available today. Jessica would offer a time and the man would take it. Sometimes a price was confirmed, sometimes it wasn't. Jessica was an independent contractor. From the beginning, Nastos had feared that Lindsay might be involved in the sex trade. If she was, she'd have learned everything she'd need to know from Jessica.

Seven calls in and there were no conversations with Jessica mentioning Nastos or Carscadden poking around, until call number eight — the first outgoing call.

"Hello?"

"Hey, it's me."

"Hey, Jess. Busy today?"

"Yeah, but they're all premature ejaculators, so it's quick money."

The other female voice laughed. Taylor continued, "Anyway, I just had two guys here looking for Lindsay."

"Cops?"

"No, guys her dad hired. You don't know where she is, do you, Beth?"

Nastos wrote down the name Beth on a scrap of paper as well as the time and date stamp from the phone call.

"Only time I ever met her was at the group session and you were there," Beth replied.

"Yeah, that's what I thought."

"You think she's in trouble?"

"Maybe. I don't know."

There was a distant sound of a doorbell. "Gotta go, Jess, there's a one-hour guy at the door."

"Okay, talk later."

The phone went dead. Nastos listened to the rest of Jessica's messages; they were all more johns booking times.

Bunting's phone was only used once, when he ordered pizza for dinner. There was nothing to rule him out.

Nastos heard glass rattle and the front door chimed open. Hopkins called out, "Nastos, you in here?"

"Yeah, I'm in the office."

She rushed into the office and tossed a copy of *Toronto Today* magazine on the desk so he could see it. "Check out the cover," she said.

Nastos angled the magazine straight and saw the front-page picture of Anthony shaking hands with a police detective at headquarters. The headline read *"Saint Anthony" Asked to Help Police*.

"You're kidding me." Nastos read some of the article, barely listening to Hopkins as she spoke.

"Yeah, right after I heard all about this guy from Kevin, I saw this at the newsstand when I was grabbing my lottery tickets."

The story was fairly short for a front-page lead.

> Shortly before this picture was taken, world-renowned psychic and native of Toronto Anthony Raines, or "Saint Anthony" to his followers, helped Toronto Police Service with a missing persons case that had left them stumped for thirty days.
>
> Rebecca Morris's remains were found shortly after a tip by Saint Anthony. Raines' career took off years ago, when he helped police with a previous investigation, bringing closure to a grieving family whose son had been murdered. While this case ended tragically, and the family wish that Anthony had become involved sooner, a police spokesperson speaking on condition of anonymity expressed relief that at least the Morris family could begin the grieving process and admitted that they should have sought his expert advice sooner.

Saint Anthony can be heard on NewsTalk radio on
Wednesday, where he'll be discussing his forthcoming
televised show at Casa Loma on October 26th.

Nastos put the paper down. It was an advertisement poorly dis-
guised as news — an advertorial. Anthony must have paid for it.

Hopkins was thinking along the same line. "Do you think he
offered to help the Bannermans just for the media coverage?"

Nastos found himself nodding. "Yeah. That guy's all about
money."

Hopkins removed her jacket off and slung it over her arm. "He's
taking a big risk. If she turns up dead, his career is over."

"These con artists just rewrite the facts anyways." Nastos closed
the paper and slid it back over to Hopkins.

"Hey, did Carscadden tell you that 'Saint Anthony' drove to my
place after leaving the Bannermans'?"

"No way! What the hell did he do that for?" Hopkins came
closer, coveting the good gossip.

"He said he wanted to offer Madeleine a free reading. Trying to
soften me up by going through her."

"That's creepy."

"Yeah. If he was a better psychic, he'd know that Maddy and I
aren't on the best terms right now. What a loser."

"Sorry about you and Maddy. She's not seeing what a catch you
are. I'll talk some sense into her."

Nastos reached for a piece of paper from his desk and wrote
something down. He slid it across to Hopkins and she read it out
loud.

"Dr. Bruce?"

Nastos said, "Yeah. That was the personalized plate of the
vehicle that Anthony drove to my house. 'DRBRUCE.' Actually,
Raines was the passenger." Nastos smiled to himself. "He had a
dude driving him — if you'll pardon the expression."

Hopkins shook her head. "You're as bad as Kevin. Want me to
run the plate?"

"Yeah, we'll run it and stick it in the file. May as well earn our twenty grand. And hey, where's your little boy-toy?"

"Oh, he had to see Viktor, then he has the meeting with the Police Services Board over your lawsuit — he won't be here till noon."

That was bad news. "Great."

"What do you need?"

Nastos picked up the office phone and dialed a number. He held up a finger for Hopkins to wait a minute.

A woman's voice answered his phone. "Records."

Nastos said brusquely, "Yeah, this is Inspector Koche, who's this?"

The woman became angry immediately. "This is Records Supervisor Sharon McLean, Inspector —"

He cut her off. "Good, now listen here, McLean. I asked for some historical CPIC returns yesterday and I don't have them yet. Where are they?"

McLean asked, "What name?"

Nastos huffed. "Listen, I don't have a photographic memory; just look through your request stack and get it to me as soon as you can. You people." He didn't like being cruel to a stranger, but he reminded himself it was out of necessity for the con game.

He waited till McLean came back to the phone. "There's nothing here for you, Inspector."

"Mother of Christ. Tell you what, Sharon, this is what I need. Every missing persons case for the last forty days."

McLean held her ground. "You can do it yourself with Versadex."

Nastos stood up. "Listen, Sharon, Versadex and me, we aren't on speaking terms. I'm going to send someone by to pick up the reports. Can you have them ready for this afternoon?"

Nastos could hear McLean sigh. "Sure thing, I'll have it at the counter, Inspector."

"Good. I think you're the only one who knows what they're doing there, Sharon."

The phone went dead. Hopkins asked, "Who's Inspector Koche?"

"Just some loser."

"What was that about?"

"Feeling better."

"Why?"

"Because I'm not a cop anymore; I'm an independent instrument of karma. And it's death by a thousand lashes for Inspector Koche."

14

WHEN CHAVEZ LURCHED HIS
way inside through the laundry room door, Anthony had heard
the van and was waiting for him. He sounded bitchier than he
intended. "And where the hell have you been?"

Chavez grunted a response and kicked his boots off by the
washing machine. He had a fresh, red scrape across his face, jagged
like a shark's tooth, running from his right cheek to his throat. His
clothes smelled of musty earth.

"I need a shower," he said. "Then I need to sleep."

Anthony peeked out the laundry room window and saw that
Chavez had parked the van in front of the garage instead of inside it.

"The police have been here. You need to think of a new place to
park. We've talked about this."

"After I sleep."

Anthony followed Chavez as he slowly climbed the spiral stairs
and trudged through to the master bathroom. "You've been
spending a lot of time up there. Is everything going okay?"

"You mean the renovation at the other property, Anthony?
That shit-hole you expect me to turn into a mansion like this?"

Anthony felt like he'd been struck. Chavez knew very well what
Anthony had meant. And the other property, when renovated, would
be worth some much-needed money — though that wasn't the real
issue, and Chavez knew that. "Do I need to go and check?"

"No. And it's best if you don't — we've discussed that."

Chavez leaned into the shower and cranked it to full heat. He leaned back out, dripping onto the floor. He peeled off his shirt and pushed down his pants, kicking his jeans off. When he was naked, he slid into the stall and hit the diverter, making sure it was turned to full heat.

Anthony watched him lean backward into the hot stream, the water pouring down his hard face and body. His big jaw tilted upward to the faucet. He needed a shave; his cheeks would be abrasive. Chavez's strong hands rubbed vainly at the sleep on his face.

Anthony opened the shower door and spoke. "Those scrapes on your thighs, where did you get them?" The steam from the water dampened Anthony's face.

Chavez lathered shampoo in his hands and rubbed it on his head, then on his chest. Anthony noted the contrast of the white suds over the tanned skin and black hair.

"I have no idea," Chavez said. He leaned back and closed the door.

It was all Anthony needed to hear. Chavez had avoided eye contact, didn't touch him when he came in the door, didn't invite him into the shower and said he needed a nap though it was daytime. Anthony put it together and understood. Chavez had raped one of the captives and he was racing to the shower to get rid of the evidence.

Dammit, Chavez, this is going to change a few things. Anthony quickly pondered the situation. Chavez had raped and potentially left DNA on one of the victims, or more. *Should we change the order in which we dump the girls? No. We have to maintain the timeline to make it appear that a methodical killer is doing this. We might need to change the way the body is dumped to help with DNA. Again, no. It all has to be the same. How long does it take DNA to decompose in a living body? How long in a dead one?* Chavez and his insatiable sexual urges had screwed the whole thing up. The only way to save the plan was to get answers from Chavez. And right now, Chavez wasn't talking.

Anthony opened the shower door a crack and spoke through it. "I don't care if one of those girls seduced you; I don't blame them for trying. But, Chavez, we have to be careful of the DNA."

Chavez paused for a moment and shrugged. Then he leaned back into the water and rinsed the soap from his body. "It's not going to be a problem." Chavez turned off the water and pointed at the towel rack.

Anthony grabbed a white towel and passed it in for him. As easily as Chavez wrapped the towel around his waist, Anthony decided that Chavez was painting himself into a corner. Only he didn't know it yet.

There was radiator fluid in the garage. He had decided from the beginning that if Chavez went out of control and threatened Anthony's calling, then he would poison him at the shack and try to make it look like an accidental overdose. He'd made up a CD of depressing songs and dug out some old pictures of Chavez dressed in drag, mugging for the camera at the Pride Parade, from years ago. That should be enough for the average heterosexual cop to think he was some fucked-up individual who wanted to die.

Chavez interrupted his train of thought. "You said we were stopping at two. So there's nothing to worry about." When Chavez saw that Anthony was trying to understand what he said, he began to recite the rhyme. "One for sorrow, two for joy, three for a girl, four for a —"

"A boy," Anthony finished.

Anthony retreated to allow Chavez out of the shower, then followed him into the bedroom.

"We only needed three. Why did you take a boy?"

Chavez smiled. "Just a toy to pass the time. You should see him, innocent-looking. It was his first time with a man."

Anthony felt his heart beat more forcefully. He was both scared and intrigued. Capturing a boy was dangerous. He wasn't needed, wasn't part of the plan. Chavez was going to have to dump one extra body, one that they could not allow to be found and linked to the others. *So that's what he was doing — a little toy to pass the time.* Pangs of jealousy made Anthony's face flush red and his stomach drop.

"How old is he?"

Chavez smiled. "Eighteen. He looks it. The prime of life." Chavez dropped the towel to the floor and pointed to the bed. "Sit down there. I'll show you what I did to him. We can re-enact it."

"No, thanks, I have to get ready for a radio interview later today."

Chavez grabbed Anthony by the arms and forced him onto the bed, on his back. He grabbed a pillow and began to smother Anthony's face with it. When Anthony blindly reached up to grab Chavez's wrists, Chavez countered with a wrist lock and rolled him face down.

"This is almost exactly how it went, Anthony." Chavez wrenched Anthony's arms, then began to punch him in the ribs. Each hollow thud was followed by a muffled grunt from Anthony. Chavez punched harder and harder. Anthony refused to give up the safe-word that would tell Chavez when it was too much. If Chavez wanted to hear it, he was going to have to earn it.

Anthony felt a hand slide under his armpit, past his shoulder and up to his neck. He felt Chavez's naked body drop down on top of him and the hand at his throat tighten. Chavez hissed in his ear, "This is what happened to the boy."

Anthony struggled to breathe. A glob of saliva became stuck in his esophagus. It burned like acid as he tried to cough it clear, but the hand crushing his throat stifled his attempts.

Chavez punched him in the back a few times, then moved to a position to where he was squatting on Anthony's shoulders. Anthony bucked, trying to breathe. He was terrified; it wouldn't be the first time Chavez choked him to unconsciousness. He'd woken up before to find Chavez finishing with him. Surprisingly, though, Chavez let go of Anthony's throat with both hands and began sliding his pants down.

Yes, Anthony decided. *I wonder what the cards would have to say about Chavez.*

ANTHONY SAT ON A STOOL IN THE BOOTH AT THE NEWSTALK 1010 radio station. The immature bruises on his back and ribs ached, but they wouldn't echo the splendour of the fall leaves for a few days yet. He body was riddled with injuries, old and new. Unlike Anthony, Chavez knew how to do the damage without the showmanship.

There was a bright green button on in front of the host, Casey Barnes. A woman was reading the traffic report in a side booth. While Barnes was in conversation with a producer, Anthony found himself fiddling with the wire from his headphones. He could feel that his face was blanched. The self-marketing industry was best suited for the narcissists of the world; he dreaded it. *If only the people of the world would search for the truth, or even just recognize it when it came to them.* He fiddled more. *And Chavez. That man has to take over everything. Such a consumer. He's like a pet vortex, a black hole that sucks up everything he's near. It's my solemn duty to bring a message to the world, and he turns it into a hedonism retreat.* Anthony tried to clear his mind. *Take a breath, Anthony. Now lure them in to the show that will change their lives. It's for their own good.*

The light in front of Barnes turned red and he began to speak. "Welcome back from the break. We're sitting here with world-famous psychic Anthony Raines. He first came on the scene in the '80s when he helped the police locate a young man who had been murdered. Shortly afterwards, Anthony found himself busy with radio and television appearances and granting readings to everyone from celebrities to the common folk. Then he stepped away from his well-known public persona and decided to practice on a much more private scale. Anthony, what made you make that sort of transition?"

Anthony adjusted his headphones. They were heavy and snug, giving his ears the feeling of being gobbled up by warm leather. Anthony made a conscious effort to smile at Barnes. Casey was famous for his stint on television, hosting a show called *Mysteries Explained*. The whole show revolved around Casey debunking so-called psychics. Anyone who watched could see that Casey acquired great personal satisfaction from exposing con artists. Anthony had come prepared. Not your basic homework here — no, Anthony was thorough.

Anthony leaned into the microphone in front of him. "I semi-retired in an effort to simplify my life, to get back to the real reason why I started in the first place. I have an ability to connect with beings that have gone beyond our earthly experience. I have learned that this ability can help people here, in the living realm. When the fame came, everything began to spiral out of control. On the one hand, my notoriety allowed me to help more people. On the other hand, though, some people were scared to come see me because they did not want their suffering to become public fodder. Returning to a more discreet practice was the right thing to do."

Barnes swivelled in his chair and leaned forward with a devilish grin. "And now you are back in the public eye. Was the discreet practitioner running out of money?"

Anthony smiled. He'd seen that one coming a mile away. "No. In fact I'd be happy to retire completely. What happened was that I received a lot of requests from friends and fans alike. So I've decided to do a big show, a one-off if you will, at Casa Loma. It'll be a night filled with rapid-fire readings, open discussions and a few predictions that I feel an urgency to share with the audience."

Barnes smiled smugly as if to say that while he didn't believe a single word, he thought it made for great radio. "Anthony, I know you get asked all of the same questions time and time again. We here at NewsTalk 1010 have informed, intelligent listeners and if I may, I'd like to take the interview up a notch and ask some really different questions."

Anthony had agreed in the pre-interview prep that he would answer callers' questions and that anything was fair game. It was his moment to step back on stage, toss in some dazzle, and knock people off their feet. "Any time you're ready, Casey."

"So you speak to the spirits of people after they have died. How do they describe the afterlife?"

"Like where they are?"

"Yes, Anthony — what does the world look like to a ghost?"

Anthony checked the time on the clock. He had ten minutes before a traffic break. "Well, let's start at the beginning. I'd like the listeners who aren't driving or looking after kids — you know, the slackers at work or people here in the station — to play along. Turn up the radio and close your eyes. You're on a planet like earth, but it seems smaller. The sun is in the sky, but it's a dark purple colour. You can see the sun spots, you can see the solar wind radiating away from the sun. You can watch it pass the earth and the moon. Some stars are there, but not as many as we see here, so the constellations appear different at night. There are animals that resemble dogs, though they look wilder. People live in things like lean-tos; there is no advanced technology. Beautiful fruit trees, lush gardens and grasses, all with darker, blander colours. It's like walking through the most beautiful parts of earth with welder's glasses on."

"Have you ever spoken to any physicists who have passed over? What do they say? How do they explain where they are?"

"In fact, I have spoken to dead physicists."

Anthony checked the production booth. There were three young people in there, two men and a woman. They seemed riveted by his answers.

"Feel like sharing?"

Anthony smiled. This debunker was at least charming. "Sure. He speculates that he is in another dimension. Gravity is weaker. The light spectrum, as I described, is very different. He feels that it is a different dimension, one that we would describe here as dark matter. Dark matter is everywhere, all around us."

"Have you spoken to any dead psychics?" Barnes chuckled.

Anthony clenched his eyes shut, as if he was in pain. It wasn't hard to fake after the beating that Chavez had given him. He pinched the top of his nose and shook his head. He'd played with the pledge of magic long enough. It was time for the turn and the prestige.

Casey asked, "Are you feeling okay, Anthony?"

Anthony rubbed his face and eyes. "Sorry. Sorry. I opened up here. I have a visitor." He looked around the room. "Who's George Sherman?"

Barnes shook his head. "No idea, I —" He stopped suddenly and cupped a hand to his earphone. "My producer, Andy there in the booth, says that George Sherman was his grandfather."

Anthony looked at the booth and saw that one of the men had an expression of surprise on his face. "Well, Andy, your granddad sends his regards. He says they don't have soccer balls where he is, but they have sticks and pebbles. He and a bunch of veterans have taken up golf. He says he loves you and that Martha has nothing to worry about — they'll be together when she's ready, no rush. If you ask me, Andy, I think he's enjoying his time with the boys."

Barnes flipped a switch on his control panel. "You're on the air, Andy — what do you have to say to Anthony?"

Andy spoke into his mic. "My granddad died two years ago. He was a big soccer fan. That was his big saying, *send my regards*."

Anthony had the show-stopper memorized. "Yes, Andy. He told me about how you and he planned to watch the World Cup in 2010; it's too bad the heart attack took him first."

Andy's eyes were as big as dinner plates. He was speechless.

Casey asked, "Is that true, Andy?"

"Yeah." He turned to Anthony. "How did you know that?"

"Come to the show on October twenty-sixth at Casa Loma, and I'll tell you, and everyone else, everything."

Casey was watching Anthony. "So what is so important about your Casa Loma appearance?"

Anthony smiled. Time to sell. "Well, it's an interesting story. A while ago, I purchased a new set of tarot cards called Oracles. These are special cards; they are very old, hundreds of years old. Not long after the dream came to me. I awoke on the other side. I was walking backward through a warm, shallow river. There was a bright sun, the darkly tinted colours. I could look back downstream and see the eddies that I had caused in the water churning around my legs, the splashes from my steps as I steadied myself on the smooth rocks.

"I tried to turn my head to look upstream, but I couldn't. That's part of the experience there, and I understood it for what it was: a metaphor for life here. The way we walk backward into our future; we can look forever backward to our past. We can only understand our history, never our future. And the further back we look, the better we understand with objectivity."

Casey said nothing. He was trying to doubt Anthony, to remain objective. Anthony continued. "And I don't think it's any great concept I came up with; I was just given this gift of understanding, and I need to share it with others."

"So how does this help us?"

Anthony cleared his throat. "Eventually, I was able to turn around. I saw everything that was coming at us down the river. I think it's time we all deal with the truth."

Casey smiled. "Let me guess, you'll tell us all about it at the Casa Loma show?"

"That's right. I'll reveal what we have to do to avoid what's coming."

15

NASTOS SAT IN CARSCADDEN'S office, flipping through the pages of the Bannerman file, hoping to see something that he might have missed before. Being alone wasn't helping. Working alone had been the annoying part of the insurance gig — no one to bounce ideas around with. Carscadden was out fighting with the Police Services Board about his lawsuit against them, and Hopkins had left to grab something to read from the used book store a few doors down and was taking her sweet time. Nastos drummed his fingers on the desk while staring at the picture of Lindsay, trying to put himself in her place.

He asked her, "So, where were you taken from? Did you see anything that can help us find you?"

Nastos anticipated dozens of missing persons reports coming from Records. Now it occurred to him that if she *had* been taken, then there might be a few suspicious vehicle calls or suspicious people called in to the police from botched abductions. *Whoever abducted her must have made mistakes previously, either in Toronto or someplace else.* He had to hope that if mistakes were made, it had been in Toronto, or he would never find her in the time remaining before she'd been gone for thirty days like that poor girl with *Sorrow* carved on her chest and *30* on her wrist.

Nastos considered the number 30. He found the newspaper article about Anthony and scanned down the page. The dead girl,

Rebecca Morris, had been missing exactly thirty days, if the article was correct. *I wonder if that's what the 30 means?*

Calling Sharon McLean back to request the suspicious persons and vehicles reports wasn't an option. He'd have to wait a long time before he could bluff her again. Further impersonating Koche might prompt her to file a complaint, and she might figure out that the real Koche had made no such inquiries.

Realizing that he needed someone else to instigate the search, he retrieved the name Jacques from his BlackBerry address book and dialed his ex-partner's number.

Jacques answered on the second ring. "Let me guess, you need something."

"Well, isn't that nice. I call to congratulate you on the Habs' embarrassing loss against Washington last night and this is how you treat me."

He heard Jacques chuckle a little. Knowing he was in good spirits was a relief; he'd probably help. "This coming from the Leafs fan. Guess you don't like someone muscling their way into your position at the bottom of the crap pile."

Nastos asked, "You near a terminal?"

"Here it comes."

He flipped the newspaper around to look at the picture of Anthony. "Anyone around?"

"This is going to be a bad one. No, go ahead."

"Listen, Jacques, did you hear about the body recovered at Morningside? Sorrow?"

"Yeah, Sorrow. The whole department knows about it. I knew it would be just a matter of time before someone blabbed to the media." Jacques must have thought Nastos had heard about it on the radio. The reporters at crime scenes always coerced someone to talk. Soon enough it would hit the internet. Then reporters would ask more and more probing questions until the implications and non-denials couldn't last. The police wouldn't have much time.

"Jacques, I only knew about it because I was there. I'm

wondering if some of the missing girls out there in the city have been abducted by the same guy. There could be more."

"If you were there, did you suggest that to Dennehy?"

"He wasn't in a receptive mood. I think he only likes his own ideas."

"Not a big deal. If he liked it, tomorrow it *will* be his idea."

"Yeah, well, the reason I called is I'd like you to run every *attempted* abduction for complainants that are approximately her age and physical appearance. I'd like to read through the reports."

"How far back?"

Nastos glanced back at Anthony's picture. "The last sixty days."

Jacques' phone made static noises, like Jacques had moved to another room. "Oh, that's all."

"No. I also want the suspicious persons or suspicious vehicles too."

"Also for the last sixty days?"

"Yeah."

"Listen, Nastos, it's not like I've gotten any better with computers since you left. This new system is a mess. What age range are we talking here? I'll do what I can and get back to you."

He tapped his pen on the paper. "Late teens, female, blond, thin."

"Nastos, you're asking me to data-mine the entire system. It would take over an hour just to print off all the reports this will generate."

Nastos was hoping Jacques would come to that conclusion. "Okay," he said, "here's an idea. Send the request down to Sharon McLean in Records. Tell her it's for Inspector Koche and that he has someone coming by to pick it up today."

Jacques made a sound like he'd been punched in the stomach. "Koche? Hearing that name makes me want to be sick."

"Tell me about it."

"Well, wait a minute. How is sending it down in his name going to help? Is he your buddy now?"

"No, I'm going to get a friend to go in and pick it up. That's if she ever gets back here."

NASTOS WAITED AROUND THE OFFICE FOR ANOTHER TWENTY minutes before deciding to forget about Hopkins; he was pissed off enough by all the waiting that he was ready to get the files himself. Now that he was no longer a cop, impersonating an officer to pick up confidential files from the records department was beyond a penalty-box infraction. If caught, he would be criminally charged and sentenced to jail — again. But Lindsay Bannerman couldn't wait for freedom of information requests and faxed reports that would be heavily redacted and illegible. He had little choice.

He put on his detective's jacket and tie, and he knew the procedure for picking up files. The real risk was being recognized.

He was halfway to the door when the phone rang and he went back to answer it. He hoped that it was Carscadden calling to stop him from doing something stupid. "Carscadden Law Firm."

A man spoke, slurring so badly he was barely understandable. He said, "Ken Carscadden."

Nastos couldn't tell if it was a statement or a question. He thought for a moment, trying to figure out what the guy wanted. Finally he said, "No, this is the law offices of Kevin Carscadden, you must have —"

"No, I'm Ken Carscadden, aren't you listening?"

Now Nastos was lost. *Who's this asshole?*

The man said, "I'm looking for my son. Who the hell are you?"

Now it makes sense. "I'm Steve Nastos, his business —"

Ken's tone relaxed considerably. "You're that cop that Kevin helped."

Nastos briefly considered pulling the chair out, but he didn't want to talk to a drunk on the phone all day, even if it was Carscadden's dad. "Yeah, your son really saved my ass. He's a good lawyer, he's just not here. So I'll tell him you —"

"Don't bother, don't bother. He never calls back anyways." The man hung up, leaving Nastos staring at the phone, wondering if the conversation had ever happened.

◻ ◻ ◻

NASTOS PARKED IN THE UNDERGROUND PARKING AT FORTY COLLEGE Street. The last time he had been there was to turn in his badge and other police gear: the gun belt that no longer fit, winter coats he'd never worn, a ticket book he rarely used, radio clips, everything except the baton, pepper spray and gun that had already been seized back when he was arrested. Barging into the chief's office with two garbage bags of gear and dumping them on his desk while he sat there slack-jawed with a phone up to his ear was a bittersweet memory. He tried to tell himself that he became an urban legend that day — as if he'd won the lottery and quit in style. Unfortunately, the truth was that he had been forced out, no matter how much he tried to take pride in the smallest of skirmishes; it was hard to ignore that he'd lost the war.

The elevator was narrow with a glass back wall. He pressed Floor Three to go to Records. When the door opened, there were half a dozen people standing there to get on. They were all civilians, except for one street cop who seemed to be on a mail run, holding a milk crate full of manila envelopes.

Nastos exited and turned right to go down the hallway. He had told himself so many times that it was urgent that he get the records as soon as possible that the idea that he might be doing this for the excitement was almost completely suppressed. He needed something to get the blood flowing again, or maybe just to thumb his nose at the organization.

The glass door had Records stencilled on it. He reached into his pocket, put his cell phone to his ear and opened the door. There were two detectives in line ahead of him and no one at the counter. Nastos recognized one cop from somewhere, but couldn't put a place to the name he remembered. When the officer saw Nastos, he smiled and hit his partner on the shoulder.

"Well, if it isn't Nasty Nastos. How the hell are you?"

"Nasty, just like always. How you doing, Phil?"

Phil turned to the other detective. "This is Steve Nastos — we used to work together in Thirty-One when we first pulled into town on the turnip truck. He was the guy with that dentist thing, you remember that?"

The cop's eyes opened in surprise. "Holy shit." He stuck his hand out. "Ian Fenton, nice to meet you."

Phil interrupted. "What brings you by, Nastos?"

He picked up a stack of Freedom of Information requests. "I work for an insurance company now. I need to order some records."

Phil exhaled and jabbed his thumb at the counter. "Good luck getting anything today. Some big wheel from upstairs has them all running around like heads with their chickens cut off. Typical bullshit."

A woman came back to the counter. She had bookish good looks, with her hair back in a bun and stylish glasses. He saw from the name tag that this was the McLean woman that he had been talking to on the phone earlier.

"Here you go guys, sorry for the delay." She avoided eye contact like she had overheard Phil's complaint and felt personally responsible.

Both Phil and Ian smiled. Ian said, "Hey, thanks."

They turned to leave. Phil held the door open for Ian, who was carrying the most files. "Nice seeing you, Nastos — gimme a call sometime if you want to grab a beer."

"You got it, Phil. See you."

Nastos had his phone up to his face with a hand over the mouthpiece like he had been in a conversation with someone. After Phil left, he put a finger up to ask the girl to wait a second and spoke into his cell.

"I'm here right now, Inspector Koche. So I should be back within the half hour. Sorry sir, traffic was . . . from who, sir?

Jacques? Lapierre? Sure, I'll get them, too. Okay, but —" He stared at the display screen on the phone, feigning confusion at an imaginary hang-up, then closed the cell phone and put it back in his pocket. He shook his head and said to the girl at the counter, "Inspector Koche is a fucking asshole, if you'll pardon my street language."

Her head tilted to one side. "You're here for him?" Nastos could see that she was wondering if she should hate him by association.

"Yeah. That narcissist, power-tripping tyrant is my boss. Lucky me. There's apparently a lot of Versadex reports here for him. He also just said something about Jacques Lapierre having something for me too, I'm just not sure if that's a first name or a last name." Nastos offered her his cell phone. "Maybe you'd like to call him and ask. I really don't feel like taking the risk of setting him off."

She recoiled from the phone as if it were covered in gonorrhea bacteria. "One second, please." She left the counter and disappeared into a back room. Nastos waited. He'd had his fun; now he just wanted to make a clean getaway. The woman came back to the desk with a banker's box. She heaved it up onto the counter. It landed with a dull thud.

She slid over the sign-in book. "The Lapierre files are in there too." Nastos wrote down something illegible and lifted the banker's box. Sharon hit a button on the counter and the power assist opened the door for Nastos. Nastos smiled. "Thanks, Sharon, you're the best."

16

NASTOS WAS RELIEVED TO EXIT the Police Records Unit. Headquarters was the kind of place that was swarming with people who were cops in name only. They carried badges and talked tough, but hadn't been on the road for years. Accommodated because they couldn't handle night shifts, promoted because they worked out, drank or golfed with the right people — whatever the reason, they had positioned themselves in HQ for straight days and light work. He'd feel more comfortable raiding a drug den or a biker clubhouse than this place.

He walked the hallway to the elevator lobby and pressed the button to go down. Once at his car, he put the box in the trunk and drove back to the office.

Traffic was starting to pick up again. On Yonge Street, the homeless had woken and taken their positions at the street corners, out front of the McDonald's, sitting in doorways, with their hats out, hands out, anything out to collect loose change. Most people ignored them. Tourists and teenagers were the most likely to even notice them and to cave in.

Nastos parked and paid the meter, returned to the car to put the white parking tag in the windshield, then brought the banker's box out of the trunk and carried it into the office. The door chimed. Hopkins was sitting in her desk, reading her mystery novel. She didn't look up from the book when she spoke.

"Don't go in the office."

Nastos put the box on the counter in front of Hopkins. "Why not?"

Hopkins folder down a page and put the book next to her keyboard.

"Kevin needs some rest."

"Rest," Nastos confirmed. "As in, he's sleeping during the day?"

She shrugged. "He arrived here in a cab, smells like a brewery, collapsed on the couch and hasn't moved since."

"Chip off the old block, eh?"

Hopkins perked up. "Huh?"

Nastos wasn't sure he'd be staying; he peeled his coat off anyway because Hopkins kept the heat at a perfectly reasonable seventy-six. "I was here earlier. His dad, Ken, called. He was wasted."

Hopkins exhaled, like she had been bracing herself for bad news.

Nastos asked, "What am I missing?"

"His mom's not doing well."

"Is she sick?"

"Yeah, sick of his dad. Ken's got the disease, and he's off the wagon, hitting it hard. The only reason that Kevin's the man he is is because of her. Kevin's a gentleman because she raised him to be one. But he drinks because of what his dad did to him." She stood up and straightened her skirt. "Buy me a water in the lunch room."

"Sure."

Nastos filled two glasses with tap water and they took seats across from each other at the lunch table. Nastos peeked out to make sure the office door was still closed. There were no signs of life.

She asked, "What do you know about his upbringing?"

Nastos sighed and rubbed his sweaty palms on his pants. "I think I first suspected something was seriously wrong when I learned that they were a pair of west-coast Leafs fans."

"Do you two take anything seriously?"

Nastos shrugged. *Looks like it's time to get serious.* He'd worked with a few cops that drank too much. Sometimes a hint or two was enough to get some people to back it off. He'd tried that with Carscadden and it hadn't worked. And being passed-out drunk in the middle of a workday was pathetic. "Well, our boy has an alcohol problem. Looks like he's having a relapse. He doesn't seem like he's addicted, though. I wonder what's going on."

Hopkins was staring through the table, lost in thought.

Nastos waved his hand in front of Hopkins to break her from her trance. "I know a guy."

"You know a guy, what?"

Nastos refilled his bottle of water from the tap, taking a long drink. "After the mess with Josie and that dead asshole, I — well, the whole family — we went to counselling with this guy who came recommended. He was really good. He's a Ph.D. in psychology. Madeleine thought he looked like Johnny Depp, except with blue eyes."

Hopkins didn't look overly disappointed by the physical description.

"We called him No Frills Mills. I'll give him a call." Nastos pulled out his phone and started scrolling through numbers.

"Why No Frills?"

"He gets right to the point. People have defense mechanisms; no one ever wants to change. He has this way of telling you that you're a big idiot without it being insulting. He deals with things quickly. He also dresses in T-shirts and jeans. His place looks like a tattoo parlour."

Hopkins looked let down. "Oh, man."

Nastos had to smile. "Did that ruin the fantasy?"

She shrugged. "I guess I don't mind a few tattoos." Now that Hopkins was warmed up, she obviously wanted to keep talking. "How are you and Madeleine doing?"

He sighed. *Here we go.* There was no woman he could talk to about Maddy except Hopkins. The two had become friends and Hopkins knew something was wrong already. "My 'selfish need for excitement' is getting in the way of our prosperity." Nastos didn't have Tara Hopkins' complete resume, but he knew she was street-smart. Her dad was a tyrant who was a self-employed plumber. She had nicknamed him Angry Angelo. He was a control freak about everything. She had bailed at eighteen and tended bar or worked retail most of her life. Meeting Carscadden was the best thing that could have happened to her.

Nastos felt a connection with her more intuitively than he did with Madeleine. Hopkins was the kind of girl who, if someone broke into her house and came at her, would pull the trigger without the slightest hesitation. Madeleine once called the police because a bat flew into the house.

"I don't think that finding a lost little girl is selfish. And hey, I work here. It's hardly exciting. I think your wife has security problems. It's like she's outsourced all of her own protective instincts to you. And when you don't do what makes her feel safe, she freaks out."

"Yeah. If I tell her to toughen up, she thinks I'm abandoning her."

Hopkins exhaled, saying nothing. After a while, she smiled. "You know, she described you to me in a way I found interesting. She said your natural instinct is to do everything yourself, just like a body that rejects a donated heart. You'd rather shun foreign intrusion, even if it means death. Trust comes slowly to you."

Nastos didn't say anything. He thought about the partners he'd had to work with over the years; there had only been two he trusted. But how many people do most people trust with both their lives and livelihood? Jacques was still in Sexual Assault; he had trained an ex-partner named Karen in the detective's office — she quit fifteen years in, to become a journalist, of all things. He was just better working alone, agile and efficient. No one else was worthy of trust.

Hopkins interrupted his thoughts. "When I first met Kevin two years ago, it was like he was my knight in shining armour. On the other hand, he's also a lost little boy, and they kind of balance each other out. Now, with the drinking — I've dated a drinker before — I know what that ride is like. Maybe I'm getting too lazy, but I want someone in my life who *wants* me, doesn't just *need* me. He needs to save me and needs me to save him. I'm not sure how much love is there sometimes."

"He loves you, Tara — hell, he's obsessed with you, and I don't blame him. I'll call Mills. You're going to like what he can do." Nastos finished his bottle of water. "Well, I'm out of here. I don't want to wake him up, so I can work from home."

"You don't mind?"

"Hmmm . . . pick Josie up from school, go home and make something for dinner, then spend the night reading a box of reports. Sure as hell beats Carscadden snoring beer breath."

17

NASTOS SAT AT THE RECEPTION
desk, reading through the files he had appropriated from the police
records department. Voices from the office, though muffled and
quiet, were still distracting. He took no pleasure in knowing that
Carscadden was being dissected by Mills while Hopkins sat there
with a front-row seat on the other side of the office door. Nastos
went to the 680 News Radio website and listened to the broadcast
to provide Carscadden some privacy. The channel advised the
upcoming repeat of the fifteen-minute news cycle. Nastos made
a point of listening. The headline story made him terrified once
more that Lindsay had been found, dead.

A reporter began, "Another body has been found in the Junction
Triangle area of Toronto, near Lansdowne Avenue and Dupont
Street. Police aren't releasing any details; however, police spokes-
person Constable Lee did not deny that there may be a link to the
previous suspicious death just a few days ago, dubbed the 'Sorrow
Slayings' by a police insider who asked not to be identified."

The voice of the police spokesperson came on. "Our investigation is in the earliest possible stages. We don't want to speculate as
to any linkage to the other body found. We aren't ruling it out
either. It's important at this stage that we keep open minds and let
the evidence lead the investigation."

Nastos turned to the reports in his hands. He flipped through

133

and found what he was looking for. Which girl had been gone for exactly thirty days? He said "Andrea Dobson" out loud to himself.

He read her complete file, then set it aside, rushing to read through the next reports. He turned to the pile dedicated to suspicious persons, which could turn out to be poorly investigated botched abductions. Two reports of suspicious persons offered some kind of a lead — two different girls, both in their teens, thin with long hair, described being creeped out while walking past a van on separate days. Both girls reported looking back over their shoulders, with a feeling that they were being watched. One girl saw nothing, only glare on the glass; the other described a man with a dark complexion staring at her. He looked to be in his forties and had a muscular frame.

If there had not been other people around, the girls said, they would have felt unsafe. Both instances had been reported as suspicious persons to police, and both had occurred before Lindsay Bannerman disappeared. One girl reported it because her dad made her, the other because she was concerned that the man seemed predatory. She described him in the report as if he were a lion from the Discovery Channel, like he was stalking a gazelle.

Nastos scanned down in the reports. The van was described in both reports as old and grey. One report suggested that one of the side mirrors had been shattered. There was a decal or writing on the sides; neither teen was able to recall what it said. One incident occurred in the Ellesmere and Meadowvale area, the other at Steeles and Morningside — ten minutes apart by car.

The door chimed. Madeleine Nastos smiled when she saw him at the front desk.

"How's it going with them in there?"

Nastos shrugged. "No yelling, no weeping; they're not giving me much to go on." Madeleine didn't take her coat off. He said, "If I had known you were coming by, I would have cleaned up."

She checked out the office and peeked into the lunch room. "Tara's done a good job with this place since I was here last." The phone rang. Nastos picked it up, and Madeleine picked up a magazine and began flipping through it. It was an old one of hers that she had donated a few months ago.

The name on the call display read *Bannerman*.

"Carscadden Law."

"Is that you, Nastos?"

"Yes, sir, it is. What's up?"

Bannerman let out his anger. "You remember that con artist psychic that my wife had over? Anthony Raines?"

Nastos wedged the phone to his ear with his shoulder and began shuffling the files together. He left the Andrea Dobson file and the two suspicious persons files on top. "Yeah. That asshole followed me home after I left your place."

Bannerman carried along as if he hadn't heard Nastos. "He's been back to the house. I just got off the phone with my wife. She had him over again. He gave her a psychic reading. He went into Lindsay's room, for Christ's sake."

Nastos had plenty of ideas regarding what to do about Raines. He reminded himself that the Carscadden Law Firm utilized a customer-based approach in decision making.

"Just tell us what you'd like to happen here, Mr. Bannerman. Our firm would be happy —"

"I want a cease and desist order issued to him today, telling him not to contact me or my wife ever again."

Nastos was disappointed. He was hoping Bannerman was pissed enough to suggest something more exciting than a letter written by a lawyer, even a harshly worded one. "Sure. It'll be delivered today. Maybe you can do me, or both of us, a quick favour?"

Bannerman sounded surprised. "What can *I* do?"

Nastos brought over a writing pad. "Check out Mr. Raines, see what kind of mortgage he owes. Do a full financial on him."

"You think he's broke? He lives in Rosedale."

"Let's find out."

Bannerman answered by pounding a keyboard. There was a

pause. "He's not with our bank. I'm doing a credit score, though. Holy shit."

"Won't you get in trouble for that?"

"We can do searches on people for security reasons in case we suspect fraud. The credit bureau will see it as an invisible search, and people with lower access will never know."

"So what's it like?"

Bannerman said, "It's like we wouldn't lend him five dollars if his life depended on it. He's in debt up to his eyeballs."

"Then there you go. He smells money, and you ended up on his radar screen." Nastos hesitated. "Other than that, how are you holding up?"

Bannerman didn't answer right away, like maybe he didn't really want to. "Up and down. I feel like I'm going crazy. At times I push her out of my mind just to function; then I remember, and I feel guilty for forgetting about her. She's all I can think about but, because it hurts, all I can't think about. We're both taking Atavan to sleep. We drank two bottles of wine at dinner last night . . . But you know . . . the people at work here are so understanding. I . . . I think they heard about the girl they found dead and think the worst. My secretary is a battle-axe. She came into my office yesterday and gave me a hug. She was crying. I asked her what was wrong and she wiped her eyes and said that they are all worried about Lindsay."

Nastos didn't want to tell him what he was thinking. With a second body found at the Junction Triangle, it was beginning to look like his suspicions of a serial abductor and killer were more accurate than he had hoped. "We're doing everything we can, Mr. Bannerman."

"I know, I know."

After they hung up, Nastos scratched a note on the writing pad, then stood up to see Madeleine. Before he could say anything to her, Mills came out of the office. When he saw Nastos, he declared, "He's cured," and smiled.

Nastos stood up and offered his hand. "Thanks again for coming in like this."

"It's nice to get out of the office."

Mills recognized Madeleine when he reached for his coat. "Hey, Madeleine, nice to see you."

She smiled. "Hey, good to see you, too."

Mills put his coat on, and with a wave of the hand disappeared out the door.

When Carscadden and Hopkins came out, Carscadden was embarrassed to see Madeleine waiting there. He said, "Holy crap, does the entire country know?"

Madeleine wrapped her arms around him. "Big deal, so you hit the booze like a sailor. Girls think sailors are cute." She finished by saying, "But back it off before you make us worried about you." She released Carscadden.

Nastos told them about Bannerman's phone call and Anthony Raines.

Madeleine said, "Sounds like he's desperate for money."

"Yeah, so Carscadden will fire off a quick letter and we'll get his address and drop it off. He's somewhere in Rosedale."

Hopkins went over to the computer and brought up Canada411. After a moment, she said, "Unlisted. I'll just go to his website." She frowned. "Only email — wait, here's a number."

She was going to dial when Nastos stopped her. "He'll see the call display if you call from here."

Madeleine suggested, "Use the Lands Registry program; that's not unlisted."

Nastos smiled appreciatively. "That's my sneaky girl."

She winked at him and blew him a kiss like Marilyn Monroe, except cuter.

Hopkins thought it was funny enough, but Nastos found himself resenting the gesture. She'd frozen him out for so long that he knew it was just a sales job for her friends. He reached back over the reception counter and produced the suspicious persons files for Carscadden to read.

Carscadden read the first page. "How did you get this, exactly?"

Nastos shook his head from side to side. Carscadden didn't really want to know.

"Two girls reported being followed. It was by an old piece-of-junk van with a decal on the side. One girl said the side mirror was busted. The driver was dark, muscular and in his forties."

Hopkins said, "You should tell the cops about it."

Nastos felt like a loser. Now he was the kind of guy who, when he had a problem, had to go running to cops for help.

"Yeah, you're right." He felt his excitement dissipate. He had been feeling like he was putting everything together; now the pieces were all over the floor again. "We'll give them a call."

Hopkins sounded keen. "Hey, check this out. Raines has two houses on record. One in Rosedale, the other — one sec."

Hopkins went to Google Maps. "Rexdale. Assessed value, two hundred thousand. A single house, it says."

Madeleine shook her head. "I'll tell you right now without looking at it that no one lives there — it'll be a boarded-up piece of garbage for that valuation."

Hopkins said, "Oh, yeah?"

Maddy said, "Guaranteed. Maybe he's going to do a reno and try to flip it. It could go for four hundred if he does a good job, so if he could do it with only a hundred in, he'd walk away with a hundred thousand."

Hopkins whistled. "Not bad for extra money."

Carscadden opened the door to the office. "Ms. Hopkins, if you could forward me the asshole's address so I can write a nasty letter."

"Sure thing, Mr. Carscadden," she said. "I'll even deliver it. Right after I have tea with Madeleine. We have some urgent matters to discuss about Dr. Mills, the rugged-looking sensitive type."

Nastos said, "We won't be here when you get back. They found a dead girl in the Junction Triangle area. Carscadden and I need to talk to the cops there. We'll leave the letter on the reception desk."

"You think it's Lindsay?" Carscadden's body tensed with dread.

"No, I think it's Andrea Dobson." Nastos held up her missing person report. "Exactly thirty days."

18

THE LAST TIME NASTOS HAD been to the Junction Triangle for work was for a call where a deranged dad had tossed his three kids from a third-floor balcony, then dismembered his girlfriend while his wife smoked a crack pipe and watched from the couch. As Carscadden drove them past brown brick low-rises and sand-coloured concrete plazas, nine-teenth-century homes, narrow and tall with tight, crooked porches, peeked out like children hiding behind a curtain. Nastos glanced at the building where the near-massacre occurred and felt sick to his stomach.

Carscadden yawned. "Remind me — they didn't release the name on the radio, did they?"

"No, you didn't miss it. The name isn't released. But she's been gone thirty days, just like the last girl, Sorrow."

"Rebecca." Carscadden reminded him. "Rebecca Morris."

"Right. And this is Andrea Dobson."

Nastos turned on the GPS and typed in the intersection of Dupont Street and Lansdowne Avenue. "There," he said. "Get on Lakeshore and exit north at Parkside. It goes —"

"Yeah, I know, right up to Dupont. With traffic we'll be there in fifteen."

Nastos exhaled.

Carscadden smiled. "Did we just finish each other's sentence?"

Nastos shuddered as he thought of Dennehy and Byrne. "That one doesn't count."

Nastos held up the Andrea Dobson report in his right hand and glanced at it. If she turned out to be the missing person they had just announced on the radio, then Lindsay Bannerman was in some serious trouble.

□   □   □

WITH THE ENVIABLE KNOWLEDGE HINDSIGHT OFFERS, ANTHONY SAT in his office, planning for overnight success for the second time in his life. The Casa Loma show was going to be his legacy. Like the prophesies of Nostradamus and Edgar Cayce. The difference was that he was going to do it live, over the internet, for all the world to see.

It was going to run two hours, which for him was a long time. He would start with cold readings for the audience; then, at the forty-five-minute mark, he would show a short video on the history of mysticism and tarot. Here he would take a piss break if needed and set up for the real purpose of the show: the enlightenment of humanity.

They had to know about the afterlife once and for all. It was going to be a turning point in human spiritualism to finally know what happens after death, where we go and what is waiting for us on the other side. The video would be replayed on YouTube millions of times. The knowledge that he would soon change the view of every organized religion on the planet was exhilarating.

He admired the image of himself on his desk: a silver-framed black-and-white picture of him and his older sister; they were six and seven at the time. A neighbour, a budding photographer in the early 1970s, had asked his mother permission to do a photo shoot with the children. He had shot them as they were, faces dirty and clothes grubby from playing, and had instructed them not to smile. The shot captured them both with forlorn expressions, their eyes gazing intently into the camera.

The image was, in a way, ominous. It was like the Anthony of the past was staring into him and in turn he was sending information back. The confidence he had always felt about his sexuality, the confidence he had always had in himself — he realized that it was at this moment of his present life that he was able to transmit it back to his past self. He had become a self-defining spirit, like the Dalai Lama.

With new eyes he appraised himself, the child he had been before the bullying and abuse at school had begun when it became obvious that he was different from the other boys. The taunts and punches were still in this young boy's future. He had gotten through it with no help from anyone, with a quiet, unstoppable resolve, the source of which he understood only now. He had taken the pain the world had served him and had overcome.

He was pulled from his reverie by a knock at the study door. *Who would knock? Do I have a reading today?*

"Hello?"

It was Greta, the dog walker. "Anthony, you have a client here."

Anthony opened the door. Behind her was a woman he had never seen before. He squinted. "I'm sorry, I don't remember having a reading booked."

The woman smiled demurely and glanced at Greta.

Greta squeezed Anthony's arm before leaving. "I'll see you in a couple days."

Anthony smiled. "Oh, right, bye."

After she had followed him down the hall, the short woman extended her hand. "Tara Hopkins." She was curvy, well dressed. Dark hair, big eyes.

He reached to take the proffered greeting. Instead of shaking his hand, she placed an envelope in it and smiled broadly. "Bad news, I'm afraid."

Anthony looked down, surprised. He opened the envelope and began reading the letter.

She said, "I've been to psychics, years ago. This is a letter from Mr. Bannerman's lawyer. It's asking you not to contact them or to enter onto their property."

Anthony smiled insincerely and waved off the psychic comment. He was trying to determine if he could still make it work with the Bannermans off-site. He could. "Is there anything else? Do I need to sign anything?"

"No. But I'll watch your show from Casa Loma." She had turned to leave when Anthony stopped her.

"Wait one second."

She paused, "Yes?"

"You work for that cute lawyer — what's his name again?"

He looked down again at the letter while she answered, "Kevin Carscadden."

He watched her face. His eyes lingered just a little too long. "Well, you don't need to be a psychic to know he's your man."

"Yeah, well, it's pretty cliché to be dating the boss."

"It just means you get to spend a lot of time with someone you love. Good for you."

She said nothing in return; she just smiled.

"Well, here, I'll show you out."

He waved an arm, inviting her to join him. "I've never been in a house in Rosedale before. This place is huge," she commented.

"Six thousand square feet. I bought it years and years ago. It's become quite the money pit. Now, Castle Frank is one of the nicest streets in the city — I'm not complaining."

"I like the built-in cabinetry. It looks so lived-in, but with such clean lines." She was checking out the décor. She had a good eye for detail. Maybe her man could buy her a house here if he was good with his money. Anthony knew with some certainty that she had grown up poor. She had probably tended bar, earned money off her looks. By now she was either divorced or was a serial dater of chronic losers. She had hit the lottery with this lawyer. Carscadden was her meal ticket and Anthony knew how that worked. In a way, she had surrendered her courage to find her own way and was dating a paycheque. Now she was allowing herself to dream about the good life.

"I had the built-ins done myself. I met a man who's good with his hands." He paused. "If you know what I mean."

Hopkins smiled.

He stopped at the front door and opened it. "Well, I'm sorry we had to meet this way. I hope this doesn't turn you off my profession."

"No. Just don't tell my boss I'll be watching your show. That has to be our little secret."

Anthony smiled. "Thank you."

He watched her go. She had a confident walk. Thick, clunky shoes that she had to clop along in; Anthony was sure she drove the boys crazy and caused traffic jams from time to time. Thinking of his expanding waist and thinning hair, he forced a smile. Lucky bitch.

A van stopped at the end of the driveway. It was Chavez, parking in right out front despite being explicitly told not to — twice. There was no getting through to him.

He was wearing jeans and a tight T-shirt, which would almost be enough to make Anthony forget the indiscretion if the stakes weren't so high.

When he glanced back at Hopkins, he knew right away that the world had come to an end. She had stopped in place, an arm's length away from her suv. She was staring at Chavez — no, at his van. Something about his arrival was obviously ringing alarm bells in her head. She knew something.

Anthony, even at twenty feet away, could see the goose bumps all over her body. She wasn't excited. She was scared out of her mind. At first he frantically appealed to himself to understand what it was that she perceived as a threat. The van was so distinct, white with the peeled decals and the smashed side mirror. It was too late to worry about what it was that caught her eye; all he had time to do was minimize the damage.

Chavez smiled at Anthony. When he noticed Hopkins, he realized something was wrong. He stopped in his tracks. It was standoff.

Anthony made an instant decision. He broke the draw, shouting, "She knows. She knows!"

Chavez reacted immediately. He charged Hopkins at full speed, racing up the long driveway. She shot a terrified glance back at

143

Anthony as she fumbled to pull the keys out of her purse. She quickly abandoned the idea, dropping the purse entirely and opening the vehicle door with the remote. She was half-inside and beginning to pull the door closed when Chavez grabbed hold of her. One hand grabbed a fistful of hair while the other wrapped around her neck. He ripped her out of the car like she weighed ten pounds and tossed her to the ground. He straddled her, his knees on either side of her head, and choked her unconscious in seconds. She never made a sound.

Anthony blinked, not believing how quickly Chavez had taken her down. He forced himself to swivel his head, checking for witnesses. No one had seen anything. Anthony ran over and crouched down next to Chavez. "Get her in your van and get her the hell out of here."

Chavez's dark eyes met Anthony's. "Others will come."

Anthony thought about that. "No. She didn't know anything until she saw you. She was totally taken by surprise. This wasn't about me, it was about you. They know about *you*."

Chavez's lips curled up as he considered that. Anthony noticed for the first time that he looked exhausted, like he hadn't slept in days. The presence of Hopkins' car gave Anthony the excuse he'd been looking for to drive up to the other house and find out what was there for himself.

Anthony opened her purse and saw the cell phone. He was about to crush it when something stopped him. A voice in his head reminded him that he might not want to disable her GPS-equipped cell phone while it was in his driveway. Instead he would toss it out somewhere along the drive.

He found her keys and sat in her SUV. Something about adjusting her seat position and the angle of the rear-view mirror made him feel that she was essentially dead. It was terrifying to drive her vehicle, even with the knowledge that Chavez would burn it out or otherwise make sure it was never found. Still, god knew what cops could do with DNA.

Before they started driving to the shack, Chavez took the

precaution of duct-taping her wrists and ankles. Anthony noticed he didn't tape her mouth. He probably wanted someone to taunt on the drive up.

Anthony tried to think about where they could possibly have gone wrong. He knew he hadn't made any mistakes, so it had to be Chavez. Hopkins had frozen in terror when she had seen the van. He'd tell Chavez to get rid of it and start driving something else.

◻ ◻ ◻

DRIVING TO A CRIME SCENE TO IDENTIFY A DEAD YOUNG WOMAN WAS not enough to make Carscadden forget about Dr. Mills crawling around inside his brain. Mills had been aggressive — a butcher, not a surgeon — and he needed quiet place to be alone, some silence to reorganize his thoughts. The more he considered what had happened, the more he thought Mills had been maddening. He had done nothing more than kick up dust and had left Carscadden to clean it all up.

Carscadden's cell phone buzzed. He jerked it out, hoping it would be Hopkins, but the display said Bannerman. He jabbed Nastos' shoulder with his elbow. "Hey — Mr. Bannerman."

Nastos turned off the car's radio, then Carscadden hit the hands-free button so Bannerman's voice would play loud enough for both of them to hear. He didn't sound happy.

"Yes, Mr. Carscadden, it looks like I have a problem here. That bitch Jessica has started a Facebook page where she has identified me as a rapist and the murderer of my daughter."

Carscadden felt like he'd found a suitable outlet for his anger. "That fucking whore."

"The media called looking for a statement — *Toronto Today* magazine. I want you to deal with this as soon as you can. One of the lawyers from work called and offered to do it, but, you know, I just want to keep some form of normalcy in my work life. They're all supportive — I don't know. This is getting to be too much."

Carscadden glanced over. Nastos had his BlackBerry out and

was trying to find the Facebook page Bannerman had mentioned. When he found it, he gave Carscadden a thumbs-up.

"Okay. It might take twenty-four hours to get Facebook to shut it down. Then I'll sue her ass off — for free."

Bannerman had a scary kind of laugh. "Oh, don't you worry, Carscadden, I'm a paying customer. You can bill me a hundred grand if you want — just promise me you'll bomb her into the fucking stone age."

Bannerman's phone call terminated so loudly it sounded like had slammed his phone through the receiver.

Carscadden took his eyes off the road to check out the Facebook page on Nastos' phone. "The broad seems like a total freak."

Nastos shrugged. "Sue her? You kidding me? She hasn't earned an honest paycheque in her entire life."

Carscadden hesitated a little before asking, "I take it you have a more practical suggestion?"

"I suggest something illegal, but no more illegal than what she did. You in?"

He thought about Bannerman being called a child molester and rapist over the internet — tainted with a stink that never goes away. You're never innocent again after something like that gets out. "Of course. After this Junction call, we'll go there next."

Carscadden drove along Dupont Street until he saw the telltale signs of a death scene. Crime scene tape cordoned off an area between two multi-residential buildings. A forensics truck was pulled up on the sidewalk, next to police vehicles up on curbs and in driveways, their lights flashing. Media trucks were farther back: huge, growling, diesel vehicles with their antennae raised only partway to the sky so they wouldn't hit the low-hanging phone and cable wires that criss-crossed the street. Carscadden pointed to a group of people by the forensics van.

"Dennehy," Nastos said. "Now's your big chance to tell him to fuck off; you missed out on that last time."

Carscadden pulled over to the side of the road and parked, blocking in a few of the residents of one of the buildings. "As much as I'd like to, the only way we're going to get anything out of him is to play nice. Let's make this quick."

They slammed the car doors shut and started toward Dennehy. It was starting to spit rain and the wind was gusting. Dennehy spotted them when they were a short distance away. He was standing with Byrne and a forensics cop who was wearing an all-white bunny suit, gloves and goggles.

Dennehy held a hand up for them to stop a minute and they did. After a moment standing in the rain, he came over to them. "Make it good, Nastos."

Nastos held out the missing person's report for Andrea Dobson. Dennehy squinted to read the sheet as if he was half-blind. He scanned both pages, then went back and read the first page again.

Dennehy said, "Joy."

Carscadden's enthusiasm deflated. "Her name was Joy?"

Dennehy almost looked human. The bully bravado was tucked away for the time being; his eyes were red with sadness. "Her name was Andrea Dobson. *Joy* — that's what was carved on her chest."

Carscadden felt his knees go weak. He rubbed his five o'clock shadow, then the back of his neck.

Dennehy said, "Okay, this is how it's going to work. Whatever you guys are on to, you're only going to talk to me about it. The homicide inspector just told me this is my project. They're going to give me bodies and resources."

Nastos said, "If we find who's doing this, we won't — hell, we *can't* — make a move without you. Your name can be all over it in the papers; we just want to find Lindsay Bannerman before it's too late."

Dennehy asked, "How long does she have?"

"Joy — Andrea — did she have the number thirty on her?"

Dennehy glanced at Byrne. "Yeah, she did."

Nastos said, "Sorrow was missing exactly thirty days. So was this girl. For Lindsay, thirty days is coming up fast — and who the hell knows who's next after her."

Carscadden said, "She has two days at the most."

Dennehy pointed back at the forensics van. A cop with a blue coat with FIU screened on the back in yellow was hanging a tarp so there would be a place to stand out of the rain. Dennehy invited him over with a wave of his hand. "Total radio silence, Nastos, got it?"

"You're running the show, Dennehy — you just remember, I'm not a cop. So I can break laws that you can't. If you need grounds for a search warrant or need something taken care of, I'm getting paid by a third party here and we both want the same thing."

Dennehy offered his hand and Nastos shook it. Dennehy held Nastos' gaze. "Piss me off, you'll regret it."

19

FOR SOMEONE AS SENSITIVE TO spirits as Anthony, approaching the death house was nerve-wracking. He wished that he had taken one of Dr. Bruce's pills. Driving Hopkins' SUV, he followed Chavez onto the property. They took the back way, further east than the abandoned driveway, where a culvert had collapsed and the ditch was too deep to navigate.

Without compacted gravel for traction, he found himself stuck in the soft field, forced to back up and floor the gas pedal to follow Chavez's tracks exactly up to the house. Anthony parked beside Chavez, where no one could see the vehicle from the roadway.

Chavez was already out, the back doors to the van open. He had Hopkins slung over his shoulder, her arms hanging limply down his back. Anthony shuddered at the thought of what was going to happen to her. He had replayed his assessment of her actions during the entire drive up. He was sure she had no suspicions of him, that it had all been Chavez, but seeing her again in the flesh still brought him back to the beginning. Either all he had planned was going to work or it wasn't. In either case, he'd make sure Chavez died and he'd blame it all on him. All he needed was an opportunity to kill him, and he'd take the first one he got. If he could get him stoned, then slip him something to drink, something like anti-freeze, he could stage everything here and it would be perfect.

Chavez pointed to the van doors and grunted something.

Anthony dutifully closed them, then followed Chavez to the front of the house. As they came around the garage he could hear the music from inside: Judas Priest's "You've Got Another Thing Coming." Chavez was supposed to use as little electricity as possible, in case Hydro picked up the usage and became suspicious. They didn't want anyone to get sent around. This was too loud.

Chavez used a key to open the door. It was dark inside, the only light coming from the red LED on the stereo. After two steps in, Chavez practically threw Hopkins to the floor, then stepped over her into the shadows, disappearing like crow into a forest fit for nightmares.

Anthony climbed the stairs, crossing the threshold. The cold he felt didn't come from the temperature; it was from the smell that animals produce when they are scared for their lives. He inched around Hopkins gingerly, not wanting her to stir, not wanting her to look at him — not when he knew that she would die here.

Chavez turned on a propane camper's lantern at the far side of the living room. The bluish cast revealed a garbage bag, half-filled with empty peel-top soup and ravioli cans. A stack of full cans lined the wall next to a clear bag filled with small cereal boxes. There was a dollar store bag of plastic spoons and a few cases of orange Gatorade. *The captives have been eating like kings.*

Through the half-light, Anthony peered around the room. His eyes fixed on two long candles, welded by their own melted wax in awkward, tilted angles, on a shelf next to the propane lantern. "You shouldn't leave the candles so close to the propane light; you could burn this place down."

Chavez picked up the lantern and came toward him. He didn't smile. The side lighting cast shadows on his face, distorting his features as if he was wearing a mask. His black eyes had the slightest flicker of blue from the burning propane, like a flame made of ice. "Don't worry, Anthony. I'll keep your pets alive long enough."

Anthony cringed at Chavez's use of his name in this place. Judging by his smile, he had done it to push Anthony's buttons, to make it clear that he was in charge here. Anthony held out a card, and with one hand Chavez grabbed it. It was a picture of Madeleine — her real estate card. She was blond and beautiful. The response in Chavez was immediate. His eyes lit up with hate. He wanted to reach through the card and kill her. "Who is this?"

Anthony was relieved to see it was going to be an easy sell. "There's a private detective poking around. I wrote his address on the back of the card. This is just his wife; don't worry about her, but you need to deal with him."

Chavez was still looking at the picture, intrigued. He said, "She looks familiar to me. I can't place her." His eyes were still filled with loathing. He tensed up like he was going to get violent.

Hopkins stirred and began to moan. The interruption was a relief to Anthony, who didn't feel like distracting Chavez with sex. He still hurt too much from the last time. Besides, Chavez preferred to decide when sex occurred. It could not be offered to him; he had to decide to take it. And there was more to Anthony's reluctance. The look on his face was terrifying.

"Let me get her." Chavez crouched down, his forearms flexing like wires on a tension bridge as he gripped Hopkins and lifted her up. Anthony was startled when she flailed her arms. She sucked in air and jolted awake, her back arching. She mumbled something from under the duct tape, something indecipherable.

Chavez slammed her against the wall. "Shut up, cunt." She made a sound that might have been a whimper. He held her with one hand and pointed to the piano with the other. "Push it aside," he commanded Anthony.

Her neck twisted. Anthony felt a bolt of fear shoot through him. He ducked back around the corner into the kitchen. If she saw him, she'd have to die right away, and he didn't think he could be here when that happened. With Dr. Bruce's sleeping pills in her system, she probably wouldn't remember leaving for his house, never mind getting there.

Chavez jabbed his head into the kitchen, scowling in disgust at Anthony's skittishness. Chavez had no idea that Anthony had changed the plans and now had to keep himself clean.

151

Seeing that Hopkins had again gone limp, Anthony stepped out and pushed the piano aside. Over the sound of the music, the scraping wasn't very loud. He lifted the hatch and when he discerned the ladder leaning against the wall in the shadows, he grabbed it and lowered it to the floor below.

Hopkins was evidently light for Chavez to carry; getting her down into the basement was smooth and fast. Anthony watched as Chavez confidently reached his foot onto the ladder and descended into the pit. A part of Anthony wanted to follow him down there, drawn by a certain allure into the core of Chavez's lair. He looked into the opening. Down at ground level he could make out a garbage bag of empty cans, like discarded animal bones, and he smelled the waft of unbathed human flesh rising up from the dark. While Anthony was on a spiritual journey to uplift humanity, at that moment he understood that Chavez had become an animal. Chavez had been descending, devolving into little more than a bone collector.

Peeking through the opening, Anthony detected rapid movement, like cockroaches scattering. A voice shouted, "Get the fuck away from me. Get the fuck away!"

Anthony froze. It was the sound of the young man's voice that stopped him — broken and defeated. Anthony tried to distract himself by examining the living area where Chavez had been spending his time. He saw more candles, scraps of food, couch cushions on a heap in the floor creating a makeshift bed. And there was the oppressively loud music. Loud enough to smother his own thoughts — hypnotically suffocating, the way it drove its way into him, like a dark magic curse.

Antony shuddered. Chavez was too predatory here. There would be no taking him down in this place, not tonight. He made the decision to leave. Right there and then. He'd have to think of another way to take him down before it was too late. As he turned to depart, he heard Chavez soothing his prey. "Oh, *mi vida*, it's not all about you. It's about me."

ONCE THEY WERE BACK IN THE CAR, NASTOS MADE TWO PHONE CALLS. The first was to Bannerman to explain that the girl at the Junction Triangle was not their daughter. The second call was to Jessica Taylor.

"Hello?"

Nastos cleared his throat, trying to sound nervous. "Hi — I saw your ad on the internet?"

"Yeah, baby?"

"Yeah, I was wondering if you have any time available this evening."

"How much time?"

Nastos waited a moment. "An hour?"

There were sounds as if she was flipping through a calendar. "Sure, I'm open for the next two hours. When can you be here?"

Nastos stammered as he realized that he wasn't supposed to know where she was. "Wait a sec, what's the exact address — the ad just says Don Mills and Eglinton?"

"Text me when you're close and I'll send you my unit number."

"Well, I can be at Don Mills and Eglinton in half an hour."

"Okay, baby, see you then."

□ □ □

CARSCADDEN STOOD BACK WHILE NASTOS KNOCKED ON JESSICA Taylor's door. Once it opened a crack, Nastos rushed her. He shouldered the door, sending it flying back full force. By the time Carscadden rounded the corner, Jessica was just getting up from the floor. Nastos grabbed her by an arm and twisted it behind her back. "Quiet, quiet. We don't want your money; we're not going to hurt you."

"Get the fuck out of here!"

Nastos wrenched her arm into a position that Carscadden thought would have been impossible. Jessica got the message and shut up. She looked them over with no expression of recognition on her face — either too many drugs or too many men. Carscadden scanned the place; there was no one else there.

He said, "Jeez, girl, you haven't spent much time tidying up, despite knowing that you had a paying customer on the way over." There were ashtrays, plastic shopping bags full of takeout boxes and dishes of raw tuna for cats on the floor. He went into the bedroom and began to rifle through the dresser drawers.

Jessica shouted, "I thought you said you didn't want money?"

Nastos twisted her wrist and she muffled a cry. "My business partner's the curious type."

Carscadden slid open the night table's drawers, not entirely surprised to find sex toys and condoms in the top two. A couple dozen dime bags of marijuana were scattered inside the bottom drawer, along with a few baggies of cocaine. He brought them out with him and dumped them on the floor in front of Jessica's face.

Nastos smiled. "Well, well, well. Looky what we have here."

"You're not cops," she said.

Nastos smiled to himself. "That's where you're wrong, Jessica. We're the Facebook Police, and it seems that you've violated our policy and slandered —"

"Libelled," Carscadden corrected.

"Libelled," Nastos continued, "a person online, and we can't have that, now can we?"

A dense scowl of utter confusion washed over her face. The accusations and the drugs on the ground in front of her were giving her too many things to think about.

When Carscadden saw her laptop computer on the kitchen table, he cleared a stack of garbage off of a chair with one kick and dragged it over. He wiggled the mouse to bring up the screen and opened her internet browser. There was a bookmark for Facebook. She didn't have the password saved, so he needed her to log in.

Nastos had been watching Carscadden and saw the problem. Keeping one hand on her wrist, he moved the other to her belt and started dragging her up to her feet. "Okay, up we go, darling."

He pushed her over to the screen. "Log in right now." He gave her arm a hard yank.

She told Carscadden her email address and the password. Her Facebook home screen opened. Carscadden found the page that she had created about Bannerman.

He spoke while he typed. *"I want to apologize for what I said about Mr. Bannerman. I was on coke and upset about my missing friend. I made it all up because I was angry and needed someone to take it out on. I'm just a pathetic, one-hundred-dollar-an-hour coke whore and I hope you'll all forgive me for saying such bad things about a good man."*

Jessica was crying. There was snot on her face, her cheeks were red and her mouth was contorted in grief rather than pain.

Carscadden navigated to the settings page and changed Jessica's password to random gibberish before logging out of her account.

Nastos let her drop to the floor, then stepped over her to reach the computer. He flipped the laptop over, slid out the battery and put it in his pocket, ensuring that she couldn't get into any more trouble for a while. Even if she had a password recovery system in place, the battery in his pocket ensured that Bannerman was safe for a while.

As much as Carscadden would rather have seen Nastos smash the computer apart, that would have been going further than he and Nastos had planned. Jessica was just an unsophisticated cokehead. They been rough enough to speak her language; no more was required.

Carscadden saw her cell phone on the counter and considered breaking it, then decided it was more valuable cloned.

Nastos straightened his shirt and tie. "We don't fight fair, Jessica, so don't get any funny ideas about calling the cops, or we'll call our friends at the Teeth Police."

They left out the front door, letting the screen swing shut behind them. Carscadden said, "I think that went well."

Nastos said, "It was a lot more effective than writing a nasty letter threatening legal action."

Carscadden pulled out his cell phone and scrolled through messages. "You mind driving?" He handed his keys to Nastos.

"Yeah, I guess."

Carscadden checked BlackBerry Messenger, email, text messages and recent calls. Hopkins had not been in touch since she had left for Anthony's place. He dialed her number and it went straight to voicemail. He hung up and dialed another number from memory.

"Hey, what's up?" Madeleine sounded surprised to hear from him. She didn't sound like she'd been drinking, which she and Hopkins usually did when they got together. *Maybe they're abstaining, for the time being, to make things easier on me.* "Is Tara with you?"

"No?" She replied as if she was asking a question. "She's not at the office?"

"She never came back. She's not answering her cell, she hasn't called, nothing."

"Is Steve with you?"

"Yeah."

"Okay. Well, tell him to call when he knows what's going on."

Carscadden hung up with a sick feeling rising in his stomach. Tara never missed calls; she lived with her phone as much as anyone. Nastos was driving south to the office. He looked thoughtful and preoccupied. Carscadden asked, "What do you think?"

"I think I feel like an asshole for having her deliver that letter."

Carscadden asked, "You think Anthony might have done something? Gay, psychic Anthony? There's not a violent bone in his body. Hell, Hopkins would kick his ass."

Nastos shrugged and sighed. "That *Toronto Today* article on Anthony was the first to put together that the first girl was missing exactly thirty days. How could they have known that?" He handed his cell to Carscadden. "Here, look up the address book and get a hold of Bannerman's buddies at the phone companies."

"Tap her cell?"

"No." Nastos merged at the Eastern Avenue exit from the Don

Valley Parkway. "No, they can trace her GPS signature. We can see where she went."

Carscadden said, "Well, we know she went to Anthony's — let's just go there."

Nastos said, "That's the point; we have no idea if she made it there. We can't assume anything."

Carscadden scrolled through the phone, then called Rod to ask for the GPS trace.

"One sec," Rod responded. There was a click as the call went on hold.

Nastos turned up Sackville Street, minutes away from the office.

□ □ □

CARSCADDEN UNLOCKED THE LAW OFFICE'S FRONT DOOR, DISAPPOINTED to find that Hopkins wasn't inside. It was close to dinner time. She was definitely AWOL. He was beginning to wonder if he should call around to the hospitals, or to the cops to see if her car had been towed or in an accident.

Nastos closed the door behind him as he came inside, speaking into his phone. "No problem, Rod. It's me, Steve Nastos — we parked so I could take the phone back. Listen, we need some help here." He gave Rod the phone number to trace, then sat down at Hopkins' desk. "We need a GPS history. You're going to see the registrant is Tara Hopkins. She works with us. As a result of the investigation, she's disappeared."

Carscadden heard Rod's voice squeak from the phone. "Really?" 157

"Yeah. The last we know she delivered something to a person of interest; now she's" — he glanced to Carscadden — "unavailable."

As Nastos sat at the desk, scribbling notes on Hopkins' writing pad, Carscadden felt for some reason that he was invading her territory. Nastos wrote down words and drew arrows at times, all upside down from his perspective so he couldn't read it. When he walked around the desk to see better, Nastos stood up and became more animated.

"Okay, Rod. Thanks. Hey, that's a great idea. We really owe you. Bye." Nastos put his phone away. "Rod's going to clone her phone. We'll hear if she has any conversations and they'll be recorded immediately."

This wasn't comforting to Carscadden. "So where has she been?"

Nastos seemed evasive. "The GPS was in and out, so at times the trace was using a triangulation from towers — it wasn't very accurate."

Carscadden stuck his hand out. "Give me the paper."

Nastos said, "No."

"Give me the fucking paper, asshole!"

Nastos picked up the office phone and dialed three numbers: nine, one, one. "Yes, I need to report a missing person." He cupped the phone. "She's transferring us to the police." He handed the phone to Carscadden. Carscadden reached for it, holding it awkwardly. He was on hold again, except this time, judging by the annoying music, it sounded more like he was on Ignore.

Nastos was leaving through the front door. He stopped to say, "I'm going to do something, Kevin, and it's best you stay out of it for now."

◖ ◖ ◖

NASTOS CLOSED THE DOOR TO THE LAW OFFICE AND STARTED FOR THE car. He noticed the air cooling; the weather was shifting. The sky to the west had a red cast as the sun retreated for the evening. Nastos dialed Madeleine's cell.

She picked up quickly. "Hey, what's up?"

Nastos asked, "Are you sitting down?"

"Yeah, I'm at the kitchen table. Jo and I are having yogurt and berries."

"Well, give her an extra berry for me."

"We split *your* berries. So what's going on?"

"I'm about to do something impulsive and stupid."

Madeleine sighed. "Oh, for god's sake, Steven."

"Exactly. Carscadden's at the office. I had to ditch him there."

"Well, why don't you want him with you?"

"Because I'm probably going to get arrested and I'll want him to bail me out."

20

holding an envelope of cash. He was parked at College and Palmerston Streets in Little Italy and was scrolling through the address book of his BlackBerry. When he found the name Damian Valentine, the man he had found on Craigslist, he dialed the number.

Damian answered, "Talk to me."

"Yes, this is Craig — we spoke earlier."

There was a pause before he spoke. "Right, right. Craig."

Bannerman sucked air. "Listen, I'm in the neighbourhood and I brought the cash with me."

Valentine perked up. "You brought the cash?"

Bannerman squeezed the envelope, feeling the thickness of it, in case the one thousand dollars in non-sequential twenties had somehow vanished into thin air.

"Yeah, that was the deal, wasn't it?"

Valentine did not respond.

"Listen, Mr. Valentine, I told you I was serious the last time we spoke. If you can't help me out, someone else will."

"Okay, okay, take it easy man, I can help you out." Valentine gave him the address and Bannerman walked the rest of the way. He had a sneaking suspicion that the address for the purchase was not going to be a sturdy, nineteenth-century mansion with original gingerbread trim like most of the houses around here. He was right. Bannerman found the small Cash Converters on College Street. Damian Valentine was sitting at the counter wearing a sky-blue shirt and white name tag.

Bannerman extended his hand. "Mr. Valentine, nice to meet you. I'm Craig Bannerman." He felt that it was important to be as professional as possible with a man like Valentine, and was irritated when Valentine looked at his hand like he'd never seen one before and smiled like a bewildered grade-school kid. Valentine shook his hand, limp-wristed and reluctantly, holding the goofy smile.

"So you came here to buy a gun? Is that right, Mr. Bannerman?"

Bannerman opened his overcoat and produced his wallet. He dropped the stack of twenties on the glass display table. The pile slowly expanded like a Slinky, ready to take the next step down.

Valentine eyed the money greedily, like it was part of a magic trick. Slowly he prodded it and began to count.

Bannerman was impatient. He heard a racket in the back room, then another man came out. White, as skinny as a pitchfork and riddled with tattoos. The way a vampire smells blood, this druggie had smelled the cash. After watching Valentine feeding on the stack of twenties, which quickly disappeared into his hand, he looked at Bannerman with profound interest. He said, "And what brings you by today? You don't need a loan, do you?"

Bannerman said, "No thanks."

Valentine said, "It's okay, boss, I've got it."

Bannerman was growing impatient. "There's the cash, where's my gun?"

The white guy smiled when Valentine said, "It's close by."

"Good, then go get it. I don't have all day."

"Hey, don't get pushy with me, old man. You don't come into my place of business and piss in the corner. You can just wait here with my colleague, and I'll be right back."

Bannerman chewed his lip. He had no idea what the standard procedure was when buying an illegal gun. Was it his imagination or did he detect a surreptitious conversation between these two men? It was as if they were communicating by telepathy, and he did not like the vibe. He stomach felt like it was up in his throat and he wanted to get out of there, fast.

"Hey, you're right. I apologize. I'm just in a hurry."

Valentine said, "Well, we run on island time. I'll be right back. Now was that the Glock seventeen or the Glock twenty-two?"

He was trying to recall the research he had done on the net. The nine-millimetre had less recoil and was easier to control. "The nine mill."

Valentine smiled broadly. "Right, the seventeen. One second."

When he disappeared into the back room, Bannerman was left out front with the skinny drug addict. He wore a name tag that said Muggy Mayhem.

"So what line of work are you in?" Pitchfork — Mayhem — asked.

"Finance," Bannerman said.

"Hey." Mayhem didn't smile. "Me too."

The silence from the back room was suspicious; this was taking too long. Walking out, however, wasn't an option; it was what they probably wanted him to do. He checked the time. His wife was at home without him. Lindsay was gone, and the man who had ultimately caused all of this, the one who had killed her mother, was somewhere out there. In that moment, Bannerman began pouring into his vision of Darius Miner all of the hurt and evil ever caused in the world. It was people like Darius who destroyed lives, sucked the life out of people and moved on, like a one-man plague of locusts, exhausting everyone and everything of all they had to offer, all of the world's beauty.

I'm not a religious person, but if there is a god, let me know in my heart that Lindsay is alive. He silenced the hateful monologue in his mind, but felt nothing other than utterly alone. *That's it,* he decided; *if God can take Lindsay, then I can send Darius to hell.* He knew where Darius was. The only obstacles stopping him from killing Darius were Valentine and Pitchfork. Once he was past them, nothing could stop him from doing his small part to make the world a better place.

Bannerman asked, "What's taking so long?" He began to walk around the counter. Pitchfork approached him with his hands up, but he was no longer intimidating. Bannerman figured if he punched him hard enough in the face, his entire head would break off.

"Hey, just wait a minute; he has a ways to go."

"He said it was close by." Bannerman inched toward Pitchfork, then shoved him back into the wall. He called out, "Valentine. Where the hell are you?" Bannerman peeked into the back room. There was a staircase that went up; Bannerman knew he had not gone up there. He glanced the other way and saw an open back door. Pitchfork staggered up, his collarbones visible through his shirt, his neck thin like an anorexic's.

Bannerman peeked out the back door and saw nothing but alleyway. He turned the other way and saw Valentine, who lunged at him right away, grabbing at his collar for leverage. Valentine fought like a hockey player, controlling Bannerman with one hand and raining punches down with the other. Bannerman instinctively ducked down to avoid the blows and dove at Valentine's waist. Out of practice from his days in Shiloh, Manitoba, Bannerman missed with one hand and had to fumble with the other until he caught a good grip of Valentine. With both hands, he pulled Valentine in tight, then picked him up and dropped him to the ground. Pitchfork came out of the store, but one hard punch in the face from Bannerman knocked him back headfirst into the steel door. He landed hard and stayed down. Valentine came at him again, so Bannerman deked to the other side of a dumpster.

"You're a piece of shit, Valentine."

"Tell that to the cops. Trying to buy an illegal gun."

"Fuck you, you piece of shit." Bannerman caught a glimpse of something on Valentine's face. The way his eyes darted to Pitchfork, lying in a heap on the ground. It was fear. Bannerman advanced from the dumpster, thrusting his hands in the air. "Here I am, tough guy." He moved toward Valentine. "Come on, tough guy, it's just you and me."

Valentine shook his head and smiled. "No, thanks. I have everything I needed from you."

Bannerman charged, "Well, I haven't."

He shoved Valentine backward into the wall, then grabbed him by the neck. He squeezed hard, until he felt that Valentine was going to slip away. So Bannerman let him — but not before pushing Valentine back into the brick wall, and hammering him with a three-punch combination. Valentine's knees buckled and he dropped to the ground next to Pitchfork, sucking air. Valentine's head sagged from side to side as he tried clumsily to push Bannerman away. Bannerman kicked him in the ribs, then noticed his fat front pocket. He reached in and seized his money back; Valentine didn't protest.

He was about to leave, but he turned back to Valentine. It was a hollow victory if he didn't get what he came for. "Where's the gun? You can still have the money."

Valentine shook his head. Bannerman pushed him to the ground and ran back into the store. He searched behind the counter until he saw a black handgrip. Two extra magazines sat next to the gun. "Fuck you, and have a nice day, Mr. Valentine."

21

NASTOS PULLED TO A STOP IN front of Anthony's house and prepared himself for what was next. He reread the sheet of paper on which he had scribbled the GPS location of Hopkins' phone before it had turned off. Rod had tried turning the feature on again, remotely, but it had failed to work. Either the battery was dead or the phone was destroyed.

From his notes, Hopkins had gone out for lunch with his wife, Madeleine, to take turns fawning over No Frills Mills the Sensitive, then gone over to Anthony's house to serve the papers. She wasn't there long. It looked like she had gone to a park around the corner and turned her phone off.

He just about jumped from the car and advanced on Anthony's front door. It was a nice place, probably cost a couple million back in the day. The brick exterior was a hundred years old; the house had a slate roof and a big garden. *Not a bad lifestyle for a professional liar and confidence man.* Telling people what they wanted to hear was probably the second-oldest profession, and more profitable than number one.

Nastos rang the doorbell — three chimes, like a subway stop. He pressed it a second time. Through the decorative glass on the door, Nastos saw a shape approaching, backlit by a crystal chandelier hanging by what looked like a spiral staircase. The prospect of going to jail for the night would normally have horrified him, but with Hopkins gone, one night didn't seem like a big risk. He'd get a cot and a reasonably warm place to sleep for a few hours; hell, he could use the break. He was more worried that it would be for nothing. Anthony made his living reading people, so trying to beat him at his own game to uncover undisputable evidence that would link him to Hopkins' disappearance was as daunting as it was critical. If Anthony didn't know anything, had nothing to do with her absence, Nastos had nothing.

Anthony opened the door. His face was unreadable, almost too composed. They watched each other for a moment, trying to decipher each other's minds.

Anthony's calculated impassiveness gave Nastos all the confidence he needed. "What did you do with Hopkins?"

Anthony hesitated, buying time to conjure a lie, but something stopped him. He stood silently. Nastos forced his way inside, pushing Anthony out of his way, and began searching through the house. He studied the walls and floor for signs of a struggle, blood, fragments of decorations that might have been broken. Any signs of a house not perfectly decorated might be an indicator of trouble. "She said she was coming here, she never came back."

"I'm calling the police." Anthony produced a cell phone and began to dial.

Nastos focused on his search. "Ask for Detective Dennehy, he's with Homicide." He saw Anthony tighten up for a moment, then proceed with the call.

"She never came here." Anthony held the phone up to his ear. "Fuck off." With his free hand he pointed to the door.

Never here? The lie was enough to embolden Nastos further. He searched the entire main floor, Anthony following at a safe distance. He was apparently talking to the emergency operator. He could have hung up, though, pretending to stay on the line.

Nastos searched the upstairs laundry room and the bedrooms, saving the master for last. He opened the dressers, starting from the bottom and leaving the drawers open as he went so he didn't have to close a drawer to search the one below. The clock was ticking. If he didn't get the entire house done before the police arrived, he'd never get a second chance.

With the self-admission of his urgency came another: the admission that he was looking for evidence of a murder. He reached down and with one hand threw back the sisal throw rugs, looking for blood. He hammered the light switch to the closet and flung the door open. He two-handed racks of clothing out, dumping them back on the bedroom floor. He made note of the clothing sizes. Something about the shoes struck him as odd. He kept looking, his desperation rising.

Then the basement. He tried to pull back the aggression, pull back the emotion, and treat the search as just business. He had to remember that by searching for something minor, he would catch something major. If all he looked for was bloodstains, he'd miss everything else. Anything out of place, missing things, broken things would do. A large portion of the floor in the basement was concrete; the rest was wood flooring. Blood was tough to clean up fast. Glare from the overhead lighting revealed no scuff marks or signs of abrasive cleaners. The seams between the boards were clean.

When the police came into the house — two uniformed officers, one older, one younger — they found Nastos in the kitchen. He was standing at the counter, reading a newspaper and drinking a Bud Light beer that he had taken from Anthony's fridge. All he had to show for his actions was his account of catching Anthony in a lie. That and something about the clothing upstairs. He had considered going up again, but when he heard the siren from the police car, he decided he'd better spend his time trying to look relaxed and unthreatening.

The older cop spoke. "Sir, there are a lot of knives and potential weapons in the kitchen. Just so there is no misunderstanding of your intentions, come out here to the lobby."

Nastos straightened up. "Of course, Officer. I used to be a cop; I understand completely. I'm just going to finish off this pathetic excuse for a beer real quick." He raised the bottle slowly, then finished off the drink. He lifted his hands up in the air. "You want me to come out backward?" He moved toward them, coming around the centre island.

"Stop there."

Nastos stopped.

"Sir, now hike up your coat and turn around slowly."

They were checking Nastos' belt line for weapons. He had been in the kitchen and could have stuffed anything into his pockets or behind his back. He considered identifying himself, then thought better of it. By trying to get them to relax, he'd only make them more cautious. These guys weren't rookies. He was better off just doing as they said and keeping his mouth shut until he was handcuffed.

After he had turned all of the way around, he followed their commands and backed out the rest of the way. He knelt down, with his hands still up, and finally was handcuffed. They double-locked the cuffs — authoritatively, not abusively. These were professionals, not thugs. Finally, they brought him up to his feet.

He saw Anthony. "Thanks for the beer." He smiled; this was his chance to crawl into Anthony's brain. "I found all I needed to see, Anthony."

The psychic shrugged. "That better not have been my last beer."

"No, and you still have the bottle for later; I'm sure you know where you can put it."

Anthony wore a mask of pity, as if Nastos was some poor love-struck fool who had taken a breakup badly.

"Maybe you're not the only psychic here. Maybe I know exactly what happened." Nastos smiled again when he saw Anthony flinch.

"Don't mock what I do, Nastos. I'm just not the type to put on a uniform and let society provide me a role so I can feel relevant, like a garbage man who wears a funny moustache to feel special in the world. I have a gift. I can bring hope to the hopeless. I can bring closure to the very depth of the deepest of wounds. My gifts deserve recognition."

Nastos said, "I'd applaud, but —" He nodded toward his cuffed hands. "Well, you know."

The older cop searched him while the other held him by the upper arm and wrist. First his belt line and pockets, the area of reach while cuffed, then the rest of his body in a four-quadrant search: upper body, left and right side, lower body, left and right side. He searched his socks and shoes, then ran his gloved fingers through his hair, as if Nastos was a crack addict hiding needles or pins to try to pick the cuffs.

He stood up and opened Nastos' wallet. He read the name. "Steve Nastos, you're under arrest for breaking and entering."

"I didn't break in, I was invited. At best this is a Fail to Leave When Directed — Trespassing."

The cop ignored the comment and opened his notebook. From the back, he read the Rights to Council. Nastos recited it along with him by memory, which made the cop more and more angry as he went.

"You have the right to retain and instruct counsel without delay . . ."

When they asked if he'd like to speak with a lawyer, he named Carscadden and gave them the phone number.

"You can do that from the station" was all the officer gave as a reply.

"You should also call Dennehy from Homicide. I have urgent information to give him. He's expecting my call." Nastos watched Anthony, disappointed to see that this time he didn't react. Anthony knew Nastos' desperate search for evidence had failed. He was relaxing so much he was even stealing a few glances at the younger cop, bigger and leaner than the other one. Anthony, it seemed, liked the beefcakes.

The cruiser was a tight fit. Nastos had to turn sideways so his feet and wrists wouldn't get crushed. The younger cop was a smooth driver, who didn't play any games like making abrupt stops or playing Black Urban Radio as psychological warfare. At Fifty-Three Division, the sally-port doors opened, then closed behind him. He was led out into a cells area, where he had to answer a series of questions on video. Had he been assaulted by the cops, did he have any injuries or medical problems or a lawyer to call? He didn't play any games or give cute answers; he was respectful.

Soon enough, he was sitting on a bench in the common holding room. His right wrist was cuffed to a metal loop sticking out of the cement wall. Passing cops sneered at him like he was a piece of trash. It was a part of rookie syndrome; young cops still care enough to make known their contempt of the arrested.

The older, arresting officer, had called Carscadden for him. The sergeant held the phone up. "Hey, Nastos, it's your lawyer." A cop came to take him to a private room, but Nastos waved him off with his free hand. "That's okay, Sarge. Can you just ask him to come down and get me out?"

The sergeant spoke to Carscadden, then put the phone down.

Nastos asked, "What about Dennehy — you get a hold of him?"

The sergeant had gone back to his paperwork. He slid his glasses up his nose and didn't look up. "Says he's coming down. No more questions."

Nastos examined the fluorescent lights and read the graffiti on the walls. *How the hell does someone put graffiti on the walls in a holding cell without the cops noticing?*

He felt a presence behind him and turned. "Dennehy, how the hell are you? Hey, and Byrne too."

Dennehy asked, "I don't suppose you and Carscadden roughed up a prostitute earlier on? Busted into her place, trashed her computer?"

Nastos asked, "Where did you hear a crazy story like that?"

"The OD we investigated in Flemingdon Park. I passed out my card to canvass for information after you and your metrosexual life partner left to buy matching underwear. She called me personally about you."

Nastos smirked at Dennehy. "You have any proof?"

"No."

"Then no, we didn't do it."

Dennehy stood with his hands on his hips, glaring at him like he had no idea what to say to an obstinate child.

Byrne asked, "And what's the deal with the psychic? I assume you hooked up for an internet date but became embroiled in a — well, let's call it an *exchange* of sorts — over who was going to be the daddy?"

Dennehy found this particularly funny. He turned to Byrne and laughed silently, his body convulsing and his face turning red, before turning back to Nastos and regaining his composure.

Nastos waited till he thought Dennehy was paying attention. "When I searched his closet —" He turned to Byrne. "Yeah, his fucking closet — I saw different-sized shoes. And different-sized pants. He's living with someone."

Dennehy replied, "The living arrangements of a gay psychic aren't of much interest to me. Did you ever think that maybe he's lost or gained weight?"

Nastos asked, "And shoe size?"

"Maybe he has a few friends who leave things there?"

Nastos was confused that they didn't think it was at least worth looking into further. "Detective Blake. The guy from the *Toronto Today* story. He did a search of Anthony's home. He might find it significant, in retrospect, that Anthony lied to him about living with someone. It's kind of a major lie. You should ask him about —"

"First time you heard of a guy lying about being in a relationship when he sees something he likes? I'm not asking anybody anything, Nastos. I thought we had a deal — now you do crazy shit like this." He shook his head like he was disgusted. Nastos found some comfort in the fact that he had at least come down rather than telling him to screw himself over the phone. There might be a vestige of hope that he could call in Dennehy again.

"We're out of here, Nastos. Good luck."

Nastos didn't say anything. He watched as Dennehy spoke to the cell sergeant and pointed to him a few times, then left without another word to him. Shortly afterwards, a uniformed cop came over and let him out of the handcuffs.

Nastos asked, "What's up?"

The cell sergeant waved him up to the counter. "Sign this." He signed it. It was a release for his property. He asked, "My lawyer get here?"

"No. Dennehy determined that it was just a misunderstanding — a he said/she said." He smiled.

Nastos rubbed his wrist and ripped open the plastic bag that contained his wallet and cell phone. "Everything's here, Sarge." The cop only responded by pointing to a special constable, who was ready to lead Nastos out to the back doors.

Nastos asked, "My lawyer's on the way. He's going to meet me at the front."

The special constable replied, "Then you can walk the fuck around to the front."

The special was over six-five and weighed at least two-forty. Some fresh air sounded like a great suggestion. Outside, it was a half-moon night, thin layers of blue clouds and a cold that felt like it was sucking the energy and concentration out of him. When he spun around to the front, Carscadden was standing there.

"What did you do this time?"

"Remember that shit-hole house that Maddy told us about in Rexdale? Come on. We're going on a drive."

22

CARSCADDEN AND NASTOS stood out front of Anthony's property in Rexdale under the dark night sky. Math had been involved in finding the exact house, since it didn't have a number on it. The house on Wansey Road was basically as described by Madeleine: 1950s, small, square-ish, twelve hundred square feet, one storey, and in serious disrepair. The front door in the centre of the house with a padlock on it, large boarded-up windows on either side. Half of the shingles were missing; the rest were peeled up at the edges. Exposed plywood on the roof had been recently replaced in parts. The boards over the windows were new, the wood almost bright coloured compared with the rest of the house. In a city of asphalt and concrete hydro poles, there was a dirt driveway leading to a garage that looked more like a lean-to. The rest the neighbourhood, although still modest, was at least cared for.

Nastos exhaled. "Why would a guy like Anthony own a piece of garbage like this place?"

Carscadden agreed. "Good question. If he's going to renovate, it'll be a totally gut job — it'd cost more than a hundred grand to fix it up."

Nastos added, "And I don't think he's the type to be handy with a nail gun."

Carscadden pointed at the ground. "Look at the tire tracks. Trucks have been in and out."

Nastos crouched down, studying the earth. It was densely compacted gravel with a layer of mud on top. "Tires are almost bald. They must be really old."

He stood up and they began walking closer to the house. Carscadden tensed when he heard a faint scream that seemed to come from the back of the house. He looked over at Nastos, and they both ran up the driveway and into the backyard.

Two pre-teen girls from the house next door were in their backyard, chasing each other with fists full of wet leaves. Nastos and Carscadden smiled at each other with relief.

"Check out the windows," Nastos said. "Boarded up here too."

Carscadden reached the back door. The padlock had been picked or left unlocked. He pushed the door and it opened slightly.

"Jesus Christ!" He recoiled from the door, putting both hands up to his mouth and nose. He took a breath and waved at Nastos to back off. Nastos had already figured that part out.

Nastos said, "What's it smell like, a body?"

"Smells worse than that, if you can imagine. Holy shit." Carscadden coughed.

Nastos tried to get a trace of the smell. He caught the scent. "Smells like a chemical."

Nastos went around the house. He sniffed near the dryer vent, then quickly recoiled, putting his hands up to his mouth.

"Solvents. Ammonia. I hope to god no one's inside." He spat onto the ground and wiped his mouth. Carscadden went over to a basement window and tried to look in. It had been painted black. "Tara! Tara! You in there?"

He pressed the door in and felt it hit something solid, like some kind of brace. It wasn't going to move.

Nastos started dialing a number on his phone as he watched Carscadden prying at boards from a window.

Nastos cupped his phone. "Good friggin' luck moving that."

Carscadden kept on pulling. "It's nailed, not screwed in." He yanked hard. The nails squealed as they began to pop out.

While Nastos waited on the line, he peered up to the roof, taking small paces backward until he could see up the roofline. "Yeah, extra vents on the roof. It's a frigging meth lab in there." Nastos spoke into his phone. "Fire department, please."

Carscadden had repositioned himself on the other side of the window, working the same board. With two hard yanks he pried the board off, nearly slipping onto his back. He tossed the board aside. "Tara! Lindsay! Anyone in there?"

There was the sound of glass shattering on the floor, like a drinking glass breaking, then a dull roar like a furnace firing up. Carscadden cocked his head to listen and examined the black window. Suddenly the glass burst out as orange and blue flames leapt from the blackness, licking at the eavestrough and roof. Black smoke trickled, then billowed out, obscuring the sky and city lights. Carscadden mouthed the words *holy shit* twice before he found his breath. "Tara! Tara!"

He looked around frantically, found another window and began ripping at the boards. Nastos shouted into his phone. "We're at an abandoned house, there's a meth lab on fire. It's a residential area. No —" He looked to Carscadden. "We were just walking past. We could smell it from the road." He gave them the address and hung up. "It won't be long."

Carscadden paid no attention to him; he was madly yanking on the boards.

Nastos joined him near the window. Carscadden said, "They could be in there — we should go in."

Nastos grabbed his arm. "If we open a door or window, we feed the flame. This is going to hurt, but we have to just wait."

Carscadden pushed him off. "Are you crazy? If she's inside — the sooner we get her out, the better." Nastos grabbed him around the chest and pulled him away. "Don't make it worse. The only way to help is to let the pros handle it." Reluctantly, Carscadden relented.

There was another squeal from the kids playing in the backyard next door. This time it wasn't because they were having fun — it was fear.

Nastos called over to them. "Get in your house! It's not safe here."

As the girls ran into their back door, he and Carscadden ran around to the front door. Empty beer cases — Moosehead — littered the cement staircase.

Nastos began pounding. "They have to evacuate."

"Good idea." Carscadden held a thousand-yard stare in the direction of the house.

A man answered the door. He was maybe forty, with skin like peeled paint and a three-day, prickly scruff on his baby face.

"Help you?"

Nastos noted the beer on his breath.

"There's a meth lab on fire next door. They're explosive. You're going to want to get your kids out of here."

The man cast a sideways glance at the house. His eyes opened wide when he saw the flames. He turned his head back. "Julie. Julie, get the kids, the house next door is on fire!" He fumbled as he put his beer down.

Nastos remembered the suspicious vehicle described in the reports. "Hey, you see an old shit-box van here?" He thumbed in the direction of the meth house.

The man grabbed a coat from the rack to his right. "An eighty-nine Dodge Caravan, sure. Something written on the side."

Nastos asked, "What did the writing say?"

"Don't know. I think it was a company name, but it's all peeled off."

"You see who was driving it?"

The man turned away, "Hey! I said grab your stuff — we're getting out of here!"

Nastos grabbed the man by the arm, "Come on, it's important."

There was commotion inside the man's house. Looking behind him, he shouted at Nastos, "I don't know!"

The man pulled his arm away and stormed off to get his family. Nastos let the screen door shut. "Hey, thanks for your time, pal."

They left the man's house and headed back in their car, Carscadden never taking his eyes from the house. "If she's in there, I'll kill him."

Carscadden moved their car to the other side of the road, pulling back a few houses to make room for the fire trucks. It was maddening to watch the fire spread, flames shooting through the roof, windows bursting out from the heat, and to think that Hopkins, Lindsay or someone else might be in there. The heat from the fire could be felt through the glass, inside the car.

Nastos watched as Carscadden stared at the flames. Carscadden said, "When someone tells you to burn in hell, it's for a reason. Burns hurt like crazy. I'd rather drown, be shot or be hit by a train than burn to death."

Nastos didn't say anything.

They were waiting in front of the house when the fire trucks screeched to a halt, the air brakes hissing. The driver of the pumper truck jumped from the cab, took a stride as he reached to a hand hold and leapt up into the landing behind the cab, where he began operating the controls while another firefighter raced around the rig and dragged the four-inch-thick, reddish hose to the hydrant. He unscrewed one of the caps at the side and attached a bar to the top square bolt. The firefighter twisted the top with an aggressive crank and when the water pouring out ran clear, he closed the faucet back up and twisted the hose on. This time when he cracked the faucet, the hose expanded with the force of the water and the pumper truck's engine throttled down under the load.

Two firemen dragged the hose from the other side of the truck and ran toward the fire. Nastos grabbed a hold, trying to help.

The firefighter in the front passenger seat wore a beige turnout coat and a white hat that Nastos understood to mean that he was the boss.

Nastos shouted over the pumper truck's engine. "I'm a private investigator. I came here to look for a deadbeat dad. We've got

177

reason to believe that there may be two women in there. Then I caught the smell — I think it's a drug lab."

The fire captain asked, "What started the fire?"

Nastos shrugged. "Your guess is as good as mine."

The captain didn't appear convinced by Nastos' answer. He turned and spoke into his radio. "Dispatch, we're going to need to another pumper here, please. Looks like a drug lab. We'll need a Hazmat truck and the police." The captain waved two of his guys over from the second truck, a rescue van. "Five houses in each direction." They turned to execute his evacuation order.

He let his radio drop. The two firefighters sprayed water all over the exterior of the house, then stopped. They waved back to the pump operator, who flipped a switch. The water from the house became thick and white and then switched to a foam fire suppressant.

Two cruisers pulled up. The cops conferenced with the fire captain.

The shorter cop asked, "So what's the deal? It's a lab?"

The captain appraised the mixed colour of the smoke and the acrid smell. "Yeah, it might be. My guys are clearing five houses to either side if you want to shut the street down. And our Hazmat truck is already coming in from downtown, so maybe you guys can move your cruisers farther down."

The fire's heat that had been apparent from inside their car was becoming unbearable from the sidewalk. The fire captain gestured for Carscadden and Nastos to join him by the pumper truck, using it as a heat shield. "It gets hot even in our coats. Unless you guys have anything more to add, you're going to have to get back behind the perimeter."

By the look on his face, he knew they weren't going anywhere. He shrugged and climbed the platform to stand next to the pump operator. He shouted down. "Suit yourself. Sooner or later it's going to become overwhelming." The man adjusted the heat-resistant balaclava tighter around his face then became involved in a conversation to his crew over his portable radio.

Carscadden peeked out to anxiously watch as a team of two

firemen kicked their way into the burning house through the front door. The heat scorched his face like an instant sunburn. Another two-man team raced around the back and out of view, presumably entering through the rear.

Thick clouds of black and green smoke billowed out of the front door, fuelled by the influx of fresh oxygen. As the thick fog of water filled the room, the smoke greyed and there was an audible hiss like water on a sauna rocks. He turned to Nastos. "If she's in there, she's dead, simple as that."

Nastos watched two firefighters at the pumper truck as they attached infrared cameras to their helmets then charged in through the front door of the house. "I cut up firemen as much as anyone, but this is their big call. They get the chance to be heroes and save someone. Don't give up hope."

It was a tense wait for Carscadden that felt like an eternity. He listened to the fire radio transmissions, listened as they cleared one room after another while the smoke grew less and less grey and finally began to dissipate. He tried to feel as if she wasn't already gone, not ready to hear the word dead and all that it meant. However, instinctively he knew that a wound like this could never heal and that he would live a lonely, broken life, knowing that Tara had suffered because of decisions that he had made.

Feeling weak, he glanced at the pumper truck for a place to sit, then decided to stand. If all he could do was watch helplessly and wait for her lifeless, blackened body to be dragged from the mouth of hell, then he would do her the honour of standing. After half an hour, the fire crew had put the fire out. The captain heard something over the radio and shouted down to Nastos. They joined him by the truck. He removed his helmet and wore an expression on his face that couldn't be read. Nastos asked, "Was anyone inside?"

He shook his head. "No. Looks like a small ecstasy lab. And there were a few pot plants."

Nastos looked at Carscadden, who was trying to decide whether he should be relieved or not. He asked Nastos, "If she's not here, where is she?"

Nastos shook his head. "When I went through Anthony's place, it looked like he had a live-in boyfriend that he didn't tell the cops about." He could tell Carscadden thought it was a pretty long shot. But Nastos wanted to provide some hope. Because with each passing moment, Hopkins was less likely to be found.

23

THEY LEFT THE CAR IN THE underground parking across from Frankie's Restaurant. Carscadden tried to ignore the nauseating worry he felt over Hopkins being unaccounted for. Nastos pulled the door open and Carscadden proceeded in the direction of the full bar. He saw the glass shelves, stacked with rum, vodka, and whisky — all would do just fine. Viktor was always well stocked in the best. He told himself, not until Tara was back; he had to keep his head clear.

"Nastos, if she had been in there, she'd be dead."

"We're going to find her, safe and sound."

"At first I was elated. I thought we had her. Then the place caught fire and I thought she was burning to death right before my eyes." He eyed a bottle of spiced rum on the mirrored wall display. "From dead, she's back to missing and presumed dead. This is torture. I wish the cops were doing more."

Nastos looked him in the eye. "That's the point of this case. Police don't go door to door looking for missing people. We're going to find her Kevin, alive. I promise."

They edged around a table of six obnoxious drunks noisily pounding back beers and shooters in the front dining area. Their behaviour was out of place here. Carscadden knew that there was no way Kalmakov was around tonight; he wouldn't tolerate that ruckus from anybody, not in his place.

The bartender was one that he had not seen before. She met all of Kalmakov's physical criteria: a beautiful, young face, large breasts, natural beauty.

"Mr. Carscadden?" she asked, not sure of the name.

"Yes. I need to speak with Viktor; he didn't answer his cell."

She was distracted by the drunks. Nastos was looking around. They both noticed that some of the customers, especially one family with two young teens, seemed offended by the behaviour. Nastos made a call on his cell while the barkeep spoke to Carscadden.

"Yeah, he's not answering for me either. I sent a text too. Nothing." She eyed the drunks again. They were toasting each other like they'd all won some corporate lottery, dressed like business executives, with matching haircuts and expensive watches. One guy, the ringleader, stood to go to the bathroom and careened into his buddy, elbowing him in the face. Buddy tipped sideways in his chair, spilling onto the floor. The drinkers became quiet, stopping mid-drink, and Carscadden thought it was going turn into a brawl. Then the guy sprang to his feet and said "Ta-da!" to the applause and cheers of the other drunks.

The bartender was frozen in place watching them, too scared to suggest they take the party elsewhere. Nastos hung up his phone and kept his eyes in the direction of the back washroom as the drunk weaved his way through the tables. Carscadden could tell that Nastos was going to start a confrontation when the guy came back.

The bartender said, "Before Viktor left he said that he'd be here by now, and he's always on time."

Nastos grabbed a menu and passed one to Carscadden. "Here. It's going to be a long night — you should eat something now." Nastos scanned the page then put it down.

When he saw the drunk coming back from the washroom, he said to Carscadden and the bartender, "Order me the burger. I'm going to deal with these guys."

Carscadden touched his elbow, but Nastos pulled away and made a hand motion to say he'd be fine. Nastos didn't have much of a reputation for taking crap from people. He was concerned about the drunk and his friends and the interior of the restaurant, not to mention the first few emergency responders if the situation escalated.

Nastos extended his hand to the man and put on a big smile. The man, in his early thirties, seemed threatened and defensive. "What?"

"Listen, I'm the night manager here. I'd like to buy you guys a round of drinks."

"Really?" He was surprised.

"Yes, really." Nastos continued, "What are you guys celebrating?"

"Oh, we closed a big deal — commissions all around."

Nastos smiled like he couldn't be happier. "Okay, now, this is the deal. Frankie's is a family place and you guys are a little loud. Let's go get your buddies' drink orders; the last round is on the house. I've already called you guys some cabs. They'll take you home, or to the strip bar, wherever you want. The taxis are on us."

The man was thinking. It wasn't a bad deal. Nastos added, "Whiskey A Go-Go has the best girls, if you're not from around here . . ."

The man shook his head. "No, we're from Ottawa. That's a good idea. Hey, thanks, man." He shook Nastos' hand.

Nastos followed him to the table to announce the good news. He made note of their drink order and returned to the bar in time to hear the cheers from the suits.

Carscadden said, "I thought you were going to cave his head in, then throw them out one by one."

Nastos looked back at them and shrugged. "Trust me, I wanted to, but we have to stay focused. Let's just get them the hell out of here. We need Viktor's help and while we wait for him I'd rather be preparing for the long night ahead than dealing with those assholes."

"Right."

After the drunks left, Nastos followed them out to the taxis and spoke to the drivers.

Carscadden watched him come back in. Nastos didn't have an

honest face and often came on aggressively — hell, he had been arrested by the cops earlier today. Nonetheless, Nastos knew exactly how to deal with the drunks. People always ended up doing what he wanted them to, even if they hated him.

He and Carscadden started on their burgers. The bartender was grateful that the drunks were gone, but was clearly uncertain about something.

Nastos asked, "What?"

Her face contorted. "Listen, I'm glad those assholes are out of here, but you're a total stranger. You gave away liquor for free and paid for taxis to Vaughan with Viktor's money."

Nastos said, "I did it because this is Viktor's place and that's what he would have done."

Carscadden added, "What he'd also do" — he pointed to the table that was the most disturbed by the drunks — "is cover their bill and apologize for the noise."

Just then, Viktor ambled through the front door, rubbing his hands together against the cold outside. He was in his mid-fifties, shorter than Carscadden but more muscular, with greying hair. When he saw Nastos and Carscadden at the bar, he smiled and came over to them, extending a hand to each. His deep voice growled through a Russian accent. "Mr. Carscadden, Mr. Nastos, great to see you." With anyone other than close friends or family, he would have gone behind the bar and used it as a barrier. With Carscadden and Nastos, he joined them on the barstools. Carscadden glanced at the bartender and saw that she noticed how informal Viktor's body language was with them. When Viktor smiled at her warmly and waved her off, she left the bar and went to the table with the family who had been disrupted by the drunks. She was offering them a discount.

Nastos leaned over to Viktor. "We need a cargo van, some odds and ends, you know — duct tape, a tool box and an expensive tinted-down automobile, preferably an suv."

Viktor's eyebrows raised and he smiled a little. "Oh, really?" He glanced at each of them again. "Are you going to tell me why?"

Nastos explained in hushed tones about Hopkins, Anthony, Bannerman, everything. Viktor silently took it all in, never asking a single question.

Carscadden could see the respect that Viktor had for Nastos. To a guy like Viktor, Nastos was a match. Viktor, the gangster, tried to live with respect and honour. Despite having ordered or caused the deaths of certain individuals over the years, he loathed the uncivilized street thugs who had no sense of purpose. He only committed violence when it was the last resort. Nastos was a cop who was analytical, dedicated and driven to help people with a singular purpose, but was also a realist who thought of violence and torture as just another couple of tools in the tool box — meaning there was a time to take the white gloves off and set them aside. And that part of both Nastos and Viktor was like a precision explosive.

The two also spoke the same language and in most cases would recommend the same course of action. Carscadden found it disappointing that while Viktor understood this and welcomed Nastos as a friend, Nastos had difficulty trusting him. Even despite the night last year at Cherry Beach.

◻ ◻ ◻

LINDSAY WOKE FROM A FRAGILE SLEEP TO PUNISHING NOISE COMING from the upstairs. It was so loud that a moment passed before she realized it was music, blasting from the ceiling. The song turned out to be "Smalltown Boy" by Bronski Beat. She had a remix of it on her iPod that Eminem had done to prove that he wasn't homophobic.

The bass was dropping beats so loudly that waves of dust were being pushed down from the floor joists above. Nails sounded like they were going to rattle out of the wood.

Lindsay crawled over to the others. The new woman was called Tara Hopkins. She was sharing a blanket with the boy, Taylor Burke. He seemed the most comfortable with her, was practically wrapped around her. Blond with dark eyes and no sign of facial hair, he said he was eighteen but acted younger, especially after what had been happening to him. Lindsay figured that he felt emasculated after the rapes. The Warden did it right in front of all of them so they had to see. It was disgusting — the gagging and the puking. Taylor's screaming was usually drowned out by the loud music. Loud music like what had just started playing.

Hopkins had her arms around Taylor like a protective mother. Lindsay was cuddled up alone and hoped she was wrong about what was about to happen.

Hopkins said loudly, "Is today another day?"

Lindsay had no idea. She was always hungry, so that was no guide. The Warden had gone off his circadian rhythm as far as she could tell. Without a watch, she couldn't even be sure of the month anymore.

Hopkins shouted in her ear. "Because if it is, my friends will be looking for me by now." Lindsay was barely paying attention. She didn't give a shit if Hopkins' friends were looking — she had bigger problems. If it was another day, then she was one day closer to her own thirty-day mark. And when the Warden played with the girls, he played for keeps. Hopkins was holding it together, trying to be strong for the boy. However, she hadn't watched him murder two people, then carve up their bodies. She might not be so tough after that.

Lindsay shook her head from side to side. "Your friends aren't going to find us. Don't you get it? We're going to die down here." Lindsay had been through it in her mind. Death was inevitable.

The song changed to "Mama" by Genesis. The reverb effect on the drums pounded through the floor, followed by the creepy, sad keyboards and then the singer, trying to speak softly but unable to contain the violence running though his mind. When the hatch flung up and back and the red flashing light shone down, Lindsay made a mental note of the exact moment in the music when all hell broke loose.

The Warden dropped the ladder into the room, then peeked down headfirst. He was wearing makeup on his face. There were black circles around his eyes and mouth, white powder over his face and red symbols on his cheeks. No, not symbols; they were poorly drawn birds. He tossed down a small black duffle bag that seemed to turn purple when the red light flashed on it. She knew what was in it. This was not the first time he had slunk down the ladder with such exaggerated movements, like he was on drugs and thought he was in a slow-motion martial arts movie. His arms stretched out, hands wide open. He was naked.

Lindsay was disgusted, but she couldn't look away from the performance. Olive skin was bathed in red light, his back, glistening with sweat, looked blood-soaked, and tufts of back hair stood out black like necrosis, as if his skin were dead and peeling away — a new, evil form of life being born in front of their eyes. His member hung heavy and thick with blood. With his lean, tight muscles, he was the worst that evolution could offer: a machine of flesh built to hunt and rape.

He jumped the last step to the ground and crouched low. The music pounded, the singer screaming, "Mama, Mama." He reached a hand out to the corner of the huddled captives, then made a "come to me" motion by slowly pulling back his index finger while staring at Taylor.

Taylor might have been screaming, but there was no way to tell with the music so loud. When Taylor didn't move, the Warden turned back to the duffle bag and slowly opened it up like he was removing the autopsy twine from a corpse's chest. He reached into the open cavity and withdrew a length of leather, thin like a shoe-lace, long like a nightmare.

He set the lace aside and withdrew several pairs of handcuffs. With his back to the captives, he stole a glance over his shoulder. Lindsay assumed he was smiling. He stood up tall, facing them. He was hard and ready for it. He came over, more determined. He wasn't going to take no for an answer. He started by grabbing Hopkins away from Taylor and forcing her to the ground. She said something to him — it might have been "No, he's just a boy" — and his only reply was a slap across her face that knocked her back.

While she tried to recover from the strike, he handcuffed her arms behind her back. When he cuffed Lindsay, he slowly licked up the side of her face, giggling when she recoiled and cried out in revulsion. He saved Taylor for last, she noted, just like last time.

They were forced to watch. He approached Taylor, again moving like he was in some performance art piece — like he was high on cocktail of rave drugs, E, Viagra, meth or acid. Taylor did nothing. Lindsay knew what was going through his mind. He was disappearing into subspace. He was praying for someone or something to make him not exist while it was happening, begging for death to take him. When your existence is shame, self-hatred, torture and horror, praying for death becomes all-consuming. She knew this first-hand.

Chavez grabbed Taylor by the back of his neck, and with a hammer fist pounded his back, like he was trying to smash him in two. Taylor didn't resist; last time it had only made things worse. Tears were pouring down his face, thick snot hung from his nose. He slowly began to crawl to the middle of the room, where the Warden had taken him last time.

The soundtrack changed to "Never Let Me Down Again" by Depeche Mode. A heavy, thick back-beat with trippy, flanged keyboards that sounded like they were rolling in a gravity-free, sickening tumble to nowhere. The Warden grabbed Taylor's pants and began yanking them down. He stopped tugging to inhale and scream into Taylor's ear like a wild animal, roaring to claim its territory. The Warden beat his own chest and slowly tightened the leather around Taylor's neck. Whether he passed out or died, Lindsay knew that to the boy either was welcome, and the sooner the better.

◻ ◻ ◻

Friday, October 26

AT MIDNIGHT CHAVEZ LAY ON THE LOUNGER ON THE BACK DECK UNDER a dark sky. The only imperfection in his body was the morphine injection he had just made in his arm, where a small drop of blood slowly clotted, the deep red colour fading to an earthy brown. The glass ampoule held only trace amounts of the clear fluid that was now pumping through his veins, courtesy of Dr. Bruce Townler. There was a wash of heat over his body, then the drug infiltrated his mind. His heart rate slowed; his veins became thick with blood, like engorged leeches. Weightless, he felt himself drift skyward, like vapour floating into the infinite blackness. From there he could hear the night animals, the scavengers and hunters prowling the landscape.

It was a crescent moon, floating among the northern constellations and the Milky Way. However, Chavez felt more drawn to the space between the stars, the dark matter. With the house lights blacked out, no neighbours or sources of light anywhere and the shadows of a cromlech — a circle of blackness made by monolithic evergreens — there was no visible difference between the world above and the one below the horizon. Just as there was no difference between where his spirit ended and the dark matter began. He felt as close to peace as he ever had in his life.

He had created a world where he was in total control. Here, in this place, there were no wars to fight, no nightmares to haunt him and no abuse to suffer. He owned the women and the boy, keeping them like pets. He provided the sustenance of his flock and they worshipped him at his pleasure. Every moment of fear the captives felt, every time they ran and cowered at his slightest flinch, it reinforced his knowledge that he had become the most feared thing in their lives, more fearful than death itself. And yet it felt empty.

The euphoria in his flesh would wane and he would take physical pleasure from the boy, who was there for him alone once more. The morphine would release his drifting spirit; he would re-enter the animal body he had perfectly sculpted, manufactured into a killing machine, and plunder the boy's body. He allowed the thought — that the fires of passion were beginning to vanish with repetition — to enter the forefront of his medicated mind. While the spectators worshipped him with their fear and fuelled his violence, it would not be enough forever. Only expanding his paradise would bring him joy.

One for sorrow, two for joy. Three for a girl and one for a boy. Five for silver and six for gold. Seven for a secret, never to be told.

Joy. The second girl had been a special sacrifice. He honoured her body by pleasuring it before freeing her spirit and returning it to the earth. For the first time, Chavez considered the need to do the same for Anthony. Maybe Anthony would be happier to return to the world of his vision rather than toil as an unfulfilled soul in this world. Anthony could never be happy on this earth, unlike Chavez, who only required physical comforts. Anthony hungered for the approval of others; the entire planet would not be enough to fill the void.

Anthony's financial support and fondness for abuse was stifling and growing tiresome. His need to save the world's savages from themselves, to unify the faiths, was pathetic and futile. He would do this one last deed to buy time to empty the bank accounts, and then return to Colombia, where he would disappear. Winter was coming and he'd had enough.

The difference between the stars and the dark was like the difference between spirit and body. Ying and yang. He had explored the balance of contrast further when he felt the gentle trembling of the frail young girl as he strangled her during the coarse act of murder.

He stood and stretched. It was time. She had already been loaded in the back of the van, and he had to go back to the city to get more drugs and food.

◌ ◌ ◌

CHAVEZ FIRED UP THE COOL ENGINE, LISTENING AS IT STRUGGLED TO roll over. The clock on the display read 4:12 a.m. The transmission lagged when he put it in drive and the throttle resisted when he pressed down the gas pedal. With a lurch, the truck jumped ahead, and he followed his tracks through the field, over the matted grass to the narrow driveway over the ditch.

When Chavez stopped at the end of the driveway to check for traffic, he was startled by a burst of activity in the bushes beside him. He opened the window and peered into the darkness. His eyes, still adjusted for the night, saw the world in black and white and were able to detect the minutiae of movement.

There was a smell in the air of fresh animal feces, but he could not identify the animal, as the odour was overwhelmed by the smell of panic. When he opened the door, the bushes again exploded with movement. A furious life or death struggle was occurring.

He craned his head and peered into the bush and saw the reason for the agitation. His van had startled a young deer. It had gotten stuck in a wire fence, unable to push through, scared to move back toward the van.

Chavez exited the van and opened the back doors. Beside the dead girl wrapped in plastic were his tools. He found what he was looking for, heavy iron bolt cutters, and approached the animal. It bucked wildly as he neared, and let out a muffled cry. As he drew closer, one of its back legs hit him, gashing his forearm open pain-lessly with sharp back toes.

Chavez shrugged off the injury — the animal was only scared for its life; it meant no offence. He made three cuts in the wire, and the animal broke free, bursting through the fence and into the field across the narrow country road. Chavez watched it until it disappeared.

24

ANTHONY HAD GIVEN UP ON sleep hours ago and found himself in his study, holding in his hands the most important and expensive artifact that he had ever purchased. It had cost him more than one hundred thousand dollars. Similar to tarot cards, Oracle cards were part of the world of cartomancy. Oracle cards, however, lacked the negativity and the dark faces of the tarot. They were the cards of angels, or of angelic mythical creatures like unicorns and mermaids. They were purified and offered clear, readable direction to the reader. What made these Oracles so valuable was their dark origin.

In the fourteenth century, in middle Europe, a group of Celtic priest called druids dreaded the coming expansion of Christianity. They had learned the power of cartomancy from Gypsy travellers and had studied the early power of divination. When the Gypsies grew suspicious that the Druids were actually more interested in the black arts, they encouraged the Druids to refrain from the tarot and to use Oracles instead. This worked only for a short time. The druids were fast learners and they advanced the science further. They developed the Devil's Blood Oracles and channelled only evil.

Anthony knew that the artwork on tarot and Oracle cards ran deep with symbolism that provided nuance to the card reading, depending on the level of the reader's understanding. These cards he had purchased were painted by Giovanni Bellini, a Gothic master painter. After they were completed, in 1516, he died under circumstances unrelated to his advanced age.

The few people who knew such cards existed were terrified of what they had been reported to do. They had summoned the deaths of generals, presidents, whole clans and families. They had inflicted plagues of cancer and other diseases on entire villages. Yet Anthony had no fear. The experiences he had had in the other world had convinced him that his spirit was strong enough. The only effect they had ever had on him was bringing him the dream, which was the path to humanity's salvation.

He opened the case, unwrapped the black cloth and lifted out the deck. There were twenty cards. He kept them face down. He had purchased the cards in Colombia five years ago from a Romanian pawnbroker, a chubby little man with a thick, gaudy birthstone ring on his pinky finger. The pawnbroker spun the ring incessantly in circles, anxious either to get the small fortune Anthony offered or to free himself from the cursed cards. Despite his girth, he appeared sickly, with sunken eyes and infected sores on his face and hands that looked like radiation poisoning.

Tired at the late hour, Anthony now shuffled the cards slowly and deliberately, not wanting to damage their images, nor the direct messages written at the bottom. He had a translation page that the pawnbroker had prepared and Anthony had had verified, still in the cards' case.

He lay out a three-card spread, face down in a single column. The top card represented Nightmare, the river of subconscious evil that flows through everyone. The second card represented Greed, the selfish trait that drives all of man's behaviour, the truth so despicable it was denied out of shame. The third card represented War, indicating that every interaction with another person was a battle of power and control, greedily taking everything from them in that moment.

Anthony meditated a moment to make his question clear and

slowly flipped the cards over one by one. The first was an angel, six-winged, with eight contorted mouths gnashing at the insects swirling around its head like a crown of flies.

The second card was a blood-soaked child with drooping arms, wailing with fright as she inched toward her mother. The mother waited with a cleaver behind her back.

The third card was an eviscerated man, feeding on his own intestines while the fires of Hell approached from behind.

The images were disturbing, painstaking in detail. Most of their meaning had sadly been lost to the ages. Anthony sat reading the lines together in context with the symbols and images, not merely as three lines of advice. The same Oracles that had told Anthony that he could bring Chavez in, could trust him to do the messy work, were now suggesting something else. He read them one more time, even considered taking a picture or writing down their message, and finally decided the evidence had to exist only in his memory.

He put the cards away, his hands trembling and his heart racing. Only after they were back on the shelf did he begin to reconcile his spirit with what the cards said and what he knew to be the path to salvation.

The way forward had nothing to do with Chavez dropping him for Bruce, nor the sex that had become too rough, nor even the fact that Chavez was attempting to co-opt Anthony's plan for his own hedonism.

The Oracles were saying it was time for Chavez to have an accident, and for Anthony to give the police enough clues to find him. The cards had said that he would be victorious. The passive sufferer, the secret dreamer, the half-impotent, middle-aged nobody would finally transform and plunder.

◻ ◻ ◻

NASTOS AND CARSCADDEN SAT IN VIKTOR KALMAKOV'S BMW DOWN the street from Anthony's house. Neither of their personal cars could have sat on the street for long without drawing attention in a neighbourhood like Rosedale. Kalmakov was much farther south, sitting a van that he claimed was used for restaurant deliveries, despite the fact that the windows were painted, not just tinted, black, there were no advertising decals on the outside, and neither Nastos nor Carscadden had ever seen it before. But Nastos didn't ask any questions; he was just glad that Kalmakov was on their side.

Anthony's house was in darkness, except for a few porch lights. It was nearly four-thirty a.m. The radio was playing *Coast to Coast*: standard-issue ghost and conspiracy radio that they had been listening to since ten last night. The host, George Noory, interviewed random crackpots with their arbitrary proclamations of global destruction caused by anything from comets or mythic monsters to nuclear war and the return of Jesus coming to punish the world for humanity's most glorious failings.

Nastos' phone rang. It was Madeleine. "Where are you?"

Nobody was particularly jubilant at four a.m. Certainly not a wife whose husband hadn't come home. He said, "I'm with Carscadden. There's still no sign of Hopkins." He hoped that saying he was doing this for Hopkins would soften her. It didn't.

"So you're hanging out with him for moral support?" It was clear that she didn't think this was a good enough reason to be out all night. Not when he'd assured her that he wouldn't go back to that lifestyle.

"I think Anthony Raines had something to do with it. We're watching his house." Nastos glanced over at Carscadden. He was listening to the conversation. It probably made a good diversion from exhaustion.

She whispered, half to herself, "I thought these days were over." Then, louder, she said, "Poor Tara. This is awful."

Nastos was still watching Carscadden to see how he was holding up. He seemed lost.

Madeleine interrupted his thought. "I wish you were here. This is giving me the creeps. When do I get to feel safe?" It was more of a statement than a question. Certainly nothing he could address without walking into a Madeleine Minefield. Marriage had taught him a thing or two. "Yeah, you're right. I'm sorry."

There was an awkward silence before he heard her make a sound, like she was sipping a drink. "Don't get me wrong, Steve, I want her back. But there are cops out there looking for her. They get paid for this, they have guns."

"That's the point, the cops aren't actively looking for her. All they did was put her name on a computer screen as missing. I phoned Jacques. She hasn't used her credit cards; the phone trace failed. They aren't going to find anything at Anthony's house without probable cause to search it and they don't have it. Not yet anyways. So the cops are out of this one for now."

Madeleine countered, "Hasn't it crossed your mind that if it could happen to her it could happen to me — or worse, Josie?"

It was something that Nastos hadn't considered. *Madeleine is so street smart.* Then he reminded himself that Tara was too. "Don't worry, we'll find her and I'll be back soon. Just keep the doors locked, the portable beside the bed. There's nothing to worry about."

She said, "Come home soon," and hung up.

Nastos looked at his phone, not believing that the relationship had deteriorated to hang-ups. *She should know more than anyone that it's up to me and Carscadden. Besides, she's got nothing to worry about.* He slid the phone into his pocket.

Carscadden changed the radio station to the news. "She doesn't like you doing this kind of work, does she?"

"It's nothing personal. Hell, she loves Tara. It's just the work. She learned the hard way what it can do to a person."

Carscadden asked, "What do you mean?"

Nastos opened his window a crack for fresh air. "It comes down to one simple sentence. The whole time you're out there, doing the job, the job is doing you. It starts by making you assume the worst about people. You begin to suspect that everyone has a dark side and any display of kindness is a façade, manufactured to deceive you, like you're some kind of idiot. Then you resent them for thinking you're an idiot."

"Not all cops are as cynical as you are, Nastos."

Nastos shrugged. "Here we are, stalking someone. I know he's scum, but still, here we are hunting a *person*. I don't know how you can hunt people and have it not change you for the worse. It can make you an asshole to live with.

"With the objectivity of time, I'd say I've done things in policing I've regretted. I've hurt people to a degree that wasn't warranted, especially considering that the only people who care about justice are the victims — no one else cares. So we corrupt ourselves. We behave like the people we hunt.

"You're away from your family," Nastos continued. "You miss important moments in your child's life. You're tired and grumpy because when you *do* get to see her, it's when you've sacrificed sleep. Invisible, odourless, no taste, no feel — whatever it is, it works its way into you like radiation. I didn't understand until I got away from it. Now here I am coming back for more."

Carscadden didn't say anything. He reached into the back and pulled out another Coke Zero, maybe his fourth, and a five-hour energy drink that he gave to Nastos.

"I didn't mean for it to come out that way. There's nothing I'd rather be doing than helping you find Tara," Nastos amended.

Carscadden asked, "I just wish we knew what we're looking for."

"We do. We're looking for whatever jacks up our blood pressure when we see it."

Carscadden opened his door. "I need to stretch my legs."

Before Nastos could ask "Where the hell are you going to go?" Carscadden was out of the car. Leaning in through the half-closed door, he told Nastos, "Before the sun comes up, I'm going to check around his place. I might peek in a few windows to see what's going on in there."

Nastos shrugged. "Be my guest."

"You're not coming?"

Nastos couldn't tell if Carscadden was disappointed or happy to be able to do something on his own. "I'm sure you can handle it, but if he sees you and offers you candy or beer or something, you're going to have to go in there and play along with his demands or you'll blow our cover."

Carscadden closed the door without saying a word and started toward Anthony's house. Nastos watched as he first skulked up the street under the city lights, going two houses past before turning back. He cut across the lawn to the side of Anthony's garage, where he disappeared out of view.

Nastos decided he'd apologize again once Carscadden returned. His cell phone buzzed. It was a text from Carscadden. *Too dark to see in the garage.* Nastos sent back, *Good, so come back.*

He looked up to see Carscadden peek around the garage and give him the finger. Carscadden went back out of view, eventually resurfacing out of the trees closest to the car. He had gone all the way around the back of the house.

When he returned, Carscadden slumped into his seat with a red nose, rubbing his hands together.

"Anthony is in the house, playing solitaire. Real exciting."

Carscadden's cell phone rang and he answered it right away. "Yes, Viktor? Okay, right, thanks." He hung up. "Viktor says he has to bail out. I guess I'll walk back and take the van."

Carscadden reached for the door, but stopped when Nastos grabbed his arm. He was beginning to tire of Nastos grabbing him instead of just talking, like he was part Neanderthal. He turned to see Anthony's garage door opening. "How did Anthony get from playing solitaire to the garage so fast?"

Nastos realized that he still had a grip on Carscadden and let go. Slowly, a vehicle pulled out of the shadows: a 1980s Dodge Caravan, with decals dried up and peeling off the sides. Nastos squinted. The writing looked like it had once said *Cuervo Perdido Carpentry.* The van slowly turned out of the driveway. The side windows were tinted too dark to see the driver as he went by, but from the outline they could tell he was too big to be Anthony.

Carscadden pulled out his phone to call Viktor.

Nastos had craned his head back and was watching as the van drove down the street toward Bloor. "Call Viktor."

Carscadden said, "I'm on it. Get driving." As the phone rang he said to Nastos, "We can do a bump and dump like they do to tourists in Florida. Viktor gets in front, hits the brakes. When the driver gets out we take him down." Carscadden shouted into the phone. "Jesus Christ, Viktor, we've got something. Pick up!"

Nastos said, "We're going to follow him." He pulled up the parking brake one notch to keep the headlights dark, then turned the car around and followed at a safe distance.

Carscadden cupped his phone. "He knows where Tara is. Let's just beat it out of him."

"It would be faster to just follow him. If we think he knows we're following, we'll go to plan B, don't you worry about that." Nastos hit the gas, closing the distance to the van.

Carscadden put his phone on speaker mode. Viktor finally answered. "Sorry, I didn't notice the vibrating."

Carscadden explained about the van. "Can you stay with us?"

"Of course."

Nastos interjected. "Okay, we're going to follow this guy smart. If we turn off and get back in behind him too many times, he might notice. This would be a lot easier with two more cars."

Viktor cleared his throat. He sounded exhausted. "I'm ahead of him now. I'll slowly let him pass, then I'll stay behind."

Nastos agreed. "Okay, then we'll drop way back. If you get burned you can turn off and we'll take the lead."

"I have to call some associates of mine to tell them I can't meet with them. Then I'll call back and we can keep the line open."

Carscadden said, "Sounds good" and ended the call.

Nastos said, "See my problem with Viktor? What associates do you think he's dealing with at this hour?" He peered ahead through the windshield as Viktor slowed and let the unknown man pass.

25

THEY LAY TOGETHER, LINDSAY with Hopkins and Taylor, touching, fingers interlocked, heads on each other's shoulders, waiting for the Warden to return and do whatever he wanted. The moments of brief silence between the songs playing on the stereo upstairs offered no reprieve to Lindsay. It felt like the pause itself was filled with the hisses of a thousand invisible snakes wrapping around her head, writhing into her brain. The speakers would soon blast again, the sounds forcibly invading her. And no matter how deep she tried to retreat into herself, there was nowhere to hide, no matter how tired she was — not even into the comfort of another nightmare.

Having a conversation was difficult because of the noise; they had to shout for everyone to hear so they spent most of the time lost in their own thoughts. It had been a long time since there had been any food or sleep.

Lindsay thought back to when the man had captured her. It was so muddy — she could remember what had happened less now than she could before. All she had to rely on was the way she had told it to herself, and she had to admit she could not trust herself to be accurate about anything.

Dust stirred in the air and she was again reminded that she was slowly being buried alive — if not literally, then certainly in the minds of her parents, who would be losing hope daily. *Maybe he killed me when he first grabbed me and this is actually hell. This is where you go after you die, to a place like this where there is no god, no hope, nothing but pain. You get raped, killed and sent some- place even worse. And it just repeats, death after death, rape after rape, forever.* She still felt the people next to her, but that didn't mean that they weren't all dead and this was just the way it goes.

She was nearly powerless, but she could have a small impact in her time in this place. She was all too aware that she had been here for twenty-nine days and that one way or the other she would be dead in less than twenty-four hours. The last thing she wanted was to have her friends have to sit and watch as she was murdered in front of them. With only one day left to live, in this place, there was one way to show the ultimate defiance to their jailor. She could kill herself and take some control back.

What if I did do it? What could he do to retaliate? He might leave me here to rot. That would be awful for Tara and Taylor. It has to be all or nothing. There was a pause in the music — the CD had hit the end of the track and needed to be manually restarted. Taylor was clearly the most likely to be suicidal; Lindsay decided to lock him down first.

In the welcome pause in the noise, Lindsay signalled that she wanted up and they unlocked from each other. She moved in front of them and made sure they were both paying attention. "It's just a matter of time before he kills us. You know that, right?"

Taylor shrugged. *That was easy.* Now it was just Hopkins. She had watched two rapes now. Maybe it was enough.

"If one of us commits suicide, it leaves a mess for the rest. If two of us do it, he'll take it out on whoever stays. It'll be brutal — you'll wish you had died."

Hopkins shook her head. "My boyfriend knows where I went; his best friend is an ex-cop. We were sent to find you and bring you back, Lindsay. They're close. They might be driving here right now."

Lindsay shook her head. It was actually a shame to see Hopkins

201

so naïve — a woman her age believing in fairy tales like hope. *What kind of world does she think this is? Things only get better so they can get worse again.*

Hopkins looked away from Lindsay, over to Taylor. She said, "If you're a woman and haven't been sexually assaulted by the time you're thirty, don't worry. You still have your eighties to look forward to, when you're in the nursing home, helpless and not considered credible. You can get past this, Taylor. Sexual assaults happen to men too — it doesn't make someone less of a man. There is always someone stronger than us out there; that's all this asshole has, strength from steroids. Trust me, when my friends get here, they'll let you put the bullet in his head yourself."

Taylor looked both skeptical and hopeful. "No they won't — you said he's an ex-cop."

Hopkins smiled. "The way he's going to treat this bag of shit, you'll know why he's an *ex*-cop."

Lindsay asked, "What do you know about being raped?"

"I've been a teenager, Lindsay. Lots of women are pressured into unwanted sex, whether it's by a boyfriend, a male friend, or a drunk who forgot what 'no' means. Taylor's strong. He can overcome this."

Lindsay only half heard what she said. She was thinking about when Jessica had found her on Facebook. It had started out well, with Jessica just offering stories about her mother, her childhood and things about the extended family she never knew. Soon after Lindsay had revealed that she lived in the Bridle Path, Jessica first suggested that they should meet up. That should have been a red flag. In retrospect, Jessica had groomed her slowly, becoming a friend, offering pot and alcohol — it was a long time before she started talking about how tight things were with money. The whole time, she had been trying to drive a wedge between Lindsay and her dad.

Watch the way he looks at you; that's how it starts. Does he take you shopping for clothes, watch you try them on?

You're wrong, Jessica, he's not like that.

Lindsay, he could have adopted anyone, but he picked beautiful you. It won't be long before he's done with that dried-up, too-posh-to-fuck religious zealot of his.

And wasn't it true that she had been afraid to tell her mom about what was going on? Jessica had connected her with confidential therapy classes, not Claire. Jessica had been able to see the truth she had buried — not pure, loving Claire who might reject her if she knew the baggage she carried inside.

Lindsay said, "A friend of mine tried to convince me of the same thing."

Hopkins asked, "Pardon?"

"Jessica," Lindsay said. "She tried to convince me that all men were like that; they're not. I lived with my birth mom until I was seven. Her boyfriend used to touch me." It had taken three months of therapy to get to the point where she could say it. This was only the second time her life that she had done so. To a degree it felt more re-victimizing than empowering. "My dad has done nothing but love me. He would never do anything like that to anyone, especially me. He'd kill anyone who ever touched me."

She turned her attention to Taylor. "There's a point when you've been through something like this, that you will yourself to remember it all. I've remembered everything that happened to me, and now I have it all straight in my mind. Now that I've done that, I can finally put a name on it and put it away. The name is Darius Miner, and I hope he suffers for what he did to me."

Taylor asked, "What's *this* guy's name — Satan?"

Lindsay leaned into Taylor, her hand finding his beneath the blanket. "I don't believe in God, but I think I'm beginning to believe in the devil."

Hopkins and Taylor both moved closer, pressing against her; it was not a claustrophobic feeling. Hot, thick tears poured down her face. Moisture she didn't think she possessed. Taylor's hands were strong. She had never noticed how beautiful he was. Gentle, she told herself — although the monster had never showed any interest in any of the girls, Taylor took the brunt of the physical abuse, and for that, in the next world she hoped to remember him as a hero.

She had gone to the therapy classes on her own, and had felt like she was getting somewhere. Like maybe she could have gotten better — and then this happened. Hope was dangerous. It opened you up to the most intimate pain.

The touch of Taylor's hands reminded her of what life could have held for her. Now only death offered the bliss that love used to — a complete escape from any uncomfortable feeling. She could return to the source of everything, leave this earth and embrace eternity. Her mom had killed herself, and in a way, like any good parent, she had lit the path to the ultimate salvation.

She saw that Hopkins and Taylor were not going to act. That was fine; she would just do it herself. She began looking around at the options. It had to be something that the other two couldn't stop, which meant she would have to hide it from them. She looked down at her filthy feet and the plan came. She peeled off her socks and rubbed her feet, putting the socks up near where she generally lay her head down. With the music loud, no one would know. Under the blanket, she would stuff them down her throat and choke to death. It would only be uncomfortable for sixty seconds; then she'd be gone. A moment later, the music began again; only this time, instead of terrorizing, it was welcome.

◊ ◊ ◊

NASTOS WOULD HAVE PREFERRED THAT CARSCADDEN DRIVE. DEALING with traffic might keep his mind from other things — like the fact that they were driving to wherever this man did what he did to the girls before they were found carved up and dead. He tried another approach, to get him busy on the phone. "Why don't you call Dennehy and see if he can come with us?"

Carscadden said, "This is day twenty-nine for Lindsay. He could be about to kill her now."

Nastos shrugged.

Carscadden continued, "Hopkins wasn't part of the plan. He might have killed her yesterday."

Nastos said nothing, not wanting any part of the conversation. Carscadden continued, "If she's dead, *he's* dead."

Nastos gulped. "It might not be easy to make it happen that way. If Lindsay is there, we'll need whoever this asshole is to bring it all back to Anthony. I don't want *him* getting away with anything."

The bug in Carscadden's ear about calling Dennehy finally worked. Carscadden reluctantly tried calling Dennehy's cell phone, but he wasn't answering so he phoned the Police Communications Centre, which would both record and log their call. Nastos listened on speaker phone.

A woman's voice said, "Communications."

Carscadden said, "Hi, this is Greg Kavanaugh. I need to speak with Detective Dennehy immediately."

There was typing. She'd be checking the screen to see if he had logged on anywhere. Detectives didn't always bother, so the task was most likely futile, unless the call-taker was just looking for a reason to dump the call.

"He's not signed on anywhere. Can you call back tomorrow?"

"I'm calling in relation to the murders he's investigating. He needs to call me in the next thirty seconds, if not sooner."

She asked, "Who is it I'm speaking to again?"

Impersonating a police officer was a crime he could easily avoid. "I'm Dr. Greg Kavanaugh of the FBI Behavioural Sciences Unit. He asked me for a consult. Well, I consulted. He needs to speak to me as soon as possible." Carscadden waited a moment. "Listen, I have the chief's home number, but I don't want to go that route. I just need you to page Dennehy, text him, call him and put a general broadcast out on all of your radio channels — do whatever it is you need to do." He reiterated, "Detective Dennehy of Homicide." Carscadden gave her his cell number and she put him on hold. Seeming fed up, he handed the phone over to Nastos.

Nastos weaved through traffic, following Viktor, who was a dozen car lengths ahead. The stayed on the 404 north out of Toronto and into York Region. Most of the high-rises were disappearing behind them. Traffic was lighter and the highway wider. Nastos looked at the speedometer; the needle was steady at 110.

The call-taker's voice burst in. "Doctor Kavanaugh, here you go."

The line sounded dead. Nastos said, "Hello?"

"Doctor Kavanaugh, do I know you?" Dennehy asked. His voice was tired, his speech slurred.

"Next time answer your fucking cell phone."

"Steve Fucking Nastos. It was in the charger, dickhead — take a Midol."

Nastos shook his head and said, "For fuck's sake," to himself. To Dennehy he said, "This is important, Dennehy. Wake up."

"It's like, five-something in the morning, Nastos. This better be important. Let's hear it."

Nastos gripped the wheel tightly and became more animated. "Try to pay attention. We know where the missing girls are. We're going there right now. You said you'd help us if we help you — well, here you go. We solved it for you. Now give your head a shake and start throwing some clothes on. We're following the suspect into York Region. We're probably forty minutes ahead of you if you leave now. Hurry up if you want to be the hero or we're going in without you."

Nastos could hear background noise on the other end of the phone.

"This better not be bullshit, Nastos."

He gave him the directions and asked Dennehy to call if he had any problems, now that his cell phone should be all charged up, then hung up the phone. He turned to Carscadden and tried to lighten the mood. "It was a lot more satisfying back in the day when you could slam a phone down on the hook to hang up. Now you have to squint your eyes to find the little red button and delicately press it in case the phone explodes in your hands."

Carscadden stared though the windshield with no reaction.

Nastos tried something else. "Not many cases of serial killers working together. I can think of the Hillside Stranglers."

He didn't think Carscadden was going to bite. Finally there was a reply, in a monotone.

"Or gay. Not too many gay killers, are there?"

Nastos started rhyming off names. "John Wayne Gacy, Jeffery Dahmer. Only they focused on male victims. Serial killers tend to choose their victims from their pool of sexual interest. Why are these two different?"

Carscadden thought for a moment. "They aren't thrill or impulsive killings. Judging by Anthony's big show coming up, it's a financial arrangement."

Nastos asked, "Okay, so which of the two is in charge, Anthony or this guy? Sure, this guy is the muscle. And Anthony is the brains."

"This guy is in charge," Carscadden said. "Anthony has money, but this one, whoever he is, has the power over life and death, and ultimately, that's all that matters." Carscadden didn't look away from the road ahead. "And I'm not waiting for shit. When I get there, I'm going in."

26

CARSCADDEN'S PHONE RANG. IT
was Viktor. "I just turned off the 404. We're going east on
Stouffville Road."

Nastos said, "Okay. Why don't you back it off and we'll move
up?"

"Traffic is only two lanes. If you want to move up, do it fast."

Nastos hit the gas and caught up as best he could. He worked
his way into a position where there were three cars between them
and the old van. They were all compacts, so Nastos and Carscadden
had a clear view.

Stouffville was little more than a village. Stouffville Road
became Main Street. Century-old row buildings, an independent
Build-All, a Legion and a Tim Hortons coffee shop. Small-town
Canada hadn't changed much in decades. Carscadden sent a text
message to Dennehy with a location update. There was no response.

The Cuervo Perdido van stopped at the York–Durham Line,
then turned north. Nastos backed right off. Even with cars in
between, he didn't want to get too close. The van turned east onto
Webb Road. Nastos decided to drive past.

"Viktor, follow him down Webb Road — I'll turn back and get
in behind you."

"Okay."

By the time Nastos did a U-turn and doubled back to Webb Road, Viktor and two other cars were in front of him.

Viktor said, "And I heard about what you did at my restaurant. If you ever want a job, just let me know. I could use a daytime manager."

Nastos shrugged. "And give up all this excitement?"

"You're the kind of man that excitement follows. Anyway, he just turned off to the south into a field. I found a safe place to stop; come meet me."

Nastos pointed to the van driving through the field up ahead. "Perfect, we're here." He hit the brakes and stopped at the side of the road. It was a narrow gravel shoulder. He peered ahead, unable to make out where the turnoff was.

Viktor said, "I've pulled in a driveway up here on the right. There's trees — he can't see me."

Nastos wasn't convinced. "Be careful."

Viktor's voice sounded excited for the first time since the pursuit began. "There's a parking area on the north side of the road farther east. Drive there. You can drop the car and it won't be as conspicuous. I'm heading there right now myself."

Nastos checked his blind spot and moved to where Viktor suggested. Once both vehicles were parked, they met up to talk face to face.

Nastos studied the scenery. Their surroundings were desolate. The road was paved but neglected, fractured and without streetlights. Tall, dark trees bordered the country road. The morning sun was still eclipsed by the horizon, leaving them in a colourless twilight, feeling like they were forgotten.

Nastos noticed the intensity on Carscadden's face. His eyes were desperately searching in every direction. He crept up to the edge of traffic, fixated on where the van had driven into the field.

Nastos joined him. He could make out the hydro lines that dropped from the top of the poles, sagging before climbing to another pole until they disappeared into distant fog.

Carscadden said, "Just up here." He pointed to the south side of the road, a hundred yards ahead.

Nastos knew what he meant. "The hydro pole. There's a line heading south. I see it."

Carscadden, Nastos and Kalmakov crossed the road and jogged up to the pole. Carscadden stood there looking up. He pointed to the hydro cable that led into the treeline. "Okay, the house is back here. Let's go before the sun burns off the fog."

The last thing Nastos wanted to do after finally finding the place was rush in blind. Somebody would get hurt. Unfortunately, cooling Carscadden down wasn't going to be easy. He'd have to think of some busywork to assign, something reasonably convincing. He looked at Viktor, who seemed to be thinking the same thing. There was a good chance that what Carscadden was going to find up there was going to send him over the line, whether it be homicidal or suicidal. Nastos started with "Listen, we have to be smart here."

"Come on, Tara's up there, for Christ's sake. Let's go."

"Let's go take a look around and see what we're dealing with. The cops are on the way —"

Carscadden didn't wait for Nastos to finish the sentence; he crossed the street, jumped the ditch and began pushing aside the low tree branches over the abandoned driveway. Nastos sighed and jumped across after him, and Viktor followed. *So much for slowing him down.*

There was a double-track trail, mostly grown over, with grass separating the two lines. The large weeping willows with their long, hanging branches alone would have been enough to shroud them from the sun. Even at nearly six in the morning the branches made these trees look melancholy. It was like walking between draglines cast by monstrous spiders. Black on grey. The distant fog suffocated any sounds outside their field of view. The fog trapped among the trees — thick, cool air — obscured them from the living world.

The trail began to bend to the east. Willows gave way to maples, partially skeletonized by the season. The sun appeared again, but as a ghost of itself, obscured by the mist. Nastos noticed a large black mass looming in the distance, blanketed by the thick greyness. The structure was the same colour as the black between the stars. It felt like they were walking into a monochrome alternate universe.

Once Carscadden could make out the house, he started for the front door. Nastos grabbed his arm, stopping him.

Carscadden wrenched his arm away. "What are you doing? We found it."

"Yeah, we found a house. Now we have to do this right. He could have a bomb rigged to blow the whole place up, for all we know. We'd take this whole mess to the grave."

Carscadden checked the signal strength on his cell phone. "Nothing."

Nastos immediately realized the mistake they had made. "Dennehy was supposed to call us when he got here. We're going to have to go back and get him." Carscadden wanted to race in; maybe this would slow him down.

"We may not have time." Carscadden squinted, looking at the house. As their eyes adjusted to the coming light, the house, its bare wood, windows like the hollowed ocular cavities of a skull, remained black. "I'll go in. You wait."

"Not a chance. We stay together. Let's check out the area before we go in."

Barely suppressing his anger, Carscadden hissed, "That's my goddamned life in there. I'm going in."

Nastos could see the tears in Carscadden's eyes and realized that there was no stopping him. Nastos was merely prolonging his misery, the possibility that Hopkins and Lindsay were dead.

Nastos exhaled. "Come on, then. It's time for answers."

211

27

NASTOS, CARSCADDEN AND Kalmakov approached the building from the north, getting as close as they could before they came through the treeline. They kept a quick, low pace across the field of waist-high grass. Kalmakov dropped a knee to the ground and offered, "We could split up, approach on three sides. We can conference call with our phones. It would be like having walkie-talkies."

Nastos felt something inside twinge at the thought. "I'd rather we stick together. I've got a bad feeling about this. I wish we had weapons."

"There are three of us, we'll be okay," replied Kalmakov.

As if to confirm Nastos' concerns, it was then that the music started. Coming from the house at the volume of a rock concert: "Mama" by Genesis. The windows were blacked out, painted on the inside. They rattled in place with the bass, their sound easily drowned out by the speakers, their movement betrayed by the way they quivered like terrified children. Nastos saw the truck parked out back. The doors were closed up. If the back doors had been left open, he'd expect the man to come out soon, probably with a body over his shoulder. Maybe he had some carving to do first.

Nastos turned to Kalmakov and Carscadden, who were both on his left. He pointed toward the house. "Must be planning to stay a while."

Carscadden said, "He won't hear us coming with that noise going on."

"You're right," Nastos said. "Looks like it's go time."

They jogged to the house in single file: Nastos, Carscadden, then Kalmakov, the older man, last. They drew up close to the north wall and began walking counter-clockwise toward the main door on the west side.

At the corner, Nastos saw that there was a long porch four feet from the ground with six-foot-tall windows. When he glanced back, he caught Carscadden's leg bouncing with anticipation. "The front door opens outward. Carscadden, you're going first. When you get to the door, have your ass to the hinges, then reach out and pull the door open toward you. Viktor and I are going to rush in full speed, then you come in right after us."

"And if it's locked?"

"I start kicking it in; I'll make noise. You stay with me and Viktor goes to another door."

Carscadden was contemplative, as if the plan wasn't to his liking, but reluctantly he agreed.

Nastos said, "On you. Go."

They ran flat out, hoping the element of surprise would give them an edge. When Carscadden pulled the door open, Nastos was amazed. He had expected it to be locked, that they would have to choose another option like jumping through the windows. Instead, he found himself going near full speed through the main door. There was a kitchen–living room common area to the left and he went to the bigger room. He felt more than saw Viktor peel off to the right, then Carscadden came to back him up.

When Nastos rounded the corner and turned into the living room, he saw the man standing near the sink, looking in a mirror and painting his face with a small brush. Nastos charged with a war cry, shoulder-tackling the man at full speed and driving him into the kitchen counter. Nastos went for a choke hold, both of his hands wrapping around the man's thick neck from behind. The man was muscular; it was like trying to strangle an ox. Shorter than Nastos and stocky, he seemed to have superhuman strength. He shoved the heel of his hand into Nastos' chest — it felt as powerful as a kick — and shoved him back. The man leapt toward him with a lightning-fast right hook that connected and spun Nastos' head at a dizzying speed. Nastos dropped instantly to the floor.

Carscadden only hesitated for a moment before jumping on the man's back and trying to force him to the ground. Viktor came around the corner and kicked the man in the right shin full force, then grabbed two fists of hair and drove his knee repeatedly into the man's face. After three strikes — which should have knocked him unconscious — the man pivoted to the side and swept Viktor's legs out from under him, taking him down to the ground. Carscadden was little more than an inconvenience, and found himself tossed on the counter and careening to the floor.

Nastos flailed against the wall, finding a gas line to the stove to pull himself up. His ass hurt from falling on the handcuffs in his back pocket. He frantically pulled them out as a plan came to him. He locked one side around the cast-iron gas pipe, leaving the other side for the wild animal.

The man was fighting for his life. When he had Viktor on the ground, he tried stomping on his face, missing narrowly. Carscadden lunged for his throat but was knocked back, kicked to the ground.

Carscadden saw what Nastos had in mind with the cuffs; all they had to do was push this man back and Nastos could hook him up to the wall. As Viktor distracted the man with a flurry of punches, Carscadden tackled him backward toward the wall. Nastos gripped his wrist, Carscadden clenched him by the hair and punched his face, and Viktor rolled over and, with some kind of wrestling move, locked up the man's legs with his own.

Nastos' shout of "I got him, I got him!" was barely audible over the music. All three of them stood back from the man. Amazingly unhurt from fighting all three of them, he could see that he was trapped by the handcuffs and the cast-iron gas line.

The man paced from side to side, able to cover maybe six feet as the handcuffs slid along the pipe. His body language taunted them, asking them to get closer to him. Nastos noticed a coat on the kitchen counter and went through the pockets, pulling out a wallet and driver's licence. "Ladies and gentlemen, introducing Mr. Chavez Vega Alvarez."

Makeup was smeared all over his face, like war paint. Chavez sucked air and tried to pull the cast-iron pipe from the wall, his tendons and veins writhing like severed worms under the skin of his neck. He wore a white, sweat-soaked shirt; a tear revealed a chiselled physique, with the kind of musculature you expect on a wild animal. Chavez's eyes were narrow and hungry.

Nastos regretted trapping him in the kitchen where there would be knives or other weapons, but at the time it had been essential. He crept forward, testing the limits of Chavez's reach, and started pulling the drawers out of the cabinets. He tossed back the cutlery, of which there turned out to be very little.

Carscadden had found the stereo and kicked it until the music stopped. When the noise stopped, the relief felt like taking the lid off a pressure cooker. He picked up a BBQ tool, the kind with two sharp four-inch prongs, and approached Chavez. "Where are they?"

Chavez didn't say anything. He paced back and forth and tried to yank the handcuffs apart. The entire house seemed to be creaking from his strength when he pulled on the pipe.

Viktor found a heavy, cast-iron frying pan. "You two go look. I'll watch our friend."

Carscadden spit a glob of blood from his cut lip at Chavez. In turn, Chavez lunged. Viktor stepped forward and swung as hard as he could. The strike hit Chavez squarely on the head, sending him to the ground.

Nastos whistled approvingly, then turned to Carscadden, "Okay, let's search the place — we'll find them."

Carscadden dropped the BBQ prongs. "Yeah, check everything, because if we don't find anything, we'll just have to go to plan B and beat it out of him."

They searched the house. Carscadden squeezed past a piano in the hallway and checked the back two bedrooms. They were empty, except for old bed frames and thin, bare single mattresses that stank from urine stains. They had been chewed by rats and left to rot. The floor had been swept, all of the rat shit and debris piled up in the closet, which had some musty clothes and damp cardboard boxes on the upper shelves. Carscadden checked the ceiling, finding no sign of an attic hatch.

He heard Nastos call him back to the hallway. Carscadden asked, "What?"

Nastos pointed to the ground. Carscadden saw the hatch under the piano. He began dragging the piano back to the bedrooms. Nastos pushed from behind.

Carscadden shouted, "Tara, can you hear me?" The piano scraped the floor so loudly that it reverberated throughout the house. Carscadden thought he heard something but could not tell over the noise.

Nastos grabbed the handle. Carscadden saw a ladder tilted back into a closest and brought it over.

The voice was muffled. "Kevin, we're down here!"

"Tara!"

Nastos pulled the hatch door open and Carscadden dropped the ladder down. It plunged into the dark. Carscadden raced down the ladder, dropping to the ground below. There was a rotten, stale sex smell in the room, and two figures emerging from blankets in the corner. Carscadden helped Hopkins to her feet then gave her a crushing hug he like he'd never let her go. The other figure was a young man. He straightened up much slower, using his hands on his knees. He refused to make eye contact with Carscadden. Tentatively he reached out for Hopkins, and she turned back to him, breaking the strength of Carscadden's embrace. "Taylor, this is Kevin."

"This is the ex-cop?" He sized Carscadden up, not convinced.

Nastos came down the ladder, but stayed back from the reunion.

Hopkins said, "He's the ex-cop." She asked Nastos, "Where's the asshole who was holding us?"

Nastos reached for Hopkins, squeezing her shoulders. "Viktor has him upstairs; you'll be sad to hear he's not feeling very well."

28

CHAVEZ WOKE WITH A JOLT TO a filthy rag stuffed in his mouth and the sound of two men speaking to each other. His head ached. His first impulse was to gag, but he maintained control of himself, breathing deeply through his nose. He resisted the temptation to open his eyes in case they were watching him; he tried to learn as much as he could before they knew he was awake.

He felt the tape around his ankles, the handcuff on one side holding him to the wall, the other arm taped down on the arm of a wooden chair. He remembered now — the fight, the old man with the frying pan.

One man asked, "Do you trust that to hold him?"

Chavez slowly flexed his forearms again, testing the strength of the binding. He wasn't going anywhere. He felt a finger running over the tape at his wrist and allowed his eyes to open a sliver.

The second male was scratching the back of his head.

"I don't trust the criminal justice system. I don't trust charities to spend money properly. I don't trust cops around my wife. I certainly don't trust lawyers, no offence."

"None taken."

"But I'll tell you, I *do* trust duct tape to hold a man while I have an honest and frank discussion with him."

Chavez opened his eyes. Both men were watching him, like he

was some kind of science experiment that was doing something unexpected. One took no offence to a lawyer joke. He made a mental note that he was a lawyer. His mind reeled with the need to identify him, to know who he was dealing with. Then he remembered that the Hopkins woman worked for a lawyer — this would be him; the other, his investigator, the ex-cop. The one he had been supposed to take care of before.

With his body coming to life, he required more oxygen than he could get through his mouth. He began to breathe more deeply, but it only made things worse. Black stars floated past and he felt weak. He was beginning to pass out when the cop ripped the rag from his mouth. He refused to retch or to show any weakness. *What's the cop's name again?*

He turned his head and spat on the ground, sucking in a few deep breaths of air. *Nastos,* he thought to himself, *and Carscadden.*

Carscadden seemed the most enthusiastic. "Okay, then. Let's get this party started. Do you recommend the easy way, or the hard way?" He slid a small table in front of Chavez. On top was a rusty, red metal tool box. Chavez watched with great interest as the man slowly undid the latch and opened it up.

Nastos asked, "You sure you want to be here for this?"

Carscadden met the man's gaze. "Hell, yeah." Then he slapped Chavez across the face as hard as he could. It stung, and the sting was made worse by the cold air. Chavez grunted and shook his head. He would use the pain to help him wake up. It only made him stronger. His eyes narrowed and focused on the lawyer. Chavez moved his head around the room, trying to find anything he could use later for when he broke free and wanted to kill them slowly.

Nastos moved directly in front of him. "Lindsay Bannerman. Where is she?"

Chavez slurred, *"No hablo ingles."*

Nastos' face squinted. "Pardon?"

"No hablo ingles."

Nastos never broke eye contact with Chavez. Instead he smiled.

219

"You see, I think you *hablo ingles* just fine. That's how you knew to say '*No hablo ingles*' when I said pardon."

Carscadden rummaged through the tool box and began removing the contents.

Nastos ran his fingers through his hair, becoming impatient. "There's the easy way, the hard way and the harder way. You're a tough guy, so you get the harder way."

On the table, Carscadden had spread out an old hacksaw, a framing hammer and a fistful of loose screws. The lawyer handed the cop the framing hammer. Nastos seized it in his right hand and traced over the various parts with his left. ·

"This part here is called the claw." He tapped the twin prongs used for pulling nails. "This is the striking face." He touched the front of the hammer's head. Then he touched the side. "This is called the cheek." He gently caressed the cool metal against Chavez's stubble.

"How's your *ingles* now, shit-for-brains?"

Nastos moved the hammer to a position in front of Chavez's face and rotated it in his hand so the claw was facing down.

Chavez said, "I don't know anything."

"Well, you better learn something pretty quick, because Lindsay's parents love her, and no piece of shit like you is going to keep us from finding her."

He lifted the hammer up in the air and swung down as hard as he could. The two prongs of the claw smashed through the middle finger of Chavez's right hand, severing the finger and sending a lone, sad spit of blood to the floor. Chavez felt the pain explode from his hand up his arm, up to his head and down to his balls. His entire body twinged and contorted. Time passed — he had no idea how much — before he could get his breath back. He forced himself to study the amputated finger, the mangled hand. He'd use the hatred to fuel his revenge. As he tried to pull his arm free, the severed finger dropped to the floor, the veins writhing under his skin like newborn snakes.

Carscadden never flinched. He never diverted his eyes from

Chavez when he leaned over to Nastos and dispassionately said, "Well, he's not denying any knowledge of Lindsay now."

Nastos gave away nothing.

Chavez considered lying, saying again that he didn't know anything, but he didn't think they'd believe him. He made a tactical decision not to lie anymore. His only hope of surviving was to give them a reason to quit what they were doing before they had crossed too far over the imaginary line of right and wrong. Becoming a liability — that would be a death sentence.

The cop tapped the claw from finger to finger on Chavez's right hand, starting with the thumb and skipping the mashed digit. "Eeny, meeny, miny, moe. Catch a tiger by the toe. If he hollers, let him go. Eeny, meeny, miny —" Instead of the last *moe*, Nastos lifted the hammer, then drove the claw through Chavez's little finger, embedding the prongs in the chair. The finger severed easily with another spout of blood squirting out to the floor, the finger rolling off of the chair's arm. Any sound it made was smothered by Chavez's screams. With a groan, the chair released the hammer from the wood as Nastos twisted it out.

Chavez tried rocking backward and forward violently, as if to tip the chair, but the cop drove his heel down on the front lip between Chavez's legs, hitting inches from Chavez's balls. It stopped the chair from rocking and got Chavez's undivided attention. "Easy now. We're just getting started with you, sunshine."

Nastos reached over to the tool box, put the hammer down and picked up the hacksaw. He held it up to Chavez's face with his right hand and gently touched a finger to the rusted, jagged blade.

"I think I'll dispense with the English lesson this time, Chavez." He plucked the saw so the vibration made a sad, metallic sound. He grabbed Chavez at the top of his head by the hair. A fist full of thick, black hair flowed from between his fingers.

Nastos asked, *"Donde está mi amiga,* Chavez? Where is my friend?" He extended his arm and rested the butt of the blade at the point where Chavez's right ear attached to his head. Chavez's face squinted shut as he braced for the pain.

221

"You work out. Your looks are probably important to you. After I saw off your ears, I'm taking off your nose and lips. I'm going to make you eat them by stuffing them in your mouth and wrapping your face in the tape. After that, I'm going to scar your cheeks with a blowtorch. When I'm done with you, this perfect body of yours is going to look like the monster you are. *Comprende?*"

Slowly, Nastos began to draw the blade back. It clunked after each jagged tooth passed over the curve of flesh and gouged into him. First a nick, then a gash. A thin red slit opened up, flecks of red rust staining his skin.

Chavez cringed and finally shouted out. "Okay, okay, stop!"

The cop crouched forward so he was nearly nose to nose with Chavez. "Stop the saw? Sure, hey, yeah. You're right about the saw. It's nowhere near as much fun as the hammer." He reached for the hammer, but the lawyer grabbed it first.

The lawyer said, "Mind if I cut in?"

The cop chuckled a little. "Oh, there's a young man here who wants to dance. Don't mind one bit. After all, Lindsay is your client; I'm just the help."

Any hopes Chavez might have had that this was a good-cop, bad-cop game were dashed. It was bad cop, worse cop. He pleaded, "But I said okay. I'll co-operate. I'll tell you everything."

The cop flung his hands up in the air like he was exasperated. "Well, Jesus Christ, Chavez, we don't have all night. Get talking."

"And you're going to let me live?"

The lawyer flipped the hammer around so the claw was facing down, hovering over Chavez's right hand. Quietly, almost to himself, he began reciting, "Eeny, meeny, miny, moe . . ."

Nastos said, "We will leave you here alive. Still cuffed to the wall, mind you, but alive. The police will be told who you are and will be looking for you. Now all I care about is finding Lindsay Bannerman. I figure the cops won't be long in finding you anyways."

"She's waiting to be found — in Toronto. In Colonel Danforth Park. If you hurry, you can save her."

Nastos and Carscadden were looking at each other, probably trying to decide whether or not to believe him.

The cop said, "Okay, deal. Now what was the situation with the boy?"

Chavez looked away. It was a mid-distance stare at the bare concrete wall. He turned back to face them.

Nastos continued, "Because he asked to kill you before we left. He doesn't want to have to testify to anything, he doesn't want anyone to know. He just wants to watch you bleed to death."

Chavez read Nastos' face and saw no signs of a bluff or of a tactic. It was just the truth.

"I swear, Lindsay is there, right down by the river, in the trees."

Nastos shook his head from side to side. "You know, I almost believed you. And if I did, I wouldn't let him do whatever it is he has planned, as sign of good faith. Unfortunately for you, I think you're full of shit. I think she's already dead and you may as well die here where the boy — Taylor is his name — can enjoy it."

The boy came around the corner. His eyes wide, his fist tightly wrapped around a small paring knife. He looked over Chavez, his eyes widening when he saw the amputated fingers on the ground, the blood dropping from the stubs.

"Go there if you want to find her." He could easily have given them the name Anthony. A name they likely already knew. He didn't — screw them. Coming to hate Anthony was one thing; giving any satisfaction to these assholes was something different. He refused to let them win. Besides, he needed to get to Anthony if he wanted to get his money, take him for all he was worth. Maybe Anthony would be kind enough to pen a suicide note, taking responsibility for everything and giving Chavez enough time to cross the border — or get on a flight to Colombia.

Nastos feigned sympathy. "Oh yeah, you've been through enough."

Carscadden tried to use his phone again, still finding there was no connection. Chavez said, "There is an electronic cell jammer in the living room. Your phones won't work until you unplug it."

223

The cop pulled out a strip of duct tape and put it over Chavez's mouth, then waved the hacksaw in his face. "If I go there and it's all bullshit, I'm coming back here to saw your balls off. *Comprende?*"

Chavez agreed, trying to look weak and frail. A part of him ached to tell them that he knew who they were, that they weren't in charge as much as they thought they were. It wasn't enough that he recognized the power he had over them; he wanted them to know it too. He made himself wait; that moment would come in time. Hopkins, the boy and Lindsay might get away. Fortunately, there were other targets out there.

"But the boy here," he waved a hand at Taylor, "You're calling him off, right?"

Nastos shook his head gravely. "No. I lied about that. Your day is about to go from bad to worse."

Nastos straightened up and turned to the lawyer. "We're not talking any chances. We're calling Dennehy again."

The lawyer said. "Fine with me."

Nastos slapped his hand on Taylor's shoulder. "Batter up." To Chavez he said, "See you in hell, cupcake."

29

THE BOY STARED AT HIM FOR A while with conflicted thoughts and feelings clashing on his face. He was tough to read. Chavez found the waiting tedious to the point of being annoying. What he had endured in his eight years in the Colombian army, watching those on either side of him — strong, brave men — die, while he survived, had forged in him a feeling of immortality. There was nothing he couldn't withstand. He had been in the *Dragoneantes*, at the rank of *Sargento Primero*, or First Sergeant. A climb through promotions that had mostly related to his lack of mercy. He had killed people with his hands, without hesitation, his heart rate never breaching seventy. Twenty-four-hour survival hikes through the mountains with only water, where eating insects while they frantically squirmed in his mouth was the price of survival. He'd snapped the necks of comrades to free them from pain, he'd sewn up his own wounds — caused by rusted, shit-covered rebel bayonets and hand knives — with needle and thread, no anesthetic.

Now the boy stood in front of him, holding the knife. He was filled with hatred, still scared and avoiding eye contact. His breathing was sharp, as if he wanted to run. After he inched a few tentative steps toward Chavez, it was clear he didn't have what it took to cut someone to pieces while they screamed.

Chavez found it challenging to not taunt him. *I targeted you because you were a bitch. Look at you. You pathetic little woman.* He needed to play this smart if he wanted to kill the cop and the lawyer. The hammer strikes to the chair had done enough to weaken it, he was sure of it. Free from the chair, he might be able to get away with enough time. All it would require was some manipulation.

Taylor's eyes were closed when he said, "You're a worthless piece of shit."

"I know."

"What you did it me . . ."

"Happened to me too. Only I was much younger."

Taylor paused, his face twisting. His eyes opened and for the first time he made eye contact with Chavez before averting his eyes to the floor. "Then why —"

"It's the way our kind breed." He wanted to smile but he found himself considering his words. "We breed like a virus that we inflict on other host animals. You will do the same now. You're now like me. The disease is growing in you right now." He paused. "Don't believe me? Look at the knife in your hands."

Taylor's hand tightened around the blade, then relaxed. The knife slowly spun in the boy's grip, the small serrated strip glinting in the light.

Chavez continued. "This will be your baptism of blood, like a praying mantis devouring its lover to nourish its future young." Chavez closed his eyes, tilting his head to the ceiling to expose his neck. "Take me, lover — I'm ready for you."

Chavez heard no rush of footsteps, sensed no push of air, felt no fear. There was the sound of clutter being shuffled around, but it was distant. He opened his eyes a sliver and smiled, quickly returning to a display of reverence for the moment — as if he still expected to die — when the boy turned back to him.

The boy knelt down and lit a candle that Anthony had left there. He had the hammer in his hand. He approached the stove, careful not to get to close the Chavez.

"I'm not like you. You're going to feel the heat in your lungs.

You're going to suck in poison and every part of your skin is going to bubble and cook off of your body. Burn in hell, you piece of shit."

Taylor brought the hammer down suddenly, smashing the top elements of the stove and fracturing a gas line. He turned back to Chavez, making sure he hadn't escaped in that brief moment, then opened the gas valve. Chavez could hear the subtle hiss in the air. The smell had not yet reached him.

Taylor put the hammer on the counter and left. Chavez heard the cop and Carscadden say to something to the boy as they led him out of the house, their voices disappearing once the front door was closed, leaving him to consider his future.

◻ ◻ ◻

CHAVEZ'S WORLD TURNED PANIC-RED. HE BUCKED WILDLY, WRENCHING the chair sideways, torquing the arm that was handcuffed to the cast-iron pipe three feet up the wall. There was no strategy other than to live — and eventually to teach Nastos and Carscadden what pain really meant.

With steroid-induced strength, Chavez used the chair and the cast-iron natural gas line against each other. The weakest of the three was by far the wooden chair. He tried twisting his arms to slacken the tape, knowing it wouldn't help much. The chair *was* damaged from the hammer strikes; the weakest point was the sides. He stole a glance at the tool box. The saw blade was the obvious choice.

Quickly, the plan came together in his mind.

Chavez began with kicking and bucking, forcing the leverage of his weight downward and sideways against the chair's arm. With the momentum he generated, he was able tip the chair sideways, plunging his weight at an obtuse angle. There was a loud snap, but the wood had not broken through. He pulled himself up partway with his cuffed wrist, then plunged back down on the chair. On the second strike, the impact broke his arm free.

Without pause Chavez continued to buck, flail and kick every muscle in his body. For decades, he had worked out, fueled by a mix of steroids and the hatred of being victimized. He had pushed and pulled metal plates, throwing them around until he could barely wipe the sweat from his brow, his muscles burning from lactic acid; he had forged a strength that mortals could only dream of. What remained of the wooden chair stood no chance. Spindles failed, first at the front lateral brace, then, as he twisted and wrenched further, at the back post. He had freed his left arm completely, and after two more spindles splintered, the chair essentially ceased to exist, becoming a bundle of sticks. But he remained cuffed to the wall, and the matter of the natural gas line was going to be a problem. Rupturing it would be a catastrophic mistake, he couldn't reach to turn off the stove, and getting through the handcuffs would take too long.

He flailed at the kitchen counter with his legs, which brought down the hacksaw. His arm ached as the edge of the cuff bit into his arm like powerful jaws. He used the pain to fuel his efforts and thrashed his legs until he reached the saw and dragged it within reach of his injured hand. The smell of gas finally hit him.

Chavez estimated that he had less than two minutes to live before the gas hit the nine-percent concentration point at which explosions occurred. He reached his arm out, put the nearest part of the blade at his left wrist and pulled back aggressively. The pain was excruciating, causing him to pant to keep himself from crying out, and the work was awkward with his mangled hand. The hacksaw's handle was slick with blood. When the teeth found the bone on the second pull, the vibrations from the sawing sent a sick tickle up to his shoulder. It was too much; he roared in agony, but only paused from his work briefly. As he sawed, the tendons and nerves severed, a feeling of cold on his fingers. The radius bone failed first, unleashing a smell from its core of weeping marrow. A vein of some significance finally opened with a thick stream of blood at first lubricating, then slowing the blade.

He considered putting down the saw and trying to slip out of the cuff, urgently deciding not to. He had to be sure. After ten more

228

seconds of aggressive, jackhammer-speed cutting, he put the saw down and snapped his hand off at the wrist. Two arteries vomited blood in long, steady streams. Worrying about blood loss was a luxury Chavez would enjoy later. He slid the back patio door open and ran as fast as he could. After maybe twenty yards he lay down in the field flat, feet toward the house, and waited for it.

The explosion vibrated though the ground, shaking the trees and sending fragments and wreckage over his head. A rush of birds was spooked into flight and quickly obscured by debris. He turned back to look. What was left of the structure had rotated nearly forty-five degrees. It was a smoldering mess, collapsed in on itself like a jack o' lantern left to rot in the sun.

Another near-death experience for Chavez Vega Alvarez. There was no time to feel relief, not yet. He was consumed with the need for revenge. There were many to blame for what had happened. Some of the injustices were longer than others, but they all ran deep. That lawyer and cop would pay with their lives, if not worse. Anthony, whose plan had been a failure, would also have to suffer.

Chavez felt his ears pop, one after the other, and the temporary reprieve from the sounds of the world was over. A hiss like from a giant snake filled his mind. Eyes wide open, he nervously glanced around him in the long grass before realizing the sound came from within him. With the hand missing from one arm and fingers from the other, his arms began to resemble snakes in his mind, as if he were being reborn as the ancient serpent that had haunted him as a child. He thought of Tio being eaten by crows and the satisfaction that it had brought. Then he felt a deep pang of unful- 229 filled rage when an image of the Child Services worker appeared, the tall thin woman with her long blond hair who had first brought him to Tio. She had escaped him. She was still out there some- where, her and others like her.

Pain brought him back to the present. He made a mental note that after torturing Anthony to death he would take his precious Oracle cards that he kept hidden in the floor of the study. Eventually he'd flee on the first plane to Colombia and disappear into her dark mountains. No, he thought, before I go, there will be time to feed the crows.

◻ ◻ ◻

AS HE PREPARED FOR THE CASA LOMA SHOW, ANTHONY APPRAISED HIS reflection in the mirror in a washroom not far from the main stage. The aging man, who could have been his father, again confronted him — a man who was just coming to his intellectual peak, while his body failed. The CBC crew were finished setting up, and this was to be his last interview before he was due on stage. Somewhere, perhaps in the creases of his deepening wrinkles, feelings of nostalgia for the love lost between him and Chavez were hidden.

Another failed relationship. He was not getting any younger. If only Chavez had listened, if only he had had cared more. Anthony decided his certainty that Chavez could change or become less selfish was where he had gone wrong. It was more than coincidence that the younger man's interest faded once the money was gone. As the wealth had disappeared, Chavez had felt his power in the relationship grow — the sex growing rougher, then mean-spirited and eventually vicious. This show would bring the power back into its natural balance. The monster within Chavez would retreat and the struggle for dominance would be over.

Anthony straightened his tie, then adjusted his collar. He composed himself and swaggered into the studio room. He told the interviewer that he was ready. The broadcaster was what Anthony

would consider the dream client. She was upper middle-class, smart; she had an innate, confident beauty earned from a healthy lifestyle and an aesthetic striving for a natural appearance. Above all she was comfortable with him.

"We'll start recording again."

Anthony re-clipped his lapel mic and breathed into it. The sound guy readjusted it, then gave a thumbs up.

"Welcome back to CBC's Special Feature on the spirits of the season. We're speaking with renowned psychic Anthony Raines, or, as he's known to many of his fans, Saint Anthony, the patron saint of missing things."

The interviewer turned to him and smiled. She was receptive; this interview was going to be an ideal advertisement for future shows. "How did you get the nickname Saint Anthony?"

He smiled. "Saint Anthony comes from a long time ago. Historically, he was the patron saint of missing things. I've helped a lot of people find missing things over the years: jewellery, mementoes, even family members or other people."

Her face adopted an expression of sympathy. "Like the young man you helped the police find so many years ago."

Anthony let his voice drop a few notes. "Yes, that was sad, very sad, but the family was in a way relieved. I really don't believe in the closure that everyone talks about. The only comfort was that at least they knew that their boy didn't abandon them. He loved them. The reason he didn't come home was something he couldn't control."

"Anthony, you speak to the spirits of people who have passed on, you read tarot cards and do public readings — how do your abilities affect your spiritual beliefs?"

"Do I believe in God?"

She laughed. "Where does faith belong in a person who already knows for a fact what is waiting for us?"

"Faith, hope — they are the most important things to have. My faith is not in God *per se*; my faith is in the ability of man to evolve into something more. When we work together, we can accomplish great things. We built pyramids thousands of years ago. The Mayans understood math and astronomy, it took millennia for our science to fully appreciate just how deeply. The problems began once our societies started encountering each other. When we saw people different from us, it made us rethink our interpretations of the world. Seeing other successful civilizations that have developed with a different religion makes us doubt our own. Then, as usual, our aggressive tendencies come out. All social progress stops until we are done waging war on each other to find who has the stronger god.

"It's time for reconciliation — not in one government, but in one system of understanding. Then we will move forward, all of us together."

"And you know the way?" the interviewer pressed.

"Simply put, I carry the burden of the truth, which throughout history has gotten more people killed than anything else. People only want their own beliefs parroted back to them. It reinforces their belief in themselves," Anthony leaned forward. "That's why messengers are shot. In a way, I envy those who let go of the immense weight of a self-dominating, self-forming life, to relax one's grip on one's own centre and yield passively to a super-ordinate power authority. That's to paraphrase Ernest Becker."

"So to clarify, as you see it, religion will not have anything to offer people going forward?"

"The fact is that religion, as it is today, exists for two simple reasons."

"And what are those?"

"To provide comfort to counter the most troubling aspect of humanity: the fear of death. If you believe in Buddha, Christ, Mohammed, Krishna — any of the gods — they all provide a chance for immortality if you believe. They alleviate the fear of oblivion and provide an escape into paradise. That can be very tempting to the type of person who thinks it unfathomable that there could be nothing more than death."

"And the second reason?"

"The second thing it provides, in its most cynical manifestation, is justifiable scapegoating. You can dump all of your sins, transgressions — whatever — onto the man who dies on the cross, onto your priest, and be reborn, cleansed of impurity. Religion uses guilt to lure you in, creates transgressions that are unavoidable — to the extent of thought crimes — and offers itself as the only source of absolution. I offer a path of freedom from the cycle of guilt."

She adjusted herself in her chair to lean forward, her hands clasped together. "Are you cynical because you think it's all wrong, or because you live an alternative lifestyle?"

232

Anthony appreciated that she was asking a pointed question in such a gentle, open way. Gays could never be totally welcome in any religious dogma, for obvious reasons. She was asking if he resented religion for rebuking him and his community.

"No. There are many believers who are gay. Some are even ministers or religious officials."

"But don't you think that religious culture provides us a sense that we are part of a meaningful universe? It gives us a sense that our lives are significant, whether we be postal workers, stay-at-home moms, janitors — we are all soldiers in Christ or Allah."

Anthony checked his watch. "It helps us avoid and deny our mortality with a fallacy of value."

She asked, "So what are you saying is the alternative?"

"During the show I'll be explaining what is actually on the other side. For now, I'll say all of the known religions are close, just not right about what's there. In fact, what they all promise is possible; only the path they require is not the proper path."

"Love each other, don't commit murder, the ten commandments — it's all wrong?" She kept the tone bright.

Anthony smiled. He liked her. She was the kind of person who loved people and enjoyed discussing such things.

"Most honest and caring interpretations of the major religions preach peace and love. That's almost the long and short of it. But when people hear the rest of the story, it will open both their minds and their hearts."

"Does the fact that there is a clear afterlife, a paradise waiting, does that send a message to people suffering here that it's okay to commit suicide as a means of escape?" she asked. "Or what about murder? If we remove someone from this life, is the crime diminished since it's not really total death?"

"This life is precious," Anthony assured her. "Only a small amount of time is spent on this earth and it's a shame for it to be taken away. Suicide causes bigger problems than to just the self; it harms the survivors. And murder? That's an awful thing. We are here to learn to work together."

233

"So, Anthony, here you are trying to recruit people to your cause. You're prophesizing a new path for humanity. Just like the other faiths."

"Yes, I know. To see others as being devoted to the same things as us, practising the same rituals, reinforces our beliefs and confidence in ourselves. If I were to tell everyone about an invisible man in the sky named Zeus who is the father of all the gods, who controls everything and talks to me, I'd be crazy. I call him God and say I need your money — then I'm a prophet. It's a lonely path to be on your own. But the fact is, I have had an experience. It came to me as a dream, where I awoke by a river in a new land. I lived an entire life in this place. I've been speaking to sprits from there since I was eight years old, but being reborn there, living there, has changed everything for me.

"I'll be starting the show with readings and a short pre-recorded video about the history of what I do; then I'm going to share nothing less than the secrets of the universe with everyone."

30

BANNERMAN CLOSED THE DOOR to his basement office and brought the laptop out of sleep mode with a shake of the mouse. When the screen was ready, he logged into the work system and began tracking records. The first check was a credit score on Darius Miner. As well as a tale of poverty, the report revealed his current address.

Nastos had found evidence that Miner had murdered Lindsay's mom, Tabitha Moreau — what he had done to Lindsay Bannerman had learned from the adoption worker.

Darius Miner started it all. He began the inevitable chain of events that had started with a perfect young girl. He filled her mind full of chemicals, molested her, then killed the mom before she could get rid of him. He abandoned the girl and left her to be adopted. Only by greasing the wheels of the adoption process and by bribing Jessica Taylor to cancel her applications for Lindsay's guardianship was Bannerman able to save her from a failed life.

He was too late to spare her from Darius, but not too late for that bitch. The jury was still out on whether the abuse from Darius would have a pervasive negative effect on Lindsay's ability to form normal, loving relationships or whether she might become highly promiscuous. The jury might be out on Lindsay, but Bannerman decided that for Darius, today was judgment day.

235

For the first time in years, Bannerman rode a subway rather than driving. A phone call to a friend at the Canada Revenue Agency confirmed that Darius Miner had been living for the last few years at a halfway house run by the Salvation Army in downtown Toronto. The gun felt heavy in Bannerman's pocket. He had to keep touching it to make sure it was still there. Glocks were mostly plastic; the only real weight came from the bullets. These were hollow points. They mushroom on impact, expanding, causing extra damage to internal organs and staying inside the body, their jagged teeth lacerating organs and arteries should the victim move while trying to flee or even just writhing in agony.

Bannerman checked his watch. Lindsay had been gone for twenty-nine days. If everything that Nastos said was true, this would be the day that she was found dead. *Sorrow, Joy.* He had Googled the words and come upon the rhyme "One for Sorrow." If Lindsay was to be found dead today, she'd have *Girl* carved on her chest. He felt sick at the thought. Having to deal with that reality was too much to bear. Even the thought of it was already too much. He was beginning to think that after he put a few bullets in Miner's head, it would be a good idea to put one in his own so he wouldn't have to experience the news of Lindsay's murder.

When the train stopped, he followed the crowd as they all exited to the right and filed up the stairs and escalators to street level. Outside it was cool and overcast, the kind of thick, fast-moving cloud that travels in ragged wisps, haunting the city.

In twenty minutes he was outside the halfway house, a restored Victorian mansion with wheelchair ramps that weaved up the sides, a black wrought-iron fence for a smoker's area to the right and a WheelTrans bus stopped at the curb.

Bannerman noted that there were no security cameras as he jogged up the steps. He marched through the front double doors and found an unstaffed reception area behind security glass. He moved impatiently, noting two residents who stumbled into reception from a side door. Two older, brain-damaged-looking men with crazy eyes and the smell of cooking sherry on their breath. They laughed heartily as they waited for the electronic door to open, then plunged down the steps toward the unsuspecting public.

Bannerman turned to see a receptionist returning to the desk. She was overweight and looked tired. She asked, "Can I help you?"

"Yes. I'm looking for Darius Miner, please."

"You're from a social agency?"

Bannerman considered whether to say yes, but he wasn't sure that he'd be able to answer jargon-laced questions. "No, I'm an acquaintance from a long time ago. I just want to see how he's making out."

This made her look at him sideways, like it was the craziest thing she had ever heard.

She hit a button under the desk and the side door where the two drunks had come out buzzed and popped open. "Room 109, end of the hall. You don't need to buzz out."

"You don't think I'll stay long?"

"No. I don't."

Bannerman grabbed the door and pulled it open to a smell of stale sweat and urine. He made his way down the hall. It looked like a neglected old-age home, the kind the government would shut down if they had any sense of compassion. It was good to know that Darius had lived here for few years. Only people like him belonged here.

A male nurse was helping a young man get into a wheelchair; they both ignored him as he passed. The smell didn't get better as he moved deeper into Darius's lair. He was expecting to see something come hobbling out at him like an undead monster, a zombie from an '80s horror movie hissing and lunging at him.

And like the heroes of the movies, he would pull the gun out and spray a hail of bullets at him, the villain's flesh peeling and dropping away, until he made a head shot and put the thing down once and for all. Darius, the vampire that had taken the purity and innocence from Lindsay, her birth mom and god knew who else.

Bannerman didn't knock on door 109. He pushed it open slowly, his right hand gripping the pistol plunged deep in his coat pocket. He began to doubt if he had racked the slide like they did in the movies to get a round in the chamber, but enjoyed the scenario in his mind of doing it slowly in front of Darius. Surely a man like him would know that the next thing Bannerman would do was blow his brains out.

He heard a slurred voice groan a question as he entered the room. Darius was sitting in a wheelchair, propped up to the window at the back of the room. He had a view of a brick wall and a sliver of a city park, where a few children were playing — poor, immigrant children, running around in circles, not knowing yet that their entire lives would be spent spinning tight circles unless they were able to stay away from men like Darius Miner.

There was no one else in the room. Bannerman came alongside Darius, not looking directly at him yet, but observing the state he was in. There was a permanent injection port in his neck and arms. He'd been in the wheelchair a long time: atrophied legs, an indwelling catheter, or piss drain.

Bannerman said, "Can you talk?"

Darius said, "I can talk." His voice was husky and dry. "Who are you?"

Bannerman detected more strength than Darius wanted to let on. He turned to Darius. "Do you remember a woman named Tabitha Moreau?"

Darius froze, which is to say his eyes stopped moving as if trying to track the children.

"You hung her to death over the closet door in her apartment."

Darius said, "I remember Tabitha."

"You remember her daughter? Lindsay?"

When Darius turned his head toward Bannerman, he looked well enough. He wasn't like a late-stage AIDS patient. He had a few good years left of this hell. "Yeah. I remember Lindsay."

Bannerman said, "You raped her."

"It wasn't like that. *I* wasn't like that."

It was a pathetic lie. It was like he was really saying, *What are you going to do about it?*

Bannerman reached into his pocket and slowly pulled out the

gun for Darius to see. Holding it in one hand and lightly tracing a finger from his other hand along the barrel like a model on a TV game show. *Look what beauty awaits you, Darius, if the price is right!*

Bannerman was happy to see that he hadn't racked the slide to charge the weapon. He did so slow and deliberately, right in Darius' face, just as he had imagined.

He pointed the gun at Darius's closest kneecap. "It's a forty-cal. Let me know if it hurts as much as they say it does on TV."

A dribble of sweat rolled down Darius' face. He said again, "It wasn't like that."

"Bullshit."

"I touched her, that's all. When I saw I had a problem, I left."

"But not before killing her mom."

"I did her a favour by killing her druggie mom. Don't kid yourself."

Bannerman smiled, not believing that the man had the audacity to say such a thing, knowing he would die for it. "You didn't think of maybe just calling Children's Aid, the cops? Anyone?"

"They would have just thrown money at Tabitha and told her to straighten up. She would have spent it on drugs. She was going to die anyways, I just moved up the date. Got Lindsay out sooner."

"And the molestation, that was just a parting gift?"

Darius said, "You're right, you're right. Just do it. Look at me. You'd be doing me a favour. Save me a few more years of living like this. In this place. I can smell the piss and shit, man — I'm not that far gone. I know the way they treat me and I know there ain't nobody coming to help."

Bannerman took a step closer and smiled. "You're right, Darius. Superman is dead." He pointed the gun at Darius's head, the muzzle boring into his temple.

Darius closed his eyes and reclined in the chair. "When you came in here, I saw your reflection in the glass. Moving slow, graceful, and shit, your coat like a cape. I prayed that you were death coming for me. Thank you."

Bannerman glanced at the piss jug tied to the bottom of the

239

wheelchair. It was filling up. He could smell the man's excitement at the prospect of being released from his hell. He was sick, a deviant trapped in his body, unable to kill himself.

Bannerman pressed the gun harder into him, wanting to leave an indentation in his skin. "You know, I came here with the specific intention of killing you. But now I see it would hurt you more to let you live."

Darius opened his eyes, "No, wait."

"No, *you* wait, you piece of shit." Bannerman spoke in an intimate whisper. "You know, all you had to do was be your usual asshole self. That would have been enough. But no, you had to talk. You had to try to tell me what to do. You tried to control me, like you've tried to control everyone else in your pathetic fucking life. Well, fuck you, Darius. Enjoy your piss bag. Enjoy eating oatmeal three times a day, and enjoy your view of bricks. Once again, you've fucked yourself."

Bannerman put the gun back in his pocket. He smiled at the distress he'd caused Darius. Crushing the man's hopes of escape was more satisfying when he saw the tears pouring down both sides of his face and heard him begin to whimper, "No, no."

The nurse heard his sobbing and appeared in the room. She looked at Bannerman with disdain, wondering what he'd done to upset a stone-cold piece of garbage like Darius Miner. She saw the tears on Miner's face and the red mark the gun's barrel had left in the side of his head. Confused, she put her hand on Miner's shoulder, but he shoved her away. "Get your hands off me, you white bitch!"

240 Bannerman smiled as he strolled down the hall, listening to the man's wailing.

31

up the van; before long, they had all gathered at the open side door. Carscadden and Hopkins held each other tightly. Viktor was standing by Taylor, not too close to his personal space, as if knew the kid felt safer with people around. Then they heard the explosion: a low thud that even through the trees was enough to feel like a punch to the chest. Black smoke appeared above the treetops. Nastos knew Chavez had to be dead, but it didn't feel like it was all over, not until Lindsay was back at home.

Carscadden dialed his phone. Nastos turned to Taylor. "I like the way you let him have it."

"Thanks." He kept his eyes down, and stole a glance at Hopkins.

Nastos reached out to touch his shoulder, feeling a twinge of guilt when the boy pulled away, so violently. "You know, they have a service at the hospital. There are nurses specially trained in helping people who —"

Taylor's face turned into a snarl. He said something under his breath to Hopkins, then looked to the ground.

Hopkins eyed him. "Nothing happened to him in there. It was just a nightmare and it's over."

Taylor added, "That piece of shit is dead and I never want to hear about him or this place ever again." He turned around, his back to Nastos and Carscadden.

241

Nastos retreated, seeing that Taylor wasn't ready or was too embarrassed to talk about what had happened to him. "I know. That's what I'm saying. People have bad dreams sometimes. So there are people who can help you."

"I'm not talking to any nurses or doctors."

The last think Taylor likely wanted was to open up to a woman, and feel more emasculated. Talking to another man might be worse.

"There's a guy I went to for my daughter — she had nightmares too. Maybe you want to talk to him?" Nastos offered.

Taylor pressed close to Hopkins, who reached out and squeezed his hand.

"You'll like this guy. Dr. Mills. He'd be good for you," Nastos continued.

Hopkins was adamant. "He's not going to hospital. He's not telling the police anything."

Nastos gave up. "That's fine with me. Your nightmares are safe with us. No one here will ever discuss a thing, not even with each other." Nastos saw that they were all in agreement. He added. "As far as the freak handcuffed to the wall in there, those were his cuffs; we just found them there."

Taylor didn't acknowledge him. He'd already started building a wall that he never wanted torn down.

Carscadden had finally gotten Dennehy on the phone. He pulled up a short time later, using the smoke from the fire as a guide. Byrne was in the passenger seat. Once they came to a stop, they heaved themselves out of their Chevy Impala and joined them at the van. Byrne had a swagger like a gunslinger, called in to save the day.

Dennehy pointed to the black smoke. "Now, who in the hell is going to explain that?" He marched up to Nastos, his chest out, finger pointing, emboldened when he saw Hopkins and Taylor — people for whom to perform.

Nastos said, "These two were held captive with Lindsay Bannerman. The guy dumped her at Colonel Danforth Park, to be found like the others."

Dennehy asked, "Dead or alive?"

"Don't know. Alive when she left here."

"What guy?"

Hopkins said, "The dead guy you're going to find in the house up there."

"Dead?" Dennehy deflated in front of them. He slumped forward, his head sagging from left to right. Then he threw his hands up in the air in exasperation. "Jesus Christ, Nastos. You leave a wake of bodies wherever you go."

"Save us the histrionics, Dennehy. The guy was a serial killer. And for the record, when we left, he was doing just fine. We handcuffed him to a gas line so he couldn't get away. No one was more surprised than me when the place blew up."

Dennehy eyed Nastos, then Hopkins. He wasn't satisfied, but Nastos didn't care. "My friend Viktor Kalmakov is going to take these two back home. You need to call out the troops to search the park for Lindsay. That's where I'm going right now."

Dennehy said, "This is Durham Region, Nastos. The Durham cops are going to have to come here and deal with this mess. They're gonna to want some answers. Our chief is going to want answers." He pointed at Taylor and Hopkins, "these two are staying for statements."

Hopkins said, "If you want a statement from me, you can wait for it. I'm going to have a shower and get something to eat."

Viktor motioned for Taylor to get into the van, and he did. Hopkins wasn't done with Dennehy. "And neither I nor Taylor will say a thing without our lawyer present."

Carscadden positioned himself between Hopkins and Dennehy as she climbed into the van with Taylor. Viktor jumped in, closed the door behind them, then crawled through to the driver's seat. It was already running and the heat was slowly warming the back.

Viktor waved at them, said something to Hopkins and Taylor, then put it in drive.

"This is the statement," Carscadden said to Dennehy as the van pulled away. "Tara Hopkins and Taylor Burke were captured by this man." He held out the driver's licence for Chavez Vega Alvarez. "I'd check his immigration, outstanding warrants with the States, South America — the works. Hell, run him with Interpol while you're at it. He beat them, starved them and emotionally tortured them. After we, umm, spoke with him, he told us that he had dumped Lindsay Bannerman in Colonel Danforth Park, near Forty-Three Division. He had told these two" — he pointed in the direction of Hopkins and Taylor in the departing van — "that she's still alive."

Byrne used his phone to call the fire department. Dennehy turned his back on Nastos and Carscadden and opened his phone. He called the Toronto Duty Inspector. "Inspector D'Arcy, ma'am. This is Dennehy from Homicide. I need a Public Order Unit search of Colonel Danforth Park in Forty-Three Division." He snarled at Nastos and covered the phone. "This better not be bullshit."

Nastos replied, "I just made your career, Dennehy — you're welcome."

32

BY THE TIME NASTOS AND
Carscadden arrived at Colonel Danforth Park, there were street
cops at the Lawrence Street bridge controlling access and the
Public Order Unit officers were walking down the Lawson Road
hill, fanning out for a line search. Chavez hadn't been clear on
where Lindsay was and the wooded park was long and winding,
covering several acres. It would take hours to get all of the way
down to Lake Ontario following the trail the way they had to
search, looking behind every tree, in the river, on both sides of the
banks. The east bank was a vertical wall at times, over a hundred
feet up to Colonel Danforth Road.

Two cadaver dogs were running off leash, their handlers barely
able to keep them in sight. Carscadden and Nastos followed behind
Dennehy's car as they drove down the Lawson hill to the police
command post. "If she's not here, Nastos, we'll never find her."

Nastos turned the radio off and dialed the heat down. "That's
why we're going to find her. If she is alive, we phone the
Bannermans right away so they can meet us at the hospital. If she's
dead, we'll tell them in person."

"Great."

Nastos watched one of the cadaver dogs run out of the woods
with part of a dead fish in its mouth. He shook his head — even
police dogs were still dogs. The other ran under the small bridge,

coming out the other side not long later. It was cold, maybe eight degrees Celsius, and windy with a setting sun. An exposed, injured person would not last long.

The Public Order Unit cops, who were more commonly noticed controlling crowds and protests at political events, were actually mandated for this type of search work, scouring fields and buildings for evidence or bodies. The search line was as many as forty cops, shoulder to shoulder, going down the east then west grass and parklands divided by the narrow, curved driveway.

The dogs had free rein; their only restriction was to maintain a position in front of the blue line of police, so they could have a clean environment to search. If it had been winter, there might have been footprints, but in fall there were dried leaves and ravaged corpses of fish and raccoons that the coyotes and foxes had left behind to distract the dogs.

Carscadden's phone rang. "Viktor, what's up?"

"We're at my place. Tara and Taylor are going to freshen up and I'll fix something for them to eat."

"Good. Don't let the cops near them; they can't force them to provide statements."

Carscadden heard clanging, as if Viktor was pulling pots out of a cupboard. "I have an unlisted number. And ever since I was wrongly accused of murder and needed you to clear my good name, I find I get nervous around the police and forget to speak English."

Carscadden smiled. The Russian mobster's house was one of the most secure places in the city. "Well, look after my girl. I hope I'll be there soon."

"I'll keep her with me tonight. She shouldn't be alone. Buzz the gate when you get here. My man will be waiting."

"Okay."

"And one more thing, my friend."

"What's that?"

Viktor paused, like he was trying to figure out how to start. "Taylor. Well, it's pretty clear what happened to him back there."

"Yeah, he was raped."

"He called his parents. I spoke to them briefly, and they have a lot of questions. Someone is going to have to tell them, but I feel that we are in the boy's confidence. If I had had children, I think I would want to know what was going on so I could be of more support."

Carscadden agreed. "But he's eighteen. He needs time. Hopefully he opens up — until then I think we just have to do as he says. Hopefully he talks to Dr. Mills."

"I suppose."

"Do you think he's upset at all about killing Chavez?"

"He hasn't said much of anything."

"Well, good luck. I'll be there as soon as I can, hopefully a few hours."

"Over and out, Mr. Carscadden."

"Over and out."

After they parked, Nastos and Carscadden assumed positions next to Dennehy and Byrne, who were slurping coffees from the command post truck.

Dennehy waved a hand. "Go get something to warm yourselves up, guys."

Nastos shook off the offer; Carscadden ignored it, his eyes searching the treeline. "Why here? The other girls were in highly populated areas."

Nastos could only guess. "The reasons these idiots do anything might never be apparent. They're just mental insects."

Dennehy asked, "Where the hell did the dogs go?"

Byrne said, "They were in front of the line." They both craned their heads around, trying to orient themselves.

Nastos motioned for everyone to follow him. "I hear barking." He began a slow jog in the direction of the search line.

One of the dog handlers sped off, running down the narrow paved bike trail that weaved along next to the river. Both dogs had run through the water and had not returned. As the cop charged through the shallows, he sank unexpectedly up to his waist and nearly lost his balance. He steadied himself and finished the crossing. He called out to the dog — "Boomer!" — but the dog didn't return. It just kept barking. A cadaver dog barking and not returning to the handler wasn't an optimistic sign. The cop climbed the far bank, the other dog handler following with two more cops.

Nastos was going at full speed. He ran down to the riverbank, found the shallowest area to cross and bulldozed into the frigid water. Lindsay had become his daughter. He felt all of the same feelings of loss and fear that he would feel if it were her. All the time he had spent staring at Lindsay's picture, seeing a face that looked like family, speaking to her and asking her where she was. Part of him didn't want to go and face his worst fear — the same reason he didn't want the case in the first place. *If she's dead, Carscadden, I'll never forgive you for dragging me into this.*

Carscadden followed him across, stride for stride. The far bank was slipperier than the first cop had made it look. Nastos had to use his hands to scramble up. From behind a thick wall of evergreens, before the terrain climbed to a nearly vertical slope, Nastos saw the two white sneakers, filthy with ground-in dirt, the kind that looked days old. Dried blood was caked on her white hands, her hair matted was and dark. The dog handler nearly shoved Nastos right off of his feet when he darted out of the bushes, keying the mic to his radio. "Get the medics here, Command. She's alive, you copy that?"

Nastos and Carscadden followed the cop back in, taking positions on either side of Lindsay. One of the dogs had cuddled against her lap, the other was standing next to her protectively. They only moved when the first handler gave a whistle through his teeth and said a command sharply in German; then they backed off. Lindsay had been drugged, her eyes unable to focus, her head rolling from side to side, a pale hand sloppily trying to push the hair out of her way.

Nastos helped her, moving her hair back and looking into her small, dirty face.

"Lindsay, we're going to get you home."

"Daddy?"

Nastos said, "Yeah, baby. Everything is going to be all right."

248

33

FOUR COPS AND TWO PARA-
medics carried the girl across the water in a canvas stretcher. A
cop had backed the ambulance as close to the water as he could
get; another was in the back, trying to find the controls to jack up
the heat. The medics loaded her in. Nastos jumped in the side door
and watched as they loaded her onto the stretcher. It was taking
a while to get an IV in. She was so cold. As they cut her clothes
off, Dennehy supervised, standing at the back of the ambulance,
making sure there was as little disruption to future evidence as
possible. She was stark naked in front of the two medics and
Nastos for a brief moment before Dennehy grabbed a blanket from
the rack and draped it on her. One medic handed the cut clothes to
Dennehy, who was waiting with paper evidence bags. Carscadden
was hanging back, watching.

Nastos felt a wave of relief, then surprise when he saw that she
didn't have a word carved on her chest. *Sorrow, Joy.* Where's *Girl*?

Lindsay was coming to, her eyes focusing. The female medic
stood up abruptly and pushed her way out to the back door,
shoving past Dennehy. When she made eye contact with the police
supervisor, she waved him over.

"You're driving — I need Gareth in back with me."

The supervisor was older, overweight, with gold epaulets on
his shoulders. He didn't respond verbally, just ran over, heaving his

249

body from side to side. He shoved his way through a bunch of cops, the entire ambulance rocking as he poured himself in the driver's seat and shoved the seat back. He craned himself to peak through the front seats and shouted back, "Centenary on Ellesmere?"

The medic checked her temperature and showed her partner the results. She shouted back, "She's going to Sunnybrook."

Nastos shook his head. Sunnybrook was the top trauma centre in the country. He asked, "Is she that how bad she is?"

The medic shook her head. "I think she'll survive the trip. The problem is that when you're really cold, movement can cause dysrhythmia. We're going to drive slow and easy. If she's still alive when we get there, I think she has a chance. Sunnybrook is the best emerg hospital; let's give her the best shot."

Nastos wanted to touch Lindsay's hand, but hesitated, hovering over her.

The medic asked, "How long has she been out here?"

Nastos shook his head. "Too long."

The medic called up to the driver, "Slow and easy, boss."

Dennehy stepped back, gave Nastos a thumbs-up to stay with Lindsay, and slammed the doors shut.

Carscadden waited for the ambulance to start its run, then returned to the car, thinking about the Bannermans.

◻ ◻ ◻

AFTER THE EXPLOSION, CHAVEZ WRAPPED HIS SHIRT AS TIGHTLY around his amputated limb as he could, using his one hand and his teeth to pull it tight. There were only two arteries in the wrist, and he was able to control the bleeding with pressure for the time being. He jogged across the fields, staying well clear of the roadways. Through lines of trees, over slanted countryside, he saw the shape of a house ahead and approached with caution from the rear. He closed the distance, mindful of the back windows. There were lights on inside, but no signs of movement. A tarped, in-ground swimming pool took up most of the backyard along with a small shack in the fenced-in area. Through the breezeway between the garage and the house he could see a red Ford pickup truck parked in the driveway.

Chavez stayed in the treeline as long as he could, then slunk up to the back wall. careful not to get any blood on the house. His arm ached; the shirt was darkened by a seeping red stain. His movement was too much for clotting to occur. There was only so much time before he lost consciousness. He needed surgery but there was no way he was going to walk in the front doors of a hospital.

A sound in the kitchen window above his head startled him. He carefully backed away from the wall and peeked in. An elderly woman was doing dishes. He exhaled. *This is going to be easy.* He straightened his back, approaching with purpose under the breezeway to the side door. Chavez watched inside through the glass pane in the door for a period of time, listening. The old woman had turned many times in the kitchen, moving from the stove to the fridge and to the counter, and never noticed him. There was no sign of anyone else and she seemed half-blind.

When her back was turned, he drove his elbow through the window in the door and reached in to undo the lock. She recoiled at the noise and turned to face him. He saw the confusion in her face; then she began to back away. Chavez considered going through her fridge for food, deciding against it. He checked the hooks in the wall next to the door, tossing coats and purses down the stairs to the basement, until he found a set of Ford vehicle keys.

"Are these for the truck?"

She peeked around the corner, an eight-inch chef's blade held up to her chest by two gnarled, liver-spotted hands. "Take it! And get the hell out of here."

"That's the general idea." He turned for the door, then stopped. "I'll be back when you're sleeping. After I rape you, I'll burn your house down."

251

◻ ◻ ◻

CARSCADDEN FOLLOWED THE AMBULANCE NORTH ON MORNINGSIDE to the 401, where it went west to the Bayview exit. After it turned south, through the red light, it pulled away and he didn't see any point in trying to keep up. He called Bannerman; his wife answered the house phone.

"Hello?"

"It's me, Claire, Kevin Carscadden."

"Yes? What is it?"

She sounded nervous, and her speech was slurred. Hell, it was during the day and she was already half-pissed. They were both probably too drunk to drive, especially the way they were going to drive.

"You're making me a promise right now, Claire, understand?"

"Is this about Lindsay? Oh, god." She was already starting to cry.

"Claire, Claire, stay with me here. Call a limo service, Claire. I need you to promise that you aren't going to drive to —"

Carscadden could hear Craig's voice in the background. He must have come in when he heard her cry out. He shouted as if he was angry and wrestled the phone from her. "Who is this?" He sounded like he'd had a few as well.

Carscadden said, "Craig, we found her." Carscadden hardly noticed the thick, hot tears pouring down his face. Blinking so he could drive, with the phone on one hand, using his sleeves to wipe his nose, he put the phone on speaker and set it down.

"Oh, god."

"She's alive, Craig. We think she's going to be okay."

"Where is she?"

"Promise me you'll call a limo. You're in no shape to drive."

"I'm okay —"

"No bullshit, Craig. This is too important. If you get in an accident —"

"Okay, okay. I won't drive."

"She's in an ambulance going to Sunnybrook. You won't get in to see her for an hour anyway, so you may as well spend the time

252

at home waiting for the limo, packing her up some fresh clothes, a toothbrush, stuff like that."

"I don't know how to thank you."

"I've got some ideas — don't you worry about that now. You just get your wife down here safe and sound. There's a girl down here who could use her mom and dad."

◘　◘　◘

NASTOS AND DENNEHY FOLLOWED THE AMBULANCE CREW IN. INSIDE there was a waiting room like any hospital's, but ambulances were in and out frequently, with the city's nightly shooting and stabbing victims. Most of the victims would be next week's suspects and even the rookie doctors treated them that way. No sympathy, slow to give narcotics for pain — this type of training ground made it easy for them to become dispassionate and adept at treating people by the statistics and numbers provided by various machines and lab results rather than by their pleas and mumbles.

When it was a legitimate victim, someone like Lindsay, who could have been anyone's daughter in the room, the approach was clearly different. A parade of specialists, pediatricians, anesthesiologists — all the instructors who would generally hang back and let the rookies learn — were the ones pushing their way to the front, showing the new recruits the way the pros do it: fast, flawless, compassionate.

Dennehy and Nastos guarded the entry point in the trauma room, their backs against the glass, curtained-off wall. Dennehy was not going to give up continuity on the off-chance she said something to identify who had dropped her. Nastos already had that part figured out; he was already trying to get it all back on Anthony.

No one in the room was paying any attention to them; they were used to cops being around. Nastos said to Dennehy, "Anthony Raines. This is all his fault."

Dennehy shrugged. "Blake searched his house, found nothing.

You went in there, found nothing and got arrested. We can't go there again without a warrant and serious evidence or we'd get our asses sued off and lose any evidence anyways."

"Bring him in for an interview. Interrogate him."

Dennehy lamented, "Tomorrow. But I need to know everything you know. If I'm going to do this and try to trip him up, I need to be prepared, and with no evidence we're basically looking for him to make a mistake."

"Yeah, I know, but it's all we've got."

Dennehy gave Nastos a sideways glance. "You're not thinking of taking matters into your own hands, are you?"

"No. Once the Bannermans get here, I'm going home, to be with my wife and daughter." Nastos glanced down at his soaking pants. "And to change my clothes. I'm a friggin' mess."

After half an hour, the hospital had a room ready for her upstairs in the ICU. She'd be in there for at least a few days as a precaution, mostly because Nastos had explained the circumstances under which she had been held. They were going to do a sexual assault kit, then get her cleaned up.

After the doctors had gone, neither Nastos nor Dennehy let Lindsay leave their sight. They sat in the ICU family room, where they could watch through the safety glass. Carscadden arrived with the Bannermans. Claire had both hands locked on her husband, one on his hand, the other his upper arm. She only left him to touch the glass and stare longingly into the ICU. Bannerman dropped a tote bag and joined her at the glass. They seemed conflicted, torn between wanting to burst through the glass to be with her and fear that in her frail state the slightest touch could cause her to break into pieces.

Nastos noticed the lights in the ICU were dim to encourage a calm, quiet environment. Only a weak overhead light illuminated her. From the waiting room, with the light over her like a halo, her head turned at an angle, her eyes closed, her index finger pointing down with a pulse oximeter, the effect was of a fourteenth-century

254

gothic painting, the kind where the Virgin Mary would be pointing down as she ascended to heaven.

Craig said, "Well, I'm not waiting here all night." He opened the door into the unit and walked up to her. To Nastos, it looked as if he was expecting to see her dead — slow, measured paces, not wanting to wake her. A nurse saw him and moved to intercept: a big, very dark Jamaican lady with blue scrubs and a pink stethoscope around her neck. Craig hesitated only slightly when she approached, trying to sidestep her. She gripped his hand and led him to Lindsay's bed, putting her arm on his back so he could get in closer.

When Bannerman touched Lindsay's hand, her eyes opened. Despite the drugs, the sleeplessness, the month she'd been through, she smiled. Nastos watched her mouth form the word *Daddy* for the second time that night.

Nastos felt the tears welling up in his eyes. He couldn't hear was they were saying and decided he didn't want to know. It was private. Claire went through the door, trying to be quiet for the other people in the ward who didn't have the same prospects of recovery that Lindsay had.

Nastos turned to Carscadden. "I think we can go."

Carscadden agreed. "Yeah, let's get out of here. You need a ride, Dennehy?"

Dennehy was reading a message on his BlackBerry. "Nastos, one sec." He dialed a number on his phone, holding a finger up for Nastos to stay a minute. "Yes this is Detective Dennehy, I just got this weird message from Detective Byrne. Right — and that's right from the forensics guys? Oh sorry, yeah, you *are* Forensics, I misunderstood. So it wasn't there. Just a hand. And it could not be explained any other way. Hacksaw? Jesus Christ, can you believe that? Okay, well, I should let you get back to it. Right, thanks. Bye."

He stuffed the phone into his pocket. "What do you say, for shits and giggles, we go accost Anthony in the middle of his tv show, just to screw with his mind?"

"Sure. What's the occasion?" Nastos asked.

"The Durham forensic cops did a search of the fire scene. No body. Just a severed hand and a hacksaw."

Nastos heard the words Dennehy had said, but found them hard to believe. "He sawed his own hand off to get away?"

"This guy must be a board-certified psychopath." Dennehy paused for a moment. "So you said you cuffed him just to hold him, right? You didn't torture him or anything, did you?"

Nastos felt his blood run cold. "Torture him — are you kidding me?"

"Well, they found a few stray fingers. It kind of makes me wonder how you persuaded him to tell you where to find Lindsay."

While Nastos could see that Dennehy had figured it out, he seemed content to play stupid for the time being. "This guy is nuts. Who knows what he was doing in those last minutes."

Dennehy smiled at him. "I need a drink. You?"

"I need one — only I need to get Anthony more."

Dennehy shook his head. "We talked about that —"

"Okay, we don't arrest him. But like you said, we can stop by his show and ask him a few questions just to screw with his mind. You'll know by one look on his face if he's our guy or not. I just want to go home to change first."

34

THE DRIVE TO TORONTO FOR Chavez was uneventful. One fire truck passed him, on its way to the house, but no police cars. He exited at Highway 48, going down to the 401, then the Don Valley Parkway to the Bayview exit. Traffic was light near Anthony's street, Castle Frank, where he went south to Gerrard. Bruce's animal clinic was closed, but he lived above it. Chavez had the phone number.

He dumped the pickup truck in a tow-away zone and rushed into the clinic. He pressed the buzzer and waited. A chill went up his amputated stump to his elbow. For the first time, he had the luxury to consider the chance of infection and of losing the rest of the arm. He hit the buzzer again, three quick presses, and finally saw the light come on. Bruce's eyes appeared in the glass, then the door swung open.

Chavez held out his bloody stump. "Got any Band-Aids?"

257

◻ ◻ ◻

SAINT ANTHONY, THE PATRON SAINT OF MISSING THINGS, SEIZED THE stage with a quick stride, his arms in the air, waving to the sold-out audience. The Conservatory Room was not large by the day's standards. The marble floor was Italian. Steam pipes had been built in to keep the flower beds warm in the winter. It was a beautiful place for an intimate audience of one hundred people. Most of the revenue would be coming from broadcast rights, both television and radio.

The cameras were HD steady-cams, so they could be close to audience members, any one of whom could expect a reading this evening. They had all paid to come, so he had no need to convert anyone. They would all be receptive to what he had to offer. His reputation spoke for itself.

After the applause waned, he began. "Thank you all for joining me tonight. We're going to have a busy program. Now, just to get things started, I want to do a few readings, get in touch with our family members on the other side. It helps me get in the zone." Anthony sipped water from a bottle on a stool near the edge of the stage. He was relaxed, warm under the lights, and surrounded by agreeable faces, excited by the possibility to reach loved ones from the other side.

"If what I'm saying sounds like you, just stand up for me, please — that way I can feel my way though the audience so I find the right person here. Now, I feel a contact with a spirit named Emily. She died in her seventies, here in Toronto." During a group reading, you couldn't play on words like in individual readings, with rainbow ruses or Barnum statements. It was far easier to use the same manipulation techniques that had made insurance companies billions of dollars: statistics.

He could have used Hazel, Ivy or Edith — with a crowd this big, any of these once-popular names would strike paydirt. One woman in the audience stood up, her face flushed red, an expression of surprise on her face as two different cameras pivoted to capture her.

Middle-aged, with a large shoulder bag still in her arms, she set down her diet ginger ale and pushed her glasses up her nose.

"Well, that was easy." Anthony smiled. He stayed on the stage, moving as close to her as he could to engage her directly. The crewman was there in no time, a microphone at the ready.

"Emily," he said. "An aunt? Mother?"

"My — my aunt," the woman said, startled by the sound of her amplified voice.

Anthony did a visual inventory, not just of her, but the woman on her left — a daughter, probably. He tapped the earpiece on the left side, a sign to drop the monitor volume.

"She's on the other side, but she's here with us now, in this place. She says that she's with someone, another relative, with a J in the name." At first the woman seemed perplexed, but Anthony was confident. Everyone from an English-speaking country had a relative with the initial J.

The reading went on. He provided her catharsis when she learned that the aunt was proud of her, proud that she had raised the children on her own — all generalities, no specifics. He used all of the classic techniques. It was good to feel alive again, to have his mojo back.

An image of the Oracle cards ran through his mind. As if they were calling to him. It was perplexing, and stopped him momentarily. He looked up when he felt the weight of the audience's gaze on him.

"I'm sorry, I just drifted off there a moment." Awkward laughter from the audience made him smile, though he was still thoughtful. The cards had never called him before.

"Listen, I think it's time I talk about my experience. In the advertisement material for this event, there was mention of a dream or vision that I had. That one night while I was sleeping, I was born into the next world.

"I was walking backward, upstream in a gentle river. The warm water bathed my feet as I made my way over the smooth rocks and cool sand. I realized that I was looking back at my history — I could see everything that I had done during my life here, just not what was waiting for me. At that time I began to understand that it was a metaphor for how we live our lives here, stumbling the wrong way into our future.

"I spent a lifetime in that world, speaking to the inhabitants. You see, on the land it was like being in a beautiful park: fruit trees, vegetables, fresh water, and cozy campfires. However, when it came to the river, we couldn't see upstream and had to walk backward.

"Well, after being there, I learned to see upstream. I could see what was coming toward us. And then I awoke here and realized that I could do the same thing in this world. I learned to turn my spirit to see the future as we can see our past now. And I have an important message for the world —" Anthony stopped in place, frozen. A feeling came over him, a mix of fear and excitement. It was as if he were on a ledge, ready to jump into a lake of fire. The moment of making magic was the turn. All of the help that Chavez had given had been to get him to this moment; the delivery had to be perfect.

He looked up at the cameras with a credible expression of fright on his face. Pale from a lack of sun and sweaty from the heat of the lights, he let his breathing grow sharp, his heart race. "I'm sorry, just give me a minute." He held a hand up to stop a non-existent stage hand from rushing to his aid. "I just had a vision of a case I'm working on. It was nothing I wanted made public; you see, I was hired to consult with a family to find their missing daughter.

"I was just overcome with a feeling of where she is. I'm sorry, this has nothing to do with the show — I know we're live, but I just have to say it as it comes or I might not remember everything. She's alive. She's in a park, across the river from the trail. It's in the east end. I have a vision of — what's the word? Military? Is it a Military Trail? No, it's a park name. Damn, does anyone here have a map? Anyone?"

A woman held up a smartphone and said, "I have GPS."

He rushed over to her, leaving the stage to enter the audience but watching to make sure the cameras followed him. "Bring up Toronto." As if flipping pages on her iPhone, he moved farther and farther east. He zoomed in. "Military Trail! It's the name of a road." He zoomed in, then stopped abruptly. He handed the phone back to the woman, staring at her, his mouth hanging open in shock. Anthony waved a stage hand over to him, a thin young man with dark hair and square glasses. He covered his microphone and said something to the young man.

The young man ran off stage and Anthony finally exhaled. He slumped forward, his hands on his knees and sucked air.

He tapped his microphone to make sure it was on and slowly straightened up. "My god, I think we found her."

Anthony noticed a disturbance off stage: people moving down the far aisle and loud voices. There were uniformed cops there. Not the hired guys for security; these were street cops. And they had two detectives with them. Anthony felt his blood run cold. Only one was a detective, he realized. The other was Nastos.

"Listen, everyone, we have a long night ahead. I am going to take a small break from the stage while a ten-minute video plays."

There was applause while Anthony left. The stage went dark, leaving the audience to turn their attention to the motion of the black curtains and the large screen dropping into position.

Anthony strutted over to the officers, putting on a façade of self-confidence and delight in their attention. "Mr. Nastos, so happy to see you."

"Save the act for someone who might believe it, Anthony." Anthony recoiled a little at the rudeness, which is what Nastos wanted him to do. It was the start of trying to make him angry and off balance; Anthony instinctively felt that it was best to play along.

"Anthony Raines, I'm homicide detective Brian Dennehy. I have some bad news."

"Oh my god, is it Lindsay? I had a feeling she was going to be okay! I was just going to call the police with some information —"

Nastos cut him off. "More like you were going to announce to your audience that you were going to give the police information."

Anthony ignored Nastos. "Is she okay, Detective?"

Dennehy tried to feign concern. "Oh, she's okay, we found her. I'm worried about you."

"About me?"

Nastos played along with Dennehy. "Oh, yeah, Anthony, if I were you, I'd be changing my underwear."

"What is it?"

"Well, we found the place where she was being held, but the guy who had her got away, for the time being."

Anthony began to go pale under his stage makeup. He looked for something to lean against, finding nothing. "What?"

Dennehy explained, "The guy who held her sawed his own

hand off to get away from a pair of handcuffs. Some guy named Chavez. You know him?"

This was going to be the critical question for Anthony. It was a yes or no, and either answer was damning. "I know a few guys named Chavez. One's an accountant, one's a carpenter."

Dennehy exchanged a look with Nastos, as if he'd seen all he needed to see. He added one more comment. "Well, if this guy is crazy enough to cut his own hand off and escape, I'd hate to be on his bad side. And you have to wonder, if he was that determined, that crazy, to saw through his own hand with a rusty saw, and if he felt that someone had screwed him over . . . Well, he might want to cut something off of that someone?"

Anthony's phony smile barely yielded. "Listen. I'm so happy that Lindsay has been found okay. As for this Chavez character, I can't believe I have much to worry about there."

Nastos said, "Glad to hear it, Anthony. I guess you won't need police protection then. So hey, good night, I hope we didn't wreck your show."

Anthony ignored him. "Good night, Detective Dennehy."

Nastos smiled. "One more thing, Anthony." Dennehy stopped his turn and waited for Nastos to continue. "Now, my feeling is that the last time you helped the police and found the body, you just got lucky. Soon enough, money started rolling in, you booked a lot of readings, but over the years the money dried up. This time you decided to make your own luck. You got Chavez to grab the girls, and rather than finding a dead one and making a modest living from it, you were going to find a *live* one. You were going to *save* her and spend the rest of your life cashing cheques and going on TV shows. Too bad you picked the wrong psycho to do the grunt work."

Anthony perked up, interested in what Nastos had to say to finish.

"Because he's got a taste for killing, Anthony, and I think he's saving the best for last. Good night — have a good show."

Saturday, October 27

NASTOS SAT IN HIS AND CARSCADDEN'S OFFICE. LINDSAY AND TARA being home safe, and every cop in North America being on a Be On the Look Out, or BOLO, broadcast for Chavez made him think that the stress of the last week was worth it. He was at his desk, flipping through the crime scene pictures of Tabitha Moreau and talking on the phone to his old friend from the force, Jacques.

"Well, Jacques, I'm glad you were able to find Darius in Toronto. I'm surprised he didn't take off years ago."

"Yeah, I got lucky. Just like I got lucky that you noticed something suspicious in the pictures."

Nastos asked, "So what about this Chavez guy? What's the latest with him?"

"They found a stolen pickup truck in Cabbagetown, but nothing further. It's been a few days, so he could be anywhere."

Nastos put the murder photos aside and flipped through the file, looking for something. He found the Ministry of Transportation return on the licence plate *DR BRUCE*. It was for Townler Veterinary Services. The address was in Cabbagetown.

His front doorbell chimed to alert him that someone had opened it. Nastos heard footsteps in the front lobby. "Hey, I should go. Swing by for lunch when you have a chance."

"Sure thing, Nastos. Bye."

"See ya." He pondered the address. If Anthony hung out with this vet, then maybe Chavez did too. *And if I was running around with my hand hacked off and I didn't want to go to a hospital, a vet would do just as well. Hell, Chavez is one rabid animal anyway.*

Carscadden came into the office, tossing his coat on a chair behind the door.

Nastos asked, "How's Hopkins?"

"Fine. She's taking Taylor to his appointment with Dr. Mills. She won't be back in today."

"Sounds like a good idea."

Nastos was going to bring up the possible lead on Chavez, but paused to watch Carscadden, who was acting unusual. He almost ran to his desk and started flipping through the pages of brochures he had brought.

Nastos asked, "Going somewhere?"

"I'm taking Hopkins on a trip. We're getting the hell out of here."

"I don't recommend South America."

"Yeah, no kidding. I was thinking Paris."

"She'll love that."

The front door chimed. Nastos, out of habit, expected to hear Hopkins' voice but then remembered that she wasn't in. He called out, "Hello?"

Craig Bannerman opened the door to their room and came in with a broad smile on his face. Nastos stood to extend his hand; Bannerman shoved it aside and gave him a hug. "I owe you guys so much."

Nastos said, "Nothing that two minutes in a bank vault couldn't clear up."

Bannerman reached a hand across to Carscadden before he sat down and threw a file on the desk. He had a smug smile on his face, giving them an I-know-something-you-don't-know smile.

Carscadden opened the file and flipped through the pages.

Nastos nudged his arm. "You normally move your lips and mumble when you read. Speak up a little."

Bannerman slid his chair forward. "Steve, I'm a top executive in a sixty-billion-dollar bank. Every politician in the city has lined up to suck my ass a little. Now, in regards your civil matter with the police service — it turns out that one of my associates knows some people on the Police Services Board."

"Bunch of communist assholes."

"You might change your attitude on them a little. A story was told to them about a cop who had been through hell with his little girl, and been wrongly terminated as a result. I told them about the man who believed a lost, grieving father when no one else would and how he brought my girl back to me. When they saw the reasonable civil remedy your lawyer Mr. Carscadden was seeking in the courts, and heard about how the police service — the ultra-right-wing, totalitarian group of thugs that they are — were sticking it to you, they were very concerned."

Nastos tried to peek at the file, but Carscadden closed it up, agreeing. "Very concerned."

Nastos asked, "Did they finally make an offer?"

Carscadden shook his head. "No."

Nastos exhaled, disappointed. Still, he found it unusual that both Carscadden and Bannerman were smiling.

Eventually Carscadden opened the file to the last page and slid it over for Nastos to read. He read it three times, turning back a few pages, then to the last page again.

Carscadden said, "Full back pay since you were fired, including pension adjustment. An amount — a little low if you ask me — for legal fees. And they are going to pay your salary until you qualify for pension. Everything we asked for."

Nastos asked, "What about the arrest records?"

Carscadden went back a few pages and pointed. "Expunged. Hell, you could probably go back and work as a cop again."

Nastos shook his head. "And give up working for you?"

Bannerman rose slowly. "I'd like to stay and have a drink with you guys — maybe we can reschedule for next weekend?"

"Sure."

"Lindsay says she wants to meet you both and thank you personally."

Carscadden stood up to show Bannerman out. "No problem. Anytime."

Bannerman was quick to leave. There was a bounce in his step that Nastos had never noticed before.

Eager to share the good news, Nastos picked up the phone and dialed Madeleine's number. There was no answer. *She must be showing a house.* He sent a quick text message: *Good news. Call right away.* After he put the phone down, he slid the MTO return for *DR BRUCE* over to Carscadden to read.

Carscadden read it. "Yeah, so?"

Nastos exhaled. "I was just on the phone to Jacques."

"You mean Polkaroo? Your invisible friend that I've never seen?"

"Yeah." Nastos had to laugh. "Polkaroo says that a burned-out pickup truck from the area of the shack was found in Cabbagetown. This asshole here lives in Cabbagetown. If I was Chavez —"

"Yeah, I'd go there too."

35

CARSCADDEN DROVE EAST ON Queen Street, then north on Parliament. In the passenger seat, Nastos hung up his cell phone and put it away. "Can you imagine if this asshole was staying right around the corner from us?"

Carscadden agreed. "Good thing he's feeling a little under the weather. He could have burst through the front door, guns a-blazing, and it would have been over."

Nastos was studying the building numbers and business names as they drove slowly up the street. When they arrived at Wellesley and Parliament, Nastos spotted a white, rectangular sign with simple blue lettering. *Veterinary Clinic.*

"There it is. Just keep driving."

Carscadden examined the business as he drove past. "How long for Dennehy?"

"He's on the way now."

Nastos could see the conflict in Carscadden. Part of him wanted the SWAT team here, part of him wanted to handle this himself. Nastos added, "And we're waiting for him. Don't get any funny ideas."

267

□ □ □

CABBAGETOWN WAS A WEIRD MIX OF RUN-DOWN AND UPSCALE. FOR two hours, they watched the entrance to the clinic from the north, parked in a tow-away zone on Parliament Street. Dennehy and Byrne were south, barely visible through the street traffic and steady waves of pedestrians. Panhandlers, the ones too lazy to be squeegee kids, sat in alcoves or on steps. Nastos saw one guy, maybe a hundred years old, wrinkled and frail at ninety pounds, holding a creased cardboard sign that read Will Work for Sex. Carscadden pointed out four different hand-to-hand drug deals with all of the enthusiasm of a nine-year-old spying tree monkeys at African Lion Safari.

It was still morning; however, the alcoholics from the nearby shelters and halfway houses — turfed out at daybreak — were roaming the streets, going through garbage bins and dumpsters looking for thrown-away food or bottles from last night's drunks.

Nastos' phone rang. He put it on speaker so Carscadden could listen.

"Yeah?"

It was Dennehy. "Yeah, Nastos. I put a call in for a surveillance team, but they aren't going to be ready to go for two more hours."

"Hey, that's not so bad."

"No. The thing is, I have court this afternoon. So I can't stick around."

"Maybe we should stir the pot. Why don't you go in there and ask some stupid questions about your dog? Try to spook him?"

"Not going to happen."

Nastos looked at Carscadden. "We'll need Viktor again. We can't do this by ourselves." Carscadden started dialing his phone. "I know he's busy. Maybe he can send over one of his tough guys."

Dennehy butted in. "I don't think you get it, Nastos — you're not sanctioned for this. Byrne and me are going; you have to go too."

Nastos read the look on Carscadden's face. It said *not a chance.* He said, "Yeah, no problem, Dennehy, whatever you say."

Dennehy wasn't falling for it. "So take a hike, Nastos. The pros will be here by one o'clock."

"Sure thing, one sec. I just have to put my seatbelt on. You guys go first."

"No, Nastos, you guys go first, you fucking asshole!"

Carscadden cut in. "Guys guys guys! Wait, I see him. I see him. Dennehy, your five o'clock position, coming up behind you on the sidewalk."

Nastos peered ahead, squinting. A large, muscular man was walking on the sidewalk, one arm in a black sling, carrying a brown grocery bag with the other. He had a satchel over his shoulder. Most people would be bogged down by the awkward weight, but to Chavez it was nothing.

Nastos saw that Dennehy and Byrne turned and looked back slowly. Maybe because they moved in unison, the motion caught Chavez's eye. He stopped in his tracks and stared.

Nastos shouted, "Carscadden, go!"

In one fluid movement, Carscadden started the car, hit the gas and veered out into traffic. Chavez initially backed away from Dennehy's car, but when the cops started to open their doors, he charged Byrne on the passenger side before Byrne could get his gun out and draw down on him. Nastos lost his view of what was happening. When Carscadden stopped at the red light, Nastos bolted from the car and ran over to the east side of the road.

From there he saw the groceries strewn across the street and Chavez punching Byrne down to the ground. His target unarmed, with only one hand, Dennehy was unjustified to shoot despite having a perfect sight over the roof of the detective car. Chavez forced his way into the passenger side of the car and began climbing into the driver's seat.

Dennehy pulled the door open and grabbed hold of Chavez around the neck. Nastos ran across the street, bulldozing through a throng of pedestrians mesmerized by the disturbance. Nastos heard a grinding from the engine as Chavez turned the key while the car was already running; repeated punches from Dennehy were having no effect on him. Dennehy was in awful physical shape, and watching him moving so frantically and being of such little use made Nastos feel that it was all on him to stop Chavez before he escaped.

Nastos was within ten paces when Chavez was able to push Dennehy free, throw the car in drive and hit the gas. Chavez lurched out into traffic, nearly running down a cyclist and speeding westbound on Wellesley Street.

Nastos shouted, "Dennehy!" to break him from his slack-jawed trance. Dennehy glanced back toward traffic, narrowly stepping out of the way of a city bus.

Nastos rushed over to Byrne and helped him up. Byrne shouted, "Go get him!"

Carscadden screeched up to Dennehy in his Ford Escape, facing the wrong way in a parking lane. He called, "Get in!"

Byrne said, "You guys go — I'll stay with the vet."

Dennehy and Nastos dove into the car. The tires squealed as he reversed, then sped west on Wellesley, cutting off traffic in all directions.

Dennehy was on his phone, calling in the stolen car — a black Pontiac Vibe with a yellow Support the Troops ribbon on the back — then, to drive the urgency home, told dispatch that it was driven by a person wanted for two murders. Nastos could barely see the car ahead with traffic so tight. When the line of cars came to a stop, Carscadden wheeled into the oncoming lane, paused at the intersection, then forced his way through. They were beginning to catch up when they arrived at Yonge Street, where they came to a dead stop.

Dennehy was in the back passenger seat with the window down and his head out, trying to catch a glimpse of his car. "He's on foot, he's on foot!" Dennehy jumped from the car despite the fact that it was still moving forward. He tried his best to maintain speed. Nastos sprang out, following. Chavez had ditched the car in the middle of the lane to stop traffic. He was going full speed into the subway access. Nastos shouted back to Carscadden, "Subway!"

Carscadden drove up on the sidewalk, getting his car clear of the road, to the horror of pedestrians, and leapt out running as well. He'd never catch up in the car with the road blocked. Nastos assumed the lead and soon enough Carscadden caught up with him. Together, the pair stormed down the concrete steps underground at top speed, slowed only by glancing collisions with pedestrians who were too slow to get to the side. Behind him Nastos heard Dennehy shouting, "Police! Watch out, coming through."

Dennehy shouted into his phone. "You need to put a call in to your management to stop all of the Yonge trains. Do it now!"

A panhandler sucked back into the wall, sliding his guitar case back with his foot. A group of teens saw them coming and pulled an elderly Asian woman out of the way.

Nastos felt his legs slow, as if he was plodding through curing cement. He pushed forward on the main level around the crowd and through the turnstile. At the subway platform, he skidded to a stop and jerked his head from side to side, scanning both directions for any telltale movement to indicate which way Chavez had gone.

Carscadden was the first to catch up to Nastos, then Dennehy. "You've got the gun, Dennehy — take left, we'll take right together. If he pops up between us, don't do anything stupid like shoot until we're clear."

"I'll try to remember that." Dennehy drew his gun out and went left down the platform. Nastos and Carscadden began searching through the crowd.

Carscadden approached a woman holding a baby who looked to be about six months old in a front pouch. "Ma'am, we have a police emergency here. You should get your little girl out of here."

She looked at Carscadden, then Nastos. "Are you serious?"

"Lady, did you notice a frantic-looking Mexican guy?"

"No."

"Good, but get the hell out of here anyway. He's wanted for murder and he's not going down without a fight."

She took the hint and started making her way out. Others stayed, including a bunch of teenaged boys who seemed more interested in getting a good view of the show.

In a moment, for Nastos, the entire concourse, the city and the planet suddenly diminished to a cone-shaped space from his eyes to Chavez, who had appeared about forty feet away. He had stopped at the end of the platform, with nowhere to go but on the tracks. Chavez stood tall, his face in a snarl, narrow dark eyes like a predator's. He was wearing all black, his pants and shirt, a black sling. His injured arm rested on a tan bag that was still slung over his opposite shoulder.

The people on the concourse seemed to understand that there was something going on between them. They backed off, a father tugging his toddler back, a teen tightening his grip on his girlfriend's hand. Carscadden appeared from behind Nastos, taking a position on his left.

Chavez smiled, like he was seeing old friends. Nastos knew what he was about to say was a waste of time, but he said it anyway. "The cops are coming, Chavez. It's over."

Chavez glanced down the train tunnel, apparently deciding that it wasn't worth the risk. He turned and began walking toward Nastos who bladed his body stance and prepared for a fight. Chavez dropped his bag to the ground, peeled off his coat, and threw it down on the tracks. He knelt down to the bag and pulled out an expandable baton, the kind cops carry, flicked it out to full length with a twist of his wrist and stood ready.

Nastos made quick judgments on the type of attack the wounded Chavez would be likely to launch but there was little time to make a counter plan.

"Nastos." Chavez lunged, swinging at him. Nastos jumped back to avoid the metal baton. Carscadden rammed his shoulder into Chavez's chest as if he was trying to push him down to the tracks but Chavez, although shorter, outweighed him and didn't budge. Instead he rammed the butt end of the baton down on Carscadden's back, driving him to the ground. Nastos leapt forward with a haymaker punch, landing it on Chavez's jaw. Chavez slowed and Nastos hit him again, as hard as he could. It must have become at least somewhat annoying, because Chavez dismissed Carscadden with a final kick to the back, then turned on Nastos.

He swung full force with the baton, striking Nastos on his side, in the ribs. Nastos collapsed forward with a feeling that his body had been snapped in half. He saw Chavez's arm raise to load for another swing, but it didn't come There was screaming from somewhere above him.

Dennehy charged with his gun out. "Down, get down, you piece of shit, you're under arrest!" Dennehy fired while running, but missed — it wasn't that close.

Most of the crowd hit the ground immediately; the teenaged kids were the first to run, obscuring another chance for Dennehy to get some shots away. A woman's two toddlers wandered away from her when she hit the deck. A big burly biker-looking guy scooped them up in his arms and carried them to the brick wall, shielding them with his body. Slowly, he scraped against the wall toward the exit. The mom followed him in a crouch, tentatively reaching for her children.

Carscadden made another attempt to push Chavez onto the tracks; again Chavez weaved and drove the baton into his back — this time, though, Chavez lost his grip on the weapon as Carscadden went down, and it clinked as it hit the subway tile. Nastos tried to reach for it, but his entire body locked up in pain when he extended his hand. He found himself bracing his arm over his ribs. It felt like he had to hold his guts in and when he breathed the pain was excruciating.

Carscadden was writhing on the floor. He rolled onto his back, unable to get up. Nastos saw that the baton had rolled to his feet and he picked it up.

He swung. Then he swung again. He aimed for Chavez's forearm in the sling, trying to smash through it, visualizing the arm splintering like a dry stick. When Chavez tried to protect himself with the other arm, Nastos swung at that one. With every movement of his upper body, Nastos felt like he was going to break apart, but he swung again, this time at Chavez's head.

The big man dropped to the ground, his face smashing into the cement platform, blood gushing from his mouth. Nastos knelt next to Carscadden.

"You'll be okay." Nastos meant it to be reassuring, but the way the words came out, it sounded more like a question.

273

Carscadden winced, but seemed comforted by having his back flat on the ground. He reached a hand up. "Help me up, would ya?"

Nastos tried to hold an arm out to help Carscadden, but it hurt his ribs too much. He found himself tucking his left arm in tight. Carscadden climbed his way up. "Cops must have found a coffee shop on the way over."

Dennehy stormed over, red-faced, sucking air. The spectators were gone. Flanked by two uniformed officers, he kept his gun pointed at Chavez, who was slowly getting to his feet. "You're under arrest for murder, Chavez."

Nastos tapped the baton on Dennehy's arm. When Dennehy saw that Nastos was offering it to him, he took it. Dennehy asked, "You going to be okay, Steve?"

Nastos nodded slowly. "Yeah, Brian. Thanks."

Dennehy turned to one of the cops. "Go get him, guys."

The cops started to advance, but Nastos stopped them. "Wait, wait! He only has one hand — you can't cuff him. If we have to fight him, he could pull us onto the tracks."

Dennehy said, "I called to have the trains stopped."

Nastos countered, "Okay, you be the first to jump down and touch the third rail and tell me it's not full of hydro. Let's wait for a road sergeant with a Taser. He can't go anywhere; he's trapped. Let's wait this out."

Howling screeches came from the darkened subway tunnel, discordant and terrifying. It confirmed Nastos' fear that the lines were still active. Chavez stood staring into the black tunnel, his arms — one shorter than the other and dripping blood — hanging by his sides. He was in rapture, his mouth hanging open, slowly reaching forward to the light on the front of the train. For the first time, Nastos noticed the scrapes, more like gouges, on his face. Fresh claw marks. A transient thought ran through his mind that the claw marks weren't from them or from Byrne during the failed takedown at street level. They must have been from before.

Chavez turned back to Nastos and shouted over the noise of the train. "She's dead. I killed her."

Nastos shouted back, "You didn't kill Lindsay; we found her. She's alive."

"Not Lindsay. You'll see, Nastos."

His words disappeared into the howls of the tracks. Nastos moved a pace after him, but Chavez was too fast. Nastos charged, reaching his hands out. "No, Chavez, *no.*"

In slow motion, he saw Chavez crouch to load his legs, like a sprinter in the starting blocks. His arms and legs exploded in motion, driving, pushing for flight. He leapt out into the path of the train, his back arched, arms thrust out in front, as if trying to fly; his black shirt, black pants, the black wrap over the amputated hand unfurling in the wind, flapping like a wing.

Later Nastos would swear that he felt Chavez's shoes brush against his fingertips. He was that close — only a stride away from pulling him back. Nastos felt a strong yank on the collar of his coat. His feet slid on the smooth surface and he fell back onto his ass as the train blurred past, coming to a stop at the end of the tunnel, too late for Chavez Vega Alvarez.

◊ ◊ ◊

IT WAS TWENTY MINUTES BEFORE THE TRAIN PULLED BACK, revealing the mess beneath it. Limbs and head severed, skin wrapped around grease-stained raw meat.

Nastos sat on a bench, Carscadden at his side. Carscadden asked, "What the hell was he talking about?"

"I have no idea. The freak was delusional."

Carscadden gulped water that a street cop had brought over from a vending machine. "He was so loaded up on drugs, it's the only reason he survived the explosion."

Nastos checked his cell phone; there were no messages. He thought of calling Madeleine, but decided to wait until he could get a better signal at ground level. Dennehy came over and joined them. "Thank Christ this mess isn't going to a trial. Holy shit."

Nastos nodded his agreement, then winced as he tried to

straighten up. "My buddy Jacques needs a transfer from the Sexual Assault Unit. I want you to bring him into Homicide."

Dennehy snorted. "That's mighty gracious of me."

"Hey, it's the least —"

"Easy, easy, Nastos. Jacques is a good guy. I'll bring him up. I owe you that."

Dennehy squeezed the button on his police radio to silence its incessant beeping. He stepped away to have a conversation.

Nastos noticed the papers — no, wait, they were cards — that littered the station. He picked a few up. It was like a tarot card, but not like one he had ever seen before. The images were horrific. Monsters with multiple mouths eating themselves, blood and entrails everywhere.

He was interrupted by Dennehy. "We checked the history on this guy. He was a glorified serial killer in the Colombian army. Beaten as a child. They say he shot his whole family the day he joined up."

Carscadden said, "Nice. To them a hero; to us a monster."

Dennehy observed, "He was just a man, a victim. If he was thirty years younger he might be the one we were saving. Instead, his abuse was rewarded with neglect; he resented the world and eventually we killed him for it."

Nastos replied, "Not every abused child becomes a psycho, and this guy was as psycho as it gets. I wish we had killed him when we had the chance." He stole a last look at what was left of Chavez and dropped the cards to the ground below. "What a mess this turned into. Sure, we saved them from death, but Lindsay will be haunted for the rest of her life — same with Hopkins."

Carscadden was bracing his lower back and trying to stretch. "If they had hired us right away, I don't know if we would have found them any sooner."

Nastos agreed. "We got lucky, I think. Anthony was trying so hard to get a consulting fee from the Bannermans that he drew our attention."

Dennehy chimed in. "When we interrogated Anthony, he held up fine — polygraph, everything we threw at him." He picked up one of the Oracle cards and grimaced at the awful image. "He said that Chavez stole these cards from him, and a few other valuables. If these are the Oracles, they're worth two hundred grand."

Dennehy pulled out his phone and said "Hello?" He held a finger up for Nastos and began to listen intently to the speaker, the whole while maintaining eye contact with Nastos. He eyes suddenly dropped, then he began fidgeting with his fingers.

Nastos asked, "This whole thing starting to get to you, Dennehy? You don't look so good."

Dennehy gulped like his throat had gone dry. He rubbed his hands on his coat.

Dennehy put his phone away. "That was Comm on the line; they asked me to clear for an attempted murder."

Nastos commiserated. "Don't they have any idea what the hell just happened here? There's this thing called paperwork."

"I'm going to go, Nastos, and I need you to come with me. I'm going to drive. You and Carscadden both need to come along."

"Why us?"

"Nastos," Dennehy said gently, "it's your wife."

◻ ◻ ◻

CARSCADDEN RUSHED TO KEEP UP TO NASTOS AS HE BULLDOZED HIS way into the emergency entrance at Sunnybrook Hospital with Dennehy trailing behind. When Nastos was held up by the locked doors into the exam area, Dennehy showed his badge to the triage nurse, who buzzed them in.

Two uniformed cops stood outside an exam room, one writing in his notebook, the other chatting up the two female medics who were repacking their kit on a hallway stretcher. To them it was a routine call, something that Nastos himself had done a hundred times — but to Nastos, this time it was personal.

Carscadden glanced back to the waiting room and noted that two distressed-looking women recognized Nastos. They were well dressed, with jewellery and blazers — they looked like real estate workers, Madeleine's colleagues probably. They covered their faces with their hands and began crying louder than they had been before. A sick, empty feeling washed over him; he could only imagine how Nastos felt.

The cops straightened up when they saw Nastos, a civilian, trying to get into the room, but Dennehy waved them off. "Dennehy, with Homicide, it's okay."

They moved back and Nastos slunk in.

Carscadden said, "You should stay back here." It was the first time he could recall seeing Nastos be tentative about anything.

Nastos had paused when he saw the state she was in. Madeleine lay unconscious on the gurney, tubes in her arms and up her nose, an oxygen mask over her face. There were four people attending to her. Carscadden couldn't tell which were the doctors and which the nurses; they were all busy. A woman rushed in between them and put X-rays up on a backlit wall. A short, red-haired woman studied the image closely and was able to discern something that didn't seem like good news.

Dennehy squeezed Nastos' shoulder as if to take him away, but Nastos pulled away and reached out to Madeleine. One of the medical staff, a guy who appeared to be no more than eighteen years old, seemed disappointed. "Who let family in?"

Nastos closed his hand around hers. "Madeleine?"

Her head rolled over to him. The red-haired woman, who seemed to be in charge, reached out and shoved Nastos up closer to the head of the bed. "Stay there and don't get in the way."

The young male — Carscadden began to think he was a nurse — stared at the redhead. He was obviously pissed off about Nastos being there. Carscadden couldn't believe it when he saw the woman slowly move her head from left to right to say *no*. His heart dropped. *No? What the hell do you mean, "no"?*

Redhead said, "Call up to surgery and tell them we'll be there in five." She glanced at Madeleine, who was beginning to stir, "And page Anesthesia stat — we can't do any more down here." Her eyes went to Nastos, but he hadn't heard her. He was staring into his wife's eyes, which had partially opened.

One of the cops came in and spoke to Carscadden. "She landed on her side. It must have been forty feet from the rooftop."

Carscadden nodded and the cop backed off. When Madeleine slowly writhed under the sheets, her head turned farther and he could see severe, black bruising on the right side of her face. It was like she had been hit with a piece of concrete — or Chavez's fist.

Nastos was holding her closer, not saying anything, just staring into her eyes. Carscadden noted the dressing on her chest was weeping through. He knew it would be a carving in her chest: the word *Girl*. She was the last of Chavez's victims. Whatever screwed-up reason he had for targeting these women was a mystery he'd never know the answer to.

Madeleine's heart monitor showed a faster rate as she tried to sit up in the bed. Both Nastos and one of the nurses put hands on her to keep her down. She tried to reach across to Nastos with her far hand, but it was held back by the tubes and a quickly reacting doctor's hand. They seemed surprised when she spoke.

"Where's . . . how's Josie?"

Nastos leaned closer and whispered, "She's safe. The guy who attacked you is dead." He seemed like he was going to remain strong, but then he said, "This is all my fault." He cracked, tears pouring down his face.

Carscadden felt like an intruder, but could not leave.

Madeleine murmured, "I'm sorry, Steve. I should have been there for you, and I wasn't."

"Don't talk, baby, just try to rest and let them help you."

"You made me so happy, so proud of you, then you gave me our little girl. Our perfect little girl."

She tried to reach for his hand again and failed. Nastos grabbed hers and squeezed. "I love you, Maddy, you've made me so happy." He brushed her hair back from her face and drew closer to her, his head lying next to hers on the stretcher.

He said again, "Just rest, let them do their thing."

"You made me so happy, Steve. I didn't know I could be so happy. You're the most honourable person I have ever known . . ."

He kissed her before her eyes closed. When the alarm sounded from the monitor, Carscadden glanced at it and saw the display had changed from what looked like inverted check marks to violent, jagged spikes. Her mouth, arms, legs, everything went slack. One of the nurses pulled Nastos aside, saying firmly, "We need to help her, sir. Why don't you wait in the family support room." Her calm demeanour was an indication of how bad it was. The patient whom the medical staff were the most concerned about now wasn't Madeleine; it was the surviving family: Nastos.

Nastos was confused. "Wait a minute. She made it here, she's going to be okay, isn't she?"

Carscadden crouched next to Nastos, guiding him backward, away from Madeleine. Dennehy stood back, remaining silent. He had no idea how to comfort someone who was watching his wife as she faded away. Neither did Carscadden.

After all of Nastos' efforts to find Lindsay, and their success saving Hopkins and Taylor — only to have his wife murdered. Carscadden wanted to get Nastos out of there, to distract him by turning his attention to his daughter Josie, but it wasn't time yet. Nastos needed to grieve until he felt he was ready to let her go.

Carscadden stepped back, next to Dennehy, whose eyes were red with tears. "Tell me Anthony is going down for this, Dennehy. Promise me."

"You're the defence lawyer, Carscadden, work through it. No physical evidence, no witness, no proof. Anthony is going to walk. This case died with Chavez."

"Nastos will never forgive you, the police service; you guys have done nothing but screw this whole thing up."

Dennehy remained silent.

Carscadden continued. "Nastos solved this. He didn't let it go, wait for managerial approval, have case conferences — he just got out there and did it." He felt the anger in himself disappear as he looked over at his grieving friend.

"They don't make them like Nastos anymore, I'll agree with you there."

Carscadden gave up on Dennehy and moved over to Nastos, who was still holding Madeleine's hand. He wrapped his arms around Nastos and held him close.

Acknowledgements

THERE ARE MANY PEOPLE I'D LIKE TO THANK FOR THEIR SUPPORT Jack, Crissy, Emily, Cat, Erin, Simon, and the entire ECW Press crew for their generous support. Karen Bhatt provided enthusiasm and guidance, and I look forward to providing her the same with her forthcoming works.

Ernest Becker's text *The Denial of Death* as well as Christopher Nolan's film *The Prestige* provided me with psychological insight into people's need to develop meaning in their lives and a theatrical approach to reveal that meaning. *The Denial of Death* is an interesting read that everyone should consider, and *The Prestige* is an earlier work from a man who has become the best filmmaker of his time.